# *Search for Valhalla*

◊ ◊ ◊

# Search for Valhalla

a novel

by
mike whicker

a Walküre imprint

This is a work of historical fiction

ISBN: 978-0-9995582-0-1

printed in the United States of America

For

Cookie and Bill Barrow

# Acknowledgements

First of all, I have to thank Lauren Jones for posing as Kay Carr for the book cover, and Amanda Reising and Shelbie Shuler of Hår Salon in Evansville, Indiana, for doing Lauren's 1940s era hair and makeup.

Thanks to photographer Jenna Roos for all her work on said book cover.

Another thanks to David Gray for his generous back cover review.

I can't leave out my friend David Jones for not only being my attorney but also serving as my advisor.

My thanks to my two professional proofreaders extraordinaire, Erin Whicker and Tim Heerdink.

I thank Dr. Susanna Hoeness-Krupsaw, a native German and friend who is a University of Southern Indiana professor, for checking my German.

A big thanks goes to Tim Walthall and Gary Weinzapfel who graciously offered their vintage 1930 automobiles for the photo shoot.

Thanks to Nona Evans, whose blonde hair represents Erika Lehmann on the cover.

Gary Klemens is a weapons expert and a friend who lives in Ohio. Gary makes sure I'm accurate on 1940s era guns.

Thank you Darrell Davis, a close friend in Terre Haute, Indiana, for critiquing this and other of my novels.

And last but not least, I thank my son, Josh Whicker, a frequent traveler to Central America and an expert on that region of the world (he wrote his masters thesis on Central American history). Josh helped me a great deal with various settings in this novel.

# Chapter 1

## The Bridge

**During World War II**
**Evansville, Indiana – Saturday, 05 June 1943**

Twilight waned as Erika Lehmann drove her car into the crowded Trocadero parking lot. The multitude of cars forced her to park farther away from the nightclub's entrance than preferred, but she expected as much. Having been to this nightclub several times, she knew the parking lot, like the club, would be crowded on a Saturday night.

Erika was there to meet Axel Ryker. A Gestapo henchman who had hunted her down in America, Ryker was an extremely unpleasant surprise three weeks ago when he broke into her apartment. Unpleasant and painful. The bull-like Ryker had given her the first true beating of her life. Now she was forced to meet with him: the purpose, an exchange. He had taken from her the top secret material she stole from the Evansville Naval Shipyard and now he was demanding money for its return. Erika knew Ryker had no intention of keeping the bargain. As soon as he had the money he would kill her. Like Ryker, she also had no intention of honoring the accord. Now she would have to take her chances with him. She gambled with fire, but if he had the materials he stole from her with him, maybe her mission could be salvaged. Before she passed through the Trocadero doorway, she stopped, bent over on the pretext of checking her shoe strap, and felt through her pant leg one last time to make sure the dagger taped upside-down to her lower leg was secure.

Inside the Trocadero, many people stood near the bar around stools that were all taken. In the dining area more of the same—all tables were occupied, and the dance floor full. It took Erika a moment to find Ryker, whom she finally spotted sitting at a small, two person table along a wall near the far side of the dining area. She worked her way through the crowd trying to keep an eye out for men who might

1

be FBI, but many men wore suits at the nicer nightclubs and she knew the American FBI agents were expert at blending in during stakeouts.

Ryker saw her approaching. He did not rise. A drink sat before him and another on the table in front of the empty seat. Without a greeting from either of them she sat down.

"I took the liberty of ordering you a drink, Lorelei," Ryker said in heavily accented English. Lorelei was her codename.

"Don't call me that in here," she admonished him sternly while leaning forward so she did not have to say it loudly. Erika Lehmann was a German spy.

Ryker seemed unconcerned. "I doubt if we will be heard above this clamor," he countered, referring to the boisterous conversations all around and the swing band music.

Axel Ryker was German but born and raised in Lithuania, so Russian was his native tongue. This gave Ryker the perfect cover in America. To anyone who needed to know, he told them he was forced out of the Soviet Union in the 1930s during one of Stalin's collectivization purges—a lie, and best of all untraceable.

"I think you are known to enjoy a brandy," Ryker motioned toward the drink in front of her. "The selections of brandies here are limited. I hope that one is acceptable."

"I don't drink with a traitor," she scorned. She looked around then added: "This meeting should have been handled much differently. You realize that the chances of us being watched are high."

Again, Ryker seemed unworried. He was a hellish apparition, a killer made more dangerous because of a total lack of fear, mercy, or regret when he had to fight his way out of trouble. Six feet tall and heavily muscled, he was a brute whose coarse facial features and dark, pitiless eyes gave him a monstrous air. Even tough men gave Axel Ryker a wide berth.

"So, you have my package, yes?" Ryker asked about the money.

"Yes."

"It is in your auto?"

"Yes, and the things of mine you took are in your car I assume?"

"Of course," Ryker said after a drink of his vodka.

"What is your plan for the exchange?" she asked.

"We will drive away in our separate autos. You will follow me. I have found a safe place for the exchange. We will make the exchange and go our separate ways."

"Very well." Erika realized he might be lying about having her items in his car, but it was the only chance she had to regain them, and she believed Ryker's confidence in his killing skills were such that he was not much concerned with her turning the tables. She reasoned that Ryker was vain enough to believe no one could best him, and that was about all she had in her favor. Erika knew she would have to strike first, and that she would have only one thrust with the knife. It would have to be true. If he survived her first strike and got hold of her, she was finished.

Ryker finished his drink and stood up. "Shall we go?"

Erika rose without answering. Normally in this type of situation she would take the man's arm as if they were a couple, but she could not bear to even act the part with Axel Ryker, so she followed him through the crowd.

Outside, night was now total with swiftly moving clouds passing now and again in front of the Ohio River moon, but the parking lot was well lit by the blinking moon and security spotlights mounted high on the building's corners and aimed toward the cars. Others were walking in and out of the nightclub, and Erika and Ryker were no more than forty feet outside the door when they heard the shout behind them.

"FBI, STOP!"

Erika spun to face the voice. A young man held out his identification in one hand with a gun in the other.

The next few seconds seemed to pass in slow motion. Ryker pulled his gun before he turned around then immediately took aim at the young agent. Two more agents rushed in and Ryker fired at them. The agents dove behind the nearest parked cars. Using the cars for cover, the FBI men took aim at Ryker, but he quickly grabbed a young woman cowering nearby and used her as a shield.

The original plan to drive separately was instantly abandoned. Erika knew her only chance of escape was to stay near the hostage. Ryker's car was nearby. He ordered the FBI men to stay where they were or he would kill the hostage, and then he dragged the screaming woman to his car, keeping her between himself and the FBI guns. Ryker opened the driver-side door and roughly pushed the young woman into the front seat. He quickly followed and started the engine. Erika rushed to the other side of the car and jumped in, forcing the hostage between her and Ryker who shifted into first gear and stomped on the accelerator, spraying gravel on the surrounding cars. As they sped from the parking lot, Erika looked behind. One of the agents stood outside a car talking into a radio.

"Please don't hurt me!" screamed the hysterical hostage.

"Shut up!" Erika ordered, then she shouted to Ryker: "Turn right! It's our only chance."

Tires squealed as the car slid out onto the highway. Ryker turned right, which took the car south and toward a bridge that crossed the Ohio River into Kentucky. The bridge was not far and with the gas pedal floored, the iron work of the bridge appeared quickly in the moonlight. In an instant, the car was on the long bridge and over the water.

"Please don't hurt me!" the young woman again begged. "I'm getting married next week."

"Kill her," Ryker told Erika.

"No! Please!" the young woman screamed.

"We need her," Erika countered.

"Kill her," Ryker repeated. "The people pursuing us will not know she is dead. Her use to us as a hostage will not change and she will be less trouble."

Their attention was immediately diverted from the hostage when they saw the flashing red lights ahead. Nearly across the bridge by now, the roadblock ahead ended any hopes of escaping into Kentucky. Ryker slammed on the brakes and the car did a half turn as the tires locked. When the car came to a stop, Erika opened the door, grabbed the hostage and pulled her across her own body and pushed her out of the car. The young woman landed on her side, rolled twice from the momentum, then sprang to her feet and ran for her life.

"You fool!" Ryker shouted. He would have killed Erika Lehmann then and there, but at that moment he had no choice other than to turn the car around and head back toward Indiana.

"Going back will do us no good," Erika said. "The FBI will be coming for us from the nightclub; they probably have the other end of the bridge already blocked. When we get to the middle of the bridge stop the car. We will have to jump. In the dark we might have a chance to swim out of the river and escape. It's our only choice."

"That fall is how many meters, Sonderführer?" Ryker almost laughed. "The fall will kill you, and I am a poor swimmer. I will take my chances on land. And if we are fated to die together, it will be a glorious death for the Fatherland. Would not our Führer be pleased?" said Ryker with heavy sarcasm. He cared nothing for patriotism, and he held no allegiance to anything.

Ryker had made a critical mistake. He told Erika Lehmann he was a poor swimmer.

The dagger was taped securely to her lower leg, but she would have to raise her pant leg and pull the tape. Ryker would see and never give her the time, so she flung herself on Ryker and tried to jerk the steering wheel to crash the car into the guard-rail, but Ryker's power was almost superhuman. He held the wheel steady with one hand and easily tossed her off of him with the other. Again she attacked. This time her thought was to block his vision for as long as she could so perhaps he would steer the car into a crash himself. Erika put him in a headlock and held on for as long as possible, using her upper body to block his vision. She looked down and pushed in the cigarette lighter with her foot, but again Ryker violently pushed her off. This time her head hit the metal dash.

She had to stop the car while it was over the water. Ahead on the bridge, two headlights grew brighter as a car raced toward them. Erika pulled the hot cigarette lighter from the dash, and pressed the business end of the lighter into Ryker's face. He barely reacted to the lighter searing his flesh, and for the third time he tossed her away like a ragdoll. But this time, when Ryker took one hand off the wheel to fend her off, she managed to kick the steering wheel hard with her left foot and the car careened left and smashed into the guard-rail.

With the car stopped, Erika fought to get out. She knew she could not last long in a close quarters fight with Axel Ryker once he was no longer driving and could focus his full attention on her. She kicked away from Ryker and managed to open the passenger door, but she did not escape cleanly. Even though Ryker was in an awkward position to deliver a punch, he managed to deliver a back-handed blow to her side that knocked the air out of her as she fell from the car. Ryker followed her out the same door. Erika saw him reach for the gun in his belt and at the same time try to kick her as she lay on the road. She rolled hard into his legs causing him to stumble, and then she kicked the heavy car door into him. The blow from the door barely jostled Ryker, but he had not yet gotten a full grip on the gun and fumbled it. The gun dropped to the road. Despite that her breath had not completely returned, Erika turned on her stomach and went for the gun but Ryker was too close and he grabbed her hair and pulled her to her feet. She saw too late his hand coming and the open-handed slap to her face from the brawny Gestapo hit man sent her reeling backward into the guard-rail. Ryker bent over and picked up the gun as a spotlight lit the area around Ryker's car.

"FBI! Stop right there, you're both under arrest!" It was the same voice from the Trocadero parking lot. Erika looked. The car that had approached them on the bridge was now stopped about fifty feet away. Erika made out a silhouette of a man standing behind the open car door with his gun aimed at Ryker. She heard other voices, but could not see the men because the FBI car's bright headlights and the spotlight were trained on her and Ryker. Ryker ignored the command.

She had to even the odds. Although she was skilled in hand-to-hand combat and in the past had won fights with many men, she had no hope of winning a blow-to-blow fight with Axel Ryker. Her side was sore from Ryker's swipe in the car, but her lungs had finally filled. She was much quicker than the heavy, muscle-bound Ryker, and she easily avoided his advance. She jumped up onto the ironwork near the edge of the road and began climbing.

Ryker followed.

Ignoring more shouts from the FBI, the two Germans climbed upward in the wind and over the water far below, their climb illuminated by the moon and the spotlight from the FBI car. The odds were now more in Erika's favor; she scaled the ironwork much faster than Ryker, but she did not want him to abandon the chase, so she slowed, adjusting her climb to stay just out of his reach.

Erika neared the top of the ironwork and put some extra distance between herself and Ryker to allow time to draw her dagger. She stopped climbing, pulled up her pant leg, ripped the dagger off her leg, and waited for him. A moment ago, her plan was simply to get him in the water, but Ryker suddenly made another error. He looked down at the FBI agents on the bridge road below. Erika saw her chance. She jumped down onto Ryker's back and sliced the knife across his throat. Blood ran from the wound onto her hand and arm. Even with his throat cut, Ryker still clung to the iron with one hand and attempted to reach back with the other to grab her. Blood continued to rush from the knife wound, soaking them both. Finally, Axel Ryker lost his grip and the two Germans began the long fall to the Ohio River. Erika held on to Ryker and the decision paid off. During the lengthy fall, gravity rotated Ryker's heavier body, and Erika entered the water on top. Still, the violent entry into the river nearly knocked her unconscious as they went to the bottom and slammed into the soft mud and silt of the riverbed. She released Ryker who was not struggling. Despite the high intensity of the moment, it flashed through her mind that the world no longer had to deal with this plague of a man.

Erika, a champion swimmer, stayed underwater as long as possible. She could feel the direction of the river current and swam with it knowing that would put more distance between her and the FBI on the bridge than if she swam against the flow. When forced to surface, she gasped as quietly as she could, and spun in the water to find the bridge. She had emerged about two hundred feet downriver. High overhead on the bridge, the FBI men had moved their car and were sweeping the river with the spotlight. They chose the correct side of the bridge, thinking bodies, dead or unconscious, would float downriver, but luckily for Erika, the sweeping light was hampered by the bridge's ironwork and brightened the river only here or there. She began a routine of swimming underwater and coming up only briefly to the salvation of the air. One time, the edge of the spotlight caught her for a moment, but she had by then moved farther away and, unknown to her, the gleaming moon was now her ally. The lunar light, instead of aiding the FBI's vision, added a sparkling shimmer to the wind-ruffled waves and prevented her white face from standing out.

At last Erika rounded a bend and left the line of sight from the bridge. Now she had to choose which state to swim toward. She reasoned the FBI might assume that a survivor (if that was possible), would seek Kentucky, away from where they came, but Erika was familiar with the area and knew if she left the river in Kentucky it would be into open farmland with miles to walk under a full moon.

She swam back to the Indiana shore.

A gang of scrub oaks welcomed her as she came out of the Ohio River. The tension of the night left her drained and the fight with Ryker sore. She sat on a log in the moonlight shadows and shivered in wet clothes. *At least the water washed away Ryker's blood.*

# Chapter 2

**[Four years later]**
**Washington, D.C.**
**Saturday, 26 July 1947**

Even though it was before lunchtime, Leroy Carr and Al Hodge sat in Carr's office with a dram of Kentucky bourbon in front of them—a celebration of sorts. This morning, the early rising and early to work President Harry Truman signed the National Security Act, making the Central Intelligence Agency an official department of the United States government.

"Finally," Carr said to Hodge, referring to the official status of an organization they had worked for 'unofficially' for over a year. The men, long time allies since the early days of World War II when they both worked for the OSS, raised their glasses. Hodge, whose title was now Director of Clandestine Operations was technically subordinate to Carr as Deputy Director, but the two men worked together more as friends than as boss and underling.

"For a while," Hodge said, "I didn't think it would ever happen."

"Now we'll get a budget," Carr said. "We won't have to go with hat in hand to the State Department asking for nickels and dimes."

"And it's certainly nice to be back at E Street," Hodge remarked.

For the past year their offices had been in the Pentagon. Now they were back in the former OSS set of buildings referred to simply as the 'E Street Complex' located in the Foggy Bottom area of D.C. near the Potomac River. The mid-summer heat outside was oppressive, over 90°. Thankfully, the building was cooled by one of the newly innovated central air conditioning units.

"ROGER that," Carr agreed. "Parking and those long walks through the Pentagon got old fast. It's great to be back at E Street." The CIA had moved out of the Pentagon a week ago, after it was assured by the White House that the president would sign the Act.

"How's Erika?" Hodge asked. "I haven't seen her in months. How much havoc has she caused at the Farm?"

At Camp Perry in Virginia, the CIA ran a training facility for field agents referred to as the 'Farm.'

"She's doing fine. She seems to be taking the job seriously. As you know, I gave her a month vacation in May. She spent it in London with her daughter."

Erika Lehmann had been a German spy during the war. Now working for the United States, she had proved a handful for Carr and Hodge but her record as a field agent was impressive. Trained heavily by the German Abwehr in weapon usage, close quarters combat, and having a multitude of clandestine expertise, Carr assigned her to serve as an instructor at the Farm between missions. Lehmann was a widow, losing her husband, Kai, on a mission in Poland while rescuing the genius inventor/Hollywood movie star Hedy Lamarr from the Russians.

It had been over six months since the former Nazi—now CIA—spy's last mission.

"Lehmann cooperating, that's a new one," Hodge said with a smirk. "Still no leads on Zhanna?"

Like Erika Lehmann, a Russian, Zhanna Rogova, was part of the four woman CIA team codenamed the *Shield Maidens.* Zhanna had gone AWOL after the last Shield Maidens mission which ended in February.

"Not a thing," Carr answered. "Zhanna has disappeared into thin air. It's now time to put Lehmann back to work."

"Another assignment? Don't tell me we're sending her to look for Zhanna. Some of my best men are already looking for her."

"No, she won't be looking for Rogova, Al, but she will be looking for someone."

"Who?"

"You better have another belt of Scotch before I tell you."

# Chapter 3

**Camp Perry, Virginia**
**Saturday, 26 July 1947**

All of the instructors in hand-to-hand combat at the CIA 'Farm' were male save one. A sturdy looking woman with bright blond hair stood among the group of coaches as the latest group of field agent wannabes lined up for that day's training. Everyone at the Farm went by a codename. The blonde's codename was *Lorelei.*

Today the instruction would be in knife fighting.

Among the plebe trainees—six total—two were women. None of the women would be matched up with Lorelei. The Farm powers-that-be decided months ago that matching up women with Lorelei served less to train them, but more to dishearten them.

Lorelei was always assigned a male trainee.

"Let's begin," barked a Marine first sergeant who was in charge of coordinating knife fighting skills at the Farm. Since it was mid-summer and the weather hot and muggy, the first sergeant had decided to move the training from the gym to a clearing in the vast woods on the Farm property.

The sergeant called on two of the male trainers first. One by one, they proceeded to instruct their plebes in slow motion how to block different types of knife thrusts, and how and when to counter an opponent's move. Rubber knives were used for the slow motion training. When the schooling elevated to full speed, a dull wooden knife with a rounded point was employed. The knife blade was covered in red caulk so any strike on an opponent could be recognized.

One of the plebes was quickly dispatched by his assigned instructor. One held his own for awhile but was eventually 'killed' by a thrust to his chest when he made the mistake of getting too cocky and moved in too quickly.

"Lorelei and 'Outrigger' (the plebe's codename) you're up," the sergeant yelled.

Outrigger stepped forward but was on his stomach, prone on the ground within seconds. Lorelei had dived into his legs like a Notre Dame linebacker, flipped over on top of his back, and 'sliced' his throat with the rubber knife. The exercise hadn't had time to progress to the wooden, caulk-covered knife.

Still on the ground, the man said in rage. "Why do I always get this bitch? She doesn't fight fair. We're supposed to go through things slow motion first."

"There is no such thing as 'fair' in a knife fight, Outrigger," the first sergeant barked. "You're dead. Now, get up and shut up or I'll let her use a real knife next time."

Before the man got off the ground, Erika stomped on his left hand and ground her heel into it, breaking two bones in his hand.


**[that evening]**

Around eight o'clock, Erika Lehmann, aka *Lorelei* at the Farm, walked into Lane's Tavern, a bar in downtown Williamsburg, Virginia. Last month a couple of her fellow Farm instructors had brought her here. Lane's served good food and was only a twenty minute drive from where the instructors billeted at Camp Perry.

Tonight she was alone—not just alone, but lonely. Her husband, Kai, had been killed over a year ago on a mission in Poland where circumstances led the CIA to team them together. After Kai's death, she made herself a promise to never again fall in love with another agent. At the age of 29, she was already a widow.

Nick, one of the bartenders at Lane's, had showed interest in her. This was not unusual for the attractive Erika Lehmann, but on her end she had also developed an attraction to him. Tonight she had agreed to a movie after his shift ended.

When she sat down, he spotted her straightaway. His eyes lit up and he came over to where she sat at the end of the bar. She smiled at him. He was tall and handsome.

"Hello, Erika," he said. "I've been looking forward to our movie for a week. Where have you been?"

"Work, Nick. You wouldn't believe the amount of paperwork a typist at Camp Perry has to keep up with. If we don't get it done during the day, we're expected to stay over for as long as it takes to finish it."

"Sounds like you work for a bunch of taskmasters at that Army base."

"Yes, it seems that way."

"What are you drinking, Erika? Your usual, brandy?"

"No, I'll have a Margarita tonight."

"Coming right up."

He walked away to begin fixing the drink.

Erika Lehmann had dark secrets unknown to Nick. For much of the war she served as a German Abwehr operative—a Nazi spy—for her homeland. Her father was a personal friend of Adolf Hitler who had joined the fledgling Nazi Party in the early years of the 1920s when Hitler and the Party were still just one of the dozens of meaningless political parties to most Germans. Through her father, Erika had known Hitler on a personal level; her father and she had been invited to the Berghof on numerous occasions. She had become friends with Eva Braun. Once, Erika had a private lunch with Adolf Hitler at his favorite Munich restaurant, the Osteria Bavaria—just she and Hitler. The Führer ordered his SS bodyguards to remain outside the private room built especially for him.

Erika's deceased husband, Kai, was a member of Otto Skorzeny's elite group of commandoes that, among other missions, rescued Mussolini from Gran Sasso after his capture by a newly formed Italian government.

Yet to Nick, all he knew about her is what she had told him. She worked as a civilian typist at Camp Perry.

Nick shortly returned with her Margarita.

"I told my boss I had to get off tonight at nine," Nick told her. "There is a ten o'clock showing of *Notorious* with Cary Grant and Ingrid Bergman downtown at the Apollo. Have you seen it?"

"No."

"Great! I also know a diner that stays open all-night where we can get something to eat if you're hungry after the show."

Erika took a sip of her drink. "Sounds like fun."

**[later]**

It had been a nice evening. Nick took her to the movie then afterwards to the all-night diner in downtown Williamsburg. There they sat and talked for a long time over apple pie and coffee. They talked some about the war. Nick had served in the South Pacific with the Navy. Erika told him she typed and filed papers at the Army base.

Finally, Nick drove her back to Lane's Tavern where she had left her car. When he pulled his car next to hers, before she got out, he gave her a long goodnight kiss.

◊ ◊ ◊

Instructors at the Farm billeted in hastily constructed wooden barracks, painted the standard white, as did the trainees. The difference being the trainees all slept in a common room on Army cots, just like military basic training. The instructors, in their building, each had his or her own cubby-hole room not much bigger than a prison cell but a place that at least afforded a measure of privacy.

The women had their own barracks. Erika was not the only woman at Camp Perry, although she was the only female instructor in combat training and swimming, many women manned jobs such as typists, file clerks, and a couple of women were instructors in field radio operation.

When Erika entered the door, the elderly building matron was sitting at the check-in desk waiting for her. Mrs. Simmons lost her son in the war and her husband died of the Spanish flu in the 20s. She had struggled to get by ever since. She took the job as a Camp Perry women's matron and was glad to get it. The job didn't pay much, but she had a small apartment in the building with no utility bills to pay. Also, she was allowed to take her meals in the camp mess hall. Erika liked the woman. It was obvious her arthritis made it painful for her at times, yet she always seemed friendly and never complained.

"It's two o'clock, Lorelei. Your date must have gone well."

"It did," said Erika. "You're up rather late, Mrs. Simmons."

"I was ordered to wait up for you. You're to report to Deputy Director Carr's office tomorrow at 0900. Now you have the message and it's off to bed for me. I'm glad you had fun on your date. I think you told me earlier that his name is Nick. I assume Nick is a nice young man."

"Yes, he is. Goodnight Ma'am."

# Chapter 4

**E Street Complex**
**Washington, D.C.**
**Sunday, 27 July 1947**

"Erika and Kathryn will be here in an hour, Al. I need a moment to talk to you before they arrive." It was eight o'clock in the morning.

"Is there a problem, Leroy?" Hodge asked. The two men sat in Carr's E Street office.

"Not a problem as far as I know. Erika is dating some guy and I want to know everything about him."

"Lehmann is dating? God help that poor slob. Who is he?"

"As far as I know, just some bartender in Williamsburg. His name is Nick. Last night, when she logged out at her barracks she wrote that she was going to Williamsburg to a Lane's Tavern. I don't know a last name, but, as I said, he's a bartender there so he won't be difficult to identify. Some of the instructors at the Farm are known to frequent the place and know him as one of the bartenders. Apparently Erika went there one night with a group of them and now she's dating the guy. Put one of your men on this. I want a full report on this guy—any political affiliations, who his first grade teacher was. The whole nine yards."

"Okay, will do. Have you told Lehmann or Fischer anything about the mission?"

"Nope. I figure you'd want to be here to see their faces when I fill them in."

Hodge chuckled. "It will be a shocker, that's for sure. Especially for Lehmann."


**[9:00 a.m.]**
Erika Lehmann and Kathryn Fischer were both on time, as they always were when called by their boss, Leroy Carr. Erika didn't always follow instruction, but she knew she owed Carr. It was the same with

Kathryn. He had protected them both from federal prosecution because of their Nazi backgrounds.

Kathryn, like Erika, was born in Germany and at the start of the war had volunteered in the German Abwehr under Admiral Canaris. She quickly was recruited as an operative. Unlike Erika, Kathryn's assignment did not involve foreign missions. Kathryn was ordered to infiltrate Heinrich Himmler's Gestapo. Canaris and Himmler were hated enemies and neither trusted the other. Both men kept tabs on the other one's organization. Kathryn Fischer was Canaris's ace in the hole. She successfully inserted herself into the Gestapo and over the course of the war rose to the officer rank of Kriminalkommissar, equal to a rank of major. In an assignment that she was not expected to survive for more than a few months, using her guile and wit, she made it through the war and survived both Canaris and Himmler.

Leroy Carr had recruited her, as was common among several U.S. government agencies after the war. No better evidence of this is the recruitment and protection offered some of Germany's top rocket scientists after the war such as Werner von Braun and dozens of others, some whose names were on the Nuremberg lists for suspected war crimes.

Between missions, Kathryn held a job as an instructor in human intelligence gathering at the Naval War College in Rhode Island. Like Erika, she was one of the four women Carr had codenamed the *Shield Maidens.* Among the other two women on the Shield Maiden team was Zhanna Rogova, a Russian sniper and assassin during the war who had gone AWOL of her own accord six months ago, and Army Major Sheila Reid, Carr's executive assistant. What led Carr to assemble the CIA's Shield Maiden team was not only the four women's toughness and skill in the world of espionage, but their bilingual talents. All four women spoke German and English. Zhanna, the missing Shield Maiden, also spoke Russian, as did Erika. Erika also spoke fluent French. The only problem presented Carr now was that none of them spoke Spanish or Portuguese, and the mission would be in South America, yet Carr felt he had found a solution.

Carr wasted no time and started the briefing as soon as Erika and Kathryn sat down. Al Hodge was already there and had been briefed beforehand. Carr addressed the women.

"Ladies, a few months ago I told you there might be an upcoming mission to South America. We weren't sure at that time if this would be something the CIA would become involved in, but we have been tasked by the State Department to look into this, so the mission is a 'go.'"

"What mission is that?" Erika asked.

"Be patient for a moment," Carr answered. "That's why you're here—to be briefed."

Carr continued. "The FBI has been looking into this for over a year, but certain important people on Capitol Hill think Hoover is not taking the inquiry seriously. That's why the CIA has been asked to get involved. Many Germans, quite a few with warrants on their heads for possible war crimes, have flocked to South America since the war. There are many small towns in the Argentine Andes where there are now more German speakers than Spanish speakers. It's a job right up your alley, but because you'll still have to deal with the Spanish language, and neither of you speak Spanish, you'll need an interpreter. I have one who will accompany you."

"Who?" Kathryn asked.

Carr paused for a moment before answering. "My wife, Kay. She took Spanish for four years in college and spent a semester in Mexico during her college days. She's quite capable as a translator, and she has clearance to do this. You made sure of that Erika with the episode in Bath during the war.

"Kay!" Erika exclaimed. "She hates me. What does she say about this?"

Carr paused again. "I haven't told her yet."

Erika laughed and shook her head. "I'd like to be a fly on the wall when you tell her this, Leroy."

"You won't have to be a fly on the wall. I'm going to tell Kay tomorrow in private, but I've booked a dinner for all of us, including Kay, for tomorrow night at the Mayflower. Hopefully we can put an end to this feud between you and my wife at the dinner. I'm going to

18

ask Kay if, after dinner, she'd be willing to meet with you on one of the hotel's secluded verandas where you and she can talk privately—just you and her with no one else around, including me."

"There is no feud on my part, Leroy," Erika replied. "I like Kay. I always have."

"That all fine, Erika, but you can't blame a wife for having hard feelings for someone who first captured her, and then her husband, when you were in cahoots with your old buddy Otto Skorzeny."

"I suppose not."

"So what is the mission?" Kathryn asked in order to get back to the main subject at hand. "You said we were here to be briefed."

"It will be your job to find out if the rumors are true." Carr then looked at Erika. "You'll be searching for your old friends, Erika. Adolf Hitler and Eva Braun."

# Chapter 5

## Washington, D.C.
## Next day—Monday, 28 July 1947

Leroy Carr and his wife Kay sat at the breakfast table in their Annapolis home. Carr was dressed and ready for work. Kay wore a blue chenille robe. Both dipped into a bowl of Kellogg's corn flakes.

"What are your plans for today, Kay?"

"I'm volunteering in the lunch serving line at St. Paul's church for veterans who have not yet found work. They can bring their families. I'll be making sandwiches. I have to be there by 10:30." It was now only 7:00.

"So you're free for dinner?" Carr asked before he took a sip of coffee.

"Yes, Leroy. I have a ham in the refrigerator. What time will you be home? Any idea?" Kay had grown very familiar with her husband staying late at the office, with middle-of-the-night telephone calls, and with him being away for days or even weeks. Unlike many CIA wives, Kay knew what her husband did for a living.

"No, I didn't mean that," Carr said. "I meant would you like to go out to eat tonight?"

Kay looked at her husband. "On a Monday night? That's unusual for you, Leroy. Has my husband suddenly become romantic? But to answer your question, sure, I'd love to go out. Where do you have in mind?"

"The Mayflower."

"Wow! The Mayflower. What's gotten into you, Leroy? You must really like this robe," Kay said grinning.

"Actually, it won't be just us."

"Oh? Who else will be there?"

"Al and Sheila will be there, and a woman you haven't met. Her name is Kathryn Fischer."

"Okay, sounds like fun."

"Uh, and one other person will be there, sweetheart. Erika Lehmann."

Kay dropped her spoon into her cereal and glared at her husband. "Well, thanks for the warning, Darling. Any thoughts I had for a romantic evening just got flushed down the toilet."

"I need your help with a mission, Kay. I need a Spanish speaker for a mission in South America. Please consider it."

"Surely the CIA has people who speak Spanish, Leroy. Why me?"

"Because you know our home number and can call me in the middle of the night if the need arises. You know I try to keep the number of people who have our home number to a minimum."

"The Nazi bitch has our phone number. She certainly calls enough. And Al has it."

"Al won't be going unless the need arises. This is a very low-risk mission. I'll tell Erika that you will be in charge of calling me to keep me updated. Sometimes she tells me everything I need to know, but sometimes she holds back. I know you'll tell me everything. That will be important on this mission because the group will be looking for a couple of people Erika and her father were close to and I don't know how Erika will react if these people are found."


**[that evening]**

The Mayflower Hotel on Connecticut Avenue was without a doubt the swankiest place to stay or dine in D.C. This is where visiting dignitaries, famous celebrities, rich lobbyists, and other people of power or influence stayed when in Washington. The hotel had three restaurants. The most expensive of which was the Capital restaurant. It was in this restaurant that Leroy Carr had ordered reservations.

The CIA and a few other government agencies used the Mayflower often, but normally for booking rooms, for which they received a 50% discount. Unfortunately, that discount did not apply to dining. Carr could declare the dinner on his expense account because it did concern an upcoming mission, but then he would have to file paperwork. For that reason, Carr decided to pick up the check himself to keep this dinner off the record.

The Capital was a spacious area with a pink-veined marble floor and a high curved copper ceiling with beautiful murals and three

21

crystal chandeliers. The walls were cherry wood with several tapestries.

Leroy, Kay, and Al Hodge arrived early. "We have reservations under the name of Carr for six," Leroy said to the maitre d'. The tuxedoed man nodded and led them to a round table for six covered by a snow white tablecloth with a beautiful arrangement of yellow Gerbera daisies as a centerpiece. Kay told Leroy what she wanted to drink then left for the ladies room. The drink waiter appeared, took their orders, and handed both Carr and Hodge the dinner menu.

Hodge opened his menu and looked it over.

"Holy cow, Leroy! Eighteen bucks for a piece of salmon. For that price the fish ought to at least blow me."

It was a typical Al Hodge joke and Carr grinned. "That was a good one, Al, but remember we have ladies with us tonight."

"Right. All except Lehmann. I haven't figured out what she is yet. I'm still not convinced she's human. She might be one of those robots who step out of those flying saucers people are starting to claim they see."

Kay returned just as the drinks were delivered.

"I see Hitler's perfect Aryan woman isn't here yet," Kay said sarcastically then took a sip of her margarita."

Carr looked at his wristwatch. "We're still a little early. They'll be here soon. I hope you'll give this a chance, Kay. I need your help."

Kay took her husband's hand. "I'll try." Then she added a caveat. "I'll try not to throw my drink on her, that is."

*This isn't going to be easy,* Carr thought to himself.

Sheila Reid arrived, then a moment later Erika and Kathryn walked in. They identified themselves as members of the Carr party of six and the maitre d' led them through the dining room. When the women arrived at the table, Carr and Hodge stood up. The maitre d' held the women's chairs, as he had done for Kay, and promised to send over the drink waiter.

The men were dressed in black tie; the women in evening gowns fitting for such a restaurant.

When everyone was seated, Carr made the introductions.

"Ladies, this is my wife, Kay. Of course you all know Al and Sheila. Kay, you know Erika." Kay ignored her husband and took a substantial swig of her drink. Carr continued, "Kay, I know you haven't met Kathryn Fischer, she's an instructor at the Naval War College in Rhode Island.

Kay looked at Kathryn and smiled. "Hello."

"Hello, Kay," said Kathryn. "It's very nice to meet you."

Kay was polite to Kathryn but she had walked in with Erika Lehmann so Kay was concerned there must be something wrong with her mind.

Erika complimented Leroy's wife. "Kay, I love your gown, you look beautiful."

Kay replied by giving Erika an icy gaze that would freeze a lake.

"Okay," Carr said quickly. "Let's order dinner."

There was not a lot of chit-chat that might relieve the obvious tension during dinner. Hodge told a couple of cleaner jokes and got a few chuckles; otherwise, the table was very solemn.

Erika finally asked Carr, "Does Kay know who we will be looking for?"

Carr replied quickly. "No, and we can't discuss anything about the mission here. It's too sensitive. It's totally up to Kay whether she accepts or rejects involvement. If she accepts, she'll be going along as a civilian aide, meaning she'll translate Spanish and that's all. Kay already has clearance to answer my phone calls at home and relay messages to Sheila if I'm not there. Getting Kay approved as a civilian aide won't be a problem. That's all we're discussing tonight. I want Kay and you, Erika, to meet on a veranda that Al has reserved and talk things over to see if it's possible for you to work together. Kay will have the night to think it over. Whether she chooses to take part or not, the rest of us will meet in my office tomorrow morning at nine o'clock and go over the details."

When everyone had finished eating, Carr looked at Al who knew that was his cue to take Kay and Erika to the private area where they could talk privately. The rest of the party remained at the table drinking coffee or brandy.

Hodge led Kay and Erika to an open air veranda over Connecticut Avenue with sliding glass doors and curtains that could be closed for privacy. These verandas were commonly used by political leaders from various countries who, after a dinner meeting, found themselves with sensitive information to discuss.

Hodge opened one of the doors to allow the women out onto the veranda then closed the door and pulled the curtains.

Earlier it had been a typical D.C. July day—hot and muggy. Now the sun had gone down and a slight breeze made it comfortable outside.

As soon as they were alone, Kay drew back and slapped Erika hard across the face. The German's first reaction was to punch Kay in the jaw, but she resisted, unclenched her fist, and gave Kay a sinister smile. Kay attempted another slap, but Erika easily blocked this one and twisted Kay's arm behind her back. Leroy's wife grimaced from the pain but refused to cry out. Kay was not a weak woman in either body or mind, but she was no match for the powerful, athletic, and highly trained Erika Lehmann. There were few women in the world who could hold their own with Erika, and not all that many average men.

Erika released Kay's arm and roughly shoved her down into one of the veranda chairs. "First of all, let me relieve your mind and let you know I don't want you on this mission," she said to Kay. "You'll just be a liability. Leroy will expect me to protect you, and I cannot guarantee anyone's safety on a mission, not even my own. So tell your husband tonight that you decline the mission."

"Fuck you!" It was a very rare obscenity from Leroy Carr's gracious wife.

"I know you hate me for what happened in Bath during the war, but you have to remember our countries were at war and the Americans had captured my husband."

"So you kidnap me in order to get to my husband so you can use him for trade bait. You put my husband's life in danger and I'm not supposed to hate you?"

"You would have done the same to save your husband. Just tell Leroy that you decline the mission. He said it is up to you. We both win. I won't have to work with some weak woman who is ruled by her emotions that I cannot depend on, and you will not have to work with me."

Erika leaned over Kay and pinned her arms to her sides with a powerful grip. She kissed Kay on the lips. Kay grimaced and tried to turn her head away, but it didn't work. The passionate kiss lasted for a long moment.

When Erika finally released her, Kay's face flushed and she gasped. "You're disgusting! If you ever do that again, I will kill you. I don't know how, but I'll find a way."

"If you don't decline the mission, I'll do other things to you that you won't like—or maybe you will like them, you'll have to decide." Erika fondled one of her breasts.

Kay screamed and said, "I despise you, you Nazi whore!"

Erika gave her another menacing look. "Your feelings about me are of no matter. If you tell your husband what happened here and accept the mission he might think you enjoyed my advances, which is what I will confirm to him. Not only that, but I will tell him it was you who made advances to me."

"My husband wouldn't believe that in a million years. He knows how much I hate you!"

"I see. So what you are saying is you would have welcomed the kiss if you liked me."

"No, that is not what I meant or said. You're twisting my words."

"Just tell Leroy that you're passing on the mission and both our problems are over. I want you out."

Erika leaned over Kay as if she would kiss her again but this time Kay managed to turn her head away. She felt Erika's warm breathe in her ear as the German whispered, "I find you alluring. You have my hazel eyes. Expect more of this if you accept the mission. Heil Hitler, my darling."

# Chapter 6

**E Street Complex**
**Washington, D.C.**
**Next day—Tuesday, 29 July 1947**

Kay tossed and turned in bed, getting perhaps two hours of restless sleep over the course of the night. Erika was ruthless and clever, Kay found herself admitting that. She was not concerned that her husband would ever believe Erika's threat that his wife had enjoyed the German's physical advances. Still, it would be embarrassing for her to admit to him that it ever happened. If she declined the assignment and said nothing about the kiss and fondling, problem solved.

She was awake when her husband arose for the day. Kay told him over breakfast that she was declining the mission.

**[9:00 a.m.]**
Al, Erika, Kathryn, and Sheila sat in Leroy Carr's office. His office on E Street was actually bigger than the one he had been assigned at the Pentagon. Both Carr and Hodge were glad to be back at E Street where they had spent the war with the OSS. The OSS signs had been taken down and scraped off office windows months ago after Truman disbanded the WWII intelligence agency shortly after the war ended.

Now new signs were going up with three different letters—CIA. A workman had painted those letters along with Carr's name and position on his office door window yesterday.

Sheila was dressed smartly in her Army uniform. Of course Al wore his everyday suit and Erika and Kathryn were outfitted in civilian attire. Both wore a blouse and a skirt.

"First of all," Carr said to the group, "after we're done here everyone needs to get their photograph taken for their official CIA I.D., and phony I.D.s and passports you might need for the mission. Sheila will have the sergeant who serves as her aide take you to the credentials room.

26

"Secondly, my wife declined the mission so it will be up to Al and me to find another Spanish interpreter. We have several agents who speak Spanish and even some associates in Central America we can call upon. We just have to find the one most suitable for this type of mission."

The buzzer on Carr's desk went off. Normally it would be Sheila at the other end, but since she was in the room, her aide was calling.

Carr pressed the intercom button. "Sergeant, I asked not to be disturbed. What is it?"

"Sir, your wife is here and would like to enter."

Carr was at a loss, but he told the sergeant to send her in. The sergeant opened the door for Kay and closed it behind her.

"Kay, what a surprise," said Carr.

"It sure is," Erika agreed.

Kay ignored Erika and said to her husband, "Leroy, I changed my mind. I accept the job you requested of me."

Erika sighed and slightly shook her head.

Kay Carr had always supported her husband. He had owned a lucrative attorney's practice before the war—until Bill Donovan called and asked him to join the newly formed OSS, the precursor to today's CIA.

Kay had supported him then, even though she wasn't enamored with moving to Washington from their beautiful ranch in Montana. This is nothing to say about the huge pay cut the OSS job would bring. But her husband was a patriot and felt bound by duty because of the war, so she endured the life changes with a smile for her husband's sake. She wouldn't let him down now, regardless of Erika Lehmann and her intimidation tactics.

Al brought up another wooden chair that had been leaning against the far wall and held it for Kay as she sat.

"So, I assume your talk on the veranda made some progress." Carr stated to Kay and Erika. "You two can work together?"

"Yes," Kay said with a straight face.

Erika stood up and walked over to the window which looked down on E Street.

"Erika, you didn't answer." Carr said.

"Sure. Kay and I can work together, Leroy. You betcha."

Carr picked up on the sarcasm but made no comment at the time.

"Then have a seat, Erika, and I'll give all of you the details we have at the present. There's little to go on but I'll give you what I have. Kay, you arrived just in time.

"The FBI has been investigating this for over a year and has gotten nowhere. The CIA has been asked by the State Department to follow up with its own investigation."

Carr told his wife what everyone else in the room already knew. The mission entailed searching for evidence that Adolf Hitler and Eva Braun were still alive.

Kay's shock was clearly evident. "We all read in the newspapers that Hitler and Braun committed suicide in his Berlin bunker, Leroy."

"Yes, but bodies were never found. When interrogated by the Russians who took the bunker during the Battle for Berlin, some SS men claimed some charred remains in the bunker courtyard were that of Hitler and Braun but identification was impossible. Stalin told both Churchill and Truman at the Potsdam Conference after the war that he firmly believed Hitler escaped. That's what started all of this. Truman ordered Hoover to investigate."

"I have the FBI documents in this folder," Carr elaborated and pointed to it on his desk. "The folder can't leave this room, but you'll all have a chance to read the documents later this afternoon."

"When do we leave?" Kathryn asked.

"I haven't decided yet. It's not an emergency, just a simple search and gather intelligence mission—low danger risk since action is not required, only information gathering. Maybe you'll leave by the end of the week. We'll see. Sheila is still putting together plans for your transportation once you get to Argentina. Many of these locations mentioned in the FBI report are very remote. The field agents will be Erika, Kathryn, and Kay. Because of their background in the Nazi Party, Erika and Kathryn might be able to open some doors. A lot of Nazis have fled to South America since the war, especially to Argentina because Peron was a huge supporter of Hitler and the National Socialists during the war. Kay will serve as your Spanish interpreter.

"Since this mission is what I would consider low-risk, Al and Major Reid will remain here in D.C. Al has other missions his men are currently working on that need his attention, and Sheila also has some important business to take care of. They'll be available to join you if you need them, but I don't foresee that happening for this simple assignment. (Carr didn't mention it, but Sheila was still recovering from a deep stab wound to her left shoulder suffered during the last mission. Her left arm was still weak).

"Any questions?" Carr asked.

No one responded.

"Good, then report back here at 1330 hours so you can read the FBI documents. I'd like to talk to Al one-on-one. Everyone else is dismissed until 1330 when we'll meet back here for more briefing and to go over the FBI reports."

Everyone else left the room.

"Do you have the report on that guy in Williamsburg that Erika is dating?"

"We're still putting his complete folder together, Leroy, but so far he looks like a straight arrow. He served on the aircraft carrier USS Bunker Hill during the war as a radar operator. As you probably remember, the Bunker Hill was struck by two Kamikazes during the Battle of Okinawa. Six hundred men died. This Nick guy, whose last name is Danvers, received a commendation for helping pull some of his shipmates out of the fires on deck."

"Okay, thanks, Al. Get me the full report when you have it ready. If you don't mind, send in Erika now."

Hodge nodded and left the room. Erika entered a moment later. Carr pointed to a chair.

"Erika, I couldn't help but notice the hesitancy in your voice when I asked you and Kay if you can work together. Give me the skinny. How did your meeting on the veranda go last night?"

"What did Kay tell you?"

"I'm asking you."

Kay had told him nothing about Erika's attempt to intimidate her off of the mission.

"You know how Kay feels about me, Leroy, but it's obvious that she's determined to take part so we'll have no choice but to try and work together."

"As I've mentioned, this should be a simple intelligence gathering assignment; otherwise, I would not have asked Kay to get involved. She has no field training. She's going along as a translator, that's all. I expect you to protect her."

"I knew you'd ask me that."

"Do you have a problem with that?"

"I don't have a problem as long as Kay will take my advice. It will be up to her if she wants to listen to me."

Carr dismissed Erika and Kay entered.

"Kay, when you changed your mind about the mission I assumed things went relatively well when you and Erika talked privately after dinner last night. But I sense there's still quite a lot of tension between you two. Did something happen last night I need to know about?"

"No, nothing happened, Leroy. Our talk went fine."

# Chapter 7

## Annapolis, Maryland
## Next day—Wednesday, 30 July 1947

One of Leroy's and Kay's favorite Chinese dishes was Cashew Chicken and rice so after he left the office that's what he brought home from the *Mandarin House,* their favorite Annapolis Chinese restaurant.

Kay used chopsticks. Leroy didn't have the patience to eat with two small sticks of wood so he always used a fork.

"Have you figured out when we leave for South America, Leroy?"

"Yes, on Monday. That will give everyone some time to prepare. Erika can finish up her training classes at the Farm this week then we'll turn her classes over to another instructor while she's gone. Same goes for Kathryn with her classes at the war college.

"Kay, as I've said, this should be a very low-risk mission, but you'll have to listen to Erika and follow her orders. She knows what's she's doing and she'll be the team leader in the field. Can you do that . . . follow Erika's orders?"

There was a brief pause, but Kay said, "Fine. Whatever you say, Leroy."

"I wouldn't ask you to be involved if I thought you might be in danger," her husband said. "Basically, you'll just accompany Erika and Kathryn around during a normal day and translate Spanish for them with shopkeepers, taxi drivers, waiters, that sort of thing. If Erika and Kathryn enter into anything dangerous you won't be around, and I've asked Erika to protect you."

Her husband had said all the wrong words. First, it sounded as if he thought she was a weakling. She had stood up to Erika Lehmann and to the feared Otto Skorzeny during the war. It hadn't done anything to improve the situation at the time, but it proved to them, and to her, that she was not some hysterical, weak woman.

And the assurance that Erika would protect her was almost funny.

Kay Carr had proved her mettle in England during the war when she was kidnapped by the famous SS commando leader Skorzeny. It had all been arranged by Erika in order to free her husband, Kai, who was one of Skorzeny's men. Kay was eventually exchanged for her husband, who in turn was traded for Kai Faust.

As fate would have it, both Erika and Kai were recruited by Leroy Carr after the war to work for the Americans. Kai was killed on a mission in Poland a year ago.

"I want to be issued a gun, Leroy. You know I've shot handguns and rifles in the past. I want a gun tomorrow so I can spend the rest of the week and weekend target practicing before we leave."

"I don't think a gun is necessary, Kay. You'll never be in a position where you have to use it."

"A gun, Leroy. It will be the middle of the winter in Argentina. Coats and jackets will be required. A handgun will be easy to conceal."

**[same day—the Farm]**

Carr had sent Erika back to the Farm to finish out the week as an instructor. Since she was the best swimmer among the instructors, and because it was mid-summer, she had been assigned to train the plebes in a lake at Camp Perry.

This evening she would say goodbye to Nick in Williamsburg.

# Chapter 8

**Flashback—1938, July**
**At Quenzsee, an Abwehr spy and SS training camp outside Berlin**

Erika Lehmann surpassed everyone in swimming at Quenzsee, instructors as well as fellow plebes. Swimming relaxed her, and most evenings she returned to the lake during her free time, as she did this evening. She changed into a Quenzsee-issued swimsuit inside the boathouse and dove from the small pier into the water. As was also the case most evenings, Kai Faust soon appeared at the lake, knowing he would find Erika here. They had entered training at Quenzsee on the same day; Erika with Abwehr, Kai with the SS. That's when they met.

He always sought her out when their groups trained together. Since the SS contingent at Quenzsee did not study to be spies, Kai had no access to her during her various classroom and laboratory sessions. Generally, their groups came together for the morning obstacle course and the afternoon fight training. It was quite obvious he was pursuing her, and on the rare occasions when they were not being watched by a Quenzsee instructor he had tried to kiss her. Once or twice she had allowed it, other times not.

Erika admitted to herself that she was attracted to him physically, but at present her interest in a relationship was zero. The grueling training schedule at Quenzsee gave her little time to think about anything but the next drill, test or manual to read. When her head hit the pillow at night, she fell asleep within minutes with no dreams of romance.

Kai had been of great help to her the past two months. He was a skilled and fierce fighter, and because of his extra tutelage in hand-to-hand, Erika now easily bested the other women in full-speed bouts, and she was beginning to hold her own with some of the men.

Kai walked out of the boathouse in swimming trunks, dove in, and began swimming toward Erika who had left the water on the opposite shore. She watched him swim and had offered him tips to improve his swimming but so far her coaching yielded only minor results. He was an acceptable swimmer, not outstanding, but the SS were not required to pass the swimming tests given the Abwehr prospects. Kai swam now only because that was the fastest way to reach her on the far shore. Walking around the lake through the high reeds and cattails would take more time, and he knew if he remained in his fatigues and circled the lake she would let him get near then take back to the water just to disappoint him.

True to form, when Faust got within 20 yards of where she stood, Erika walked back into the lake and submerged. He stopped and treaded water, spinning to see where she surfaced. But Erika remained underwater for such a long time he grew concerned and ducked his head to find her. The water was clear enough to see her on the bottom, only 10 feet down. She gripped a rock to stay submerged and watch him. As soon as he saw her, she pushed off the bottom and rocketed toward him. When she broke the surface she laughed.

"When you swim you splash like a Panzer fording a stream," she said.

He reached out for her, but she easily eluded him and kept her distance, teasing. "What is it you want?" She pivoted in the water and headed toward the boathouse pier, backstroking so she could watch him and laugh at his futile attempts to catch her. When Kai finally made it back across the lake, Erika had been out of the water for several minutes and sat on the pier dangling her feet in the water.

As he neared, he looked past her and asked, "Why is your drill master here?"

When she turned to look, her drill master was nowhere to be seen, but then she felt a strong grip on her ankle and was yanked back into the lake. He had her now and drew her to him. They stood on the sandy bottom chest high in the water. His arms and shoulders were as hard as the rock she had gripped at the bottom of the lake. She felt tempted to let him have his way.

"It's getting dark," she said, "and I have a great deal of reading assigned."

He kissed her neck. It took all of her willpower to refuse him. "Let me go, Kai."

His hands held her waist and he left them there, refusing to release her. "Tomorrow is my last day here," he said. "Then I have three days furlough. I found out that if Abwehr recruits pass their tests this week they'll be granted an evening leave Saturday night. Is that true?"

He was right. The first leave since her group arrived in June would be granted this weekend for recruits in good standing.

"It's for only a few hours," she said. "Anyone earning leave has to be back by midnight."

"Will you join me for dinner? But before you answer, you should know I'll happily stand in this water all night with my hands on you until you say *yes.*"

"I don't have a dress with me here appropriate for a dinner out."

"It doesn't matter. I believe your leave will begin at six o'clock that evening?" He had done his research.

"Yes," she said.

◊ ◊ ◊

"How did you find this restaurant?" Erika asked as Kai parked his 1938 Horch Sport Cabriolet. The restaurant was in Genthin, a small town about 20 minutes east of the Quenzsee estate.

"A comrade in my detachment grew up near here and assured me this is a good place. I know a very good restaurant in Potsdam and several in Berlin I would like to take you to, but since we have only a few hours I didn't want to waste half our time driving." He stepped out and came around to open her door. Rain had been forecast for the area, but so far none had fallen.

Once inside, they were shown to a table. The small restaurant was charming rather than elegant, and all but two of the eight tables were occupied. Kai helped Erika remove her coat. Despite the August warmth, she had worn her thin, Quenzsee-issued rain slicker because of the forecast. He laid her jacket over a spare chair and pulled another out for her.

Erika's body was changing. The soft arms and legs of two months ago had grown toned and firm. And despite the vigorous daily

35

exercise, she ate heartily at Quenzsee and had gained weight. She had borrowed a dress, a size 10. She now wished she had a size 12. The red and white cotton summer dress felt tight and revealed more cleavage than Erika would have chosen. She wasn't surprised when she noticed Kai looking at her chest. He noticed her noticing him and looked up quickly, a bit sheepish that she caught him staring. He cleared his throat and looked for something to say.

"Wine?" he asked quickly.

"That would be nice."

He opened the wine list, but knew nothing about wines and admitted it. "You should decide. I'll pick the wrong one." He handed her the list. "Your dress is beautiful."

She smiled. It was just a polka-dot summer dress. "Thank you. You look dashing." He wore his SS parade dress uniform. "You didn't tell me you were an officer. Twenty-one is young for an Untersturmführer."

"Don't be too impressed; I didn't earn it. I was an enlisted man in the Heer but was offered the lieutenant rank to join the SS. Many others have gotten the same offer."

"You surprised me the other day at the lake when you told me your training was finished," Erika commented. "I don't know why, but I assumed SS training lasted as long as ours."

"I wish it did. I'd still see you every day. Most of our training takes place elsewhere. Our Quenzsee program is only six weeks. I asked my group leader and he told me the Quenzsee training program for Abwehr lasts a lot longer."

"Yes, and after Quenzsee I'll have a series of practice missions to complete that will take several months."

"What determines how long you'll be at Quenzsee?"

"Test scores—in both physical training and classroom instruction."

"The long program at Quenzsee, then the practice missions, and add to that the time you've already spent at Tegel—that's a lot of training time."

"And all this is just the initial program that determines if they want to accept me," Erika added. "If accepted, I'm not sure the training ever ends. I'll be sent back to Quenzsee for advanced training and eventually to Potsdam for shortwave transmission school." A waitress approached. "I'll order a red," she told Kai, then ordered a bottle of Spätburgunder. Before the waitress walked away, she left menus.

"My comrade who told me about this place says the Rouladen is very good."

"Ah, that's my father's favorite dish."

"What does your father do?"

"He works at the Ministry of Enlightenment."

Kai was impatient to learn more about her. "Tell me about yourself, Erika. What got you involved with Abwehr?"

"I think my recruitment had a lot to do with the fact I speak Russian, English, and French. I was working at the Seehaus translating foreign radio broadcasts when I was approached."

"How did you learn all those languages?"

"My mother was British and spoke French, so I learned English and French from her. I learned Russian while working at the Seehaus. It seems I have a knack for languages and can pick them up fairly quickly. I know this is very unscientific, but I've always thought my musical background—being able to read music—aides me with languages."

"Interesting. First time I've heard that. So what do your parents think of your move from the Seehaus to Abwehr?"

"My father was not happy when I told him my decision. My mother died last year in America, an auto accident. We lived there for four years. My father served as press secretary to our ambassador in Washington."

"I'm sorry about your mother."

"And your family?" she asked.

"My father was a German hero killed in the Great War. My mother lives in Cologne where I grew up. I have a brother in the Kriegsmarine. Do you have brothers or sisters?"

"No."

The waitress returned with the wine and to take their orders. Erika ordered a Schnitzel, Kai the Rouladen.

"So you are to be one of our Führer's bodyguards," she said as he poured two glasses of the wine.

"Yes. I have actually spoken with the Führer," he said proudly. "He insists on meeting beforehand any man who will undergo training for his personal guard. I met him at the Berghof in Bavaria. Three of us being considered for the Führer's detail were taken there. Our conversation was very brief. He had read the report containing the military service information about my father and told me he fought in some of the same battles. He shook my hand and that was the end of it. The meeting lasted perhaps two minutes."

"That's exciting." Erika didn't tell Kai that her father was a trusted friend of the Führer and that she had visited Adolf Hitler many times, or that she was on friendly terms with Eva Braun. She wondered if Kai knew of Eva. Most Germans had never heard of her, but if he had been to the Berghof perhaps he knew who she was. "Do you know a woman named Eva Braun?"

Kai shook his head. "No. I don't recall the name. Who is she?"

"A friend of mine. Once you are assigned to the Führer I'm sure you'll eventually meet her."

Kai nodded then asked her opinion about a current event much in the news of late. "Do you think the Jews are trying to start a war?"

"I don't know," she answered. "Certainly they are according to the newspapers. My father thinks the Anschluss of Austria last spring will go a long way toward ensuring peace, but he feels problems in Czechoslovakia need to be addressed. Germans living there are treated badly, but Father is confident that the Führer will find a solution, and that should end talk of a possible war."

When their dinner arrived, further talk of politics ceased. They ate slowly and spoke of pleasant things. It turned out that Kai could be quite funny and he made Erika laugh several times. By the time the waitress delivered the strudel, they had been at the restaurant well over two hours.

"I know of a beer hall that's on the way back to Quenzsee; it's in Rossdorf. We have the time. Would you like to stop there?"

"I would love that."

After dessert, as Kai paid for their meal, another customer walked up to their table.

"Untersturmführer," the man said. He held an ink pen and piece of paper. "It is an honor. My son recently turned ten years old and is now in the Hitler Youth. Would you mind signing an autograph for him? I know it will thrill him to have the autograph of an SS officer. His name is Stefan."

Kai took the paper and pen, wrote a brief note to the boy and signed it.

"Thank you, Untersturmführer."

"My best wishes to your son," Kai replied.

As the man walked away, Erika teased, "I didn't realize I shared dinner with a movie star." She thought she noticed him blush slightly.

"That is the first time that has happened to me."

"It won't be the last, I'm sure. A suave young officer who will be one of the Führer's personal escorts—you'll have to fend off the Fräuleins with a stick, their hearts aflutter."

"Suave? Now you're making fun of me."

She smiled.

On the way to the tavern in Rossdorf, as twilight waned, Kai pulled over to put down the convertible top. While he worked, Erika walked down to a shallow brook a few yards from the road, removed her shoes and waded in ankle deep. When he finished he walked down to join her.

"You're always in the water," he said from the edge of the stream. "I think you're part mermaid or the Lorelei of the Rhine who bewitches men and lures them to their doom."

"The Lorelei. I like that." She walked out of the water and put her arms around his neck. "Maybe you're right. You might be doomed."

The kiss lasted ten minutes. The forecasted rain never fell and they spent the rest of their time together by the brook, never making it to the beer hall in Rossdorf.

# Chapter 9

**[Back to Present]**
**Williamsburg, Virginia**
**Friday, 01 August 1947**

Since civilians without clearance were not allowed to enter Camp Perry, Erika always had to drive to Williamsburg to see Nick. Most of his family lived in the Williamsburg area; in fact, Lane's Tavern was a family business owned by Nick's father. Last night they went to a local play in which Nick's female cousin had a part.

Tonight she was tired after spending half of the day in the Farm lake instructing plebe agents in swimming.

Friday was a busy night at Lane's Tavern so Nick would have to work late. Erika sat in her usual place at the end of the bar. As she sipped on a beer while waiting for him to go on break, an obviously inebriated man wearing overalls staggered over and sat down beside her.

"It's your lucky night, sister," he slurred. "You've got me now."

"Go away or it will be your unlucky night." Erika had a small dagger in an ankle sheaf but she knew she wouldn't need it. *Just breaking one of his fingers should take care of the problem.*

Nick was fixing drinks at the other end of the bar, but glanced over and saw what was happening. He sat the bottles down and walked over.

"Ernie, are you making a pest of yourself again?" Nick asked the man.

"What's it to you, Nick? I was just talking to the lady."

Nick looked at Erika. "Do you want to talk to this guy, Erika?" Nick didn't want to interfere if he was wrong that she was being hassled.

"No. I told him to go away. He's drunker than Cootie Brown."

"Okay, scram, Ernie. In fact, scram all the way out the door. It's easy to tell that you've had several too many. See you tomorrow night."

"Up yours, Nick. You're not kicking me out of here." Then he hiccupped.

"Ernie, I kick you out about once a week," Nick said with a grin. "You should be used to it."

"Oh, that's right. I forgot," said Ernie. "Okay, I'll see you tomorrow night, Nick."

Ernie got off the bar stool and almost fell as he headed for the door.

"You're too drunk to drive, Ernie," Nick told him. "Leave your car here and take the bus home."

"Okay, Nick," Ernie slurred.

Nick and Erika looked at each other and laughed.

"He's harmless," Nick said. "Ernie and I went to school together."

"Thanks for saving me," Erika smiled. Unknown to Nick, it was Ernie that he saved. Most men who bothered Erika Lehmann in a bar ended up regretting it from the hospital emergency room.

"I get a twenty-minute break at nine," Nick told her. (It was 8:45).

"Can we go for a short drive?" Erika asked.

"Sure."

Tomorrow morning Erika would report back to D.C. and she was here tonight to tell Nick she was leaving. Of course, she wouldn't be able to tell him why she would be gone. She would have to come up with a cover story—a spy euphemism for a lie.

After Nick went on break and they were in his car, Erika waited until he pulled out of the parking lot.

"Nick, I have a few things to tell you. I know you have to be back in twenty minutes so I'll make it brief. I have a seven-year-old daughter."

"A daughter? Why didn't you tell me? I love kids. When can I meet her?"

"She's staying with my maternal grandparents in London. My husband was killed in a car crash a little over a year ago."

"I'm sorry, Erika. I mean that. So Lehmann is your married name?"

"No, I took back my maiden name after . . . Ken died. I want you to move on with your life, Nick."

"What do you mean 'move on'? You having a daughter doesn't bother me at all. In fact, I think it's great."

"It not just that. I'm being transferred. Today was my last day at Camp Perry, at least for a while."

"Transferred? Why? Where?"

"It seems there is a severe shortage of typists at Fort Hood in Texas. The Army is transferring some typists from other places. Camp Perry is one of those places and I was picked because I'm single."

"This is a . . . temporary thing . . . right?" Nick stuttered.

"I don't know if it's temporary or not. Even if it's not, I have no idea how long I'll be gone."

"We can call each other and exchange letters. Better than that, I'm sure there are plenty of bars around Fort Hood. Bartenders can always find a job."

Erika smiled at him. "Don't be ridiculous, Nick. All of your family is here and your father owns Lane's. Nick, move on. You're young and have too much to offer some lucky girl. You shouldn't wait around for me when I have no idea if I'll be returning."

◊ ◊ ◊

### [late Saturday morning—E Street ]

Since Leroy Carr called her to Washington from her home in Rhode Island, Kathryn Fischer had stayed nights in Sheila Reid's apartment. Now, she and Kay Carr were in the E Street basement target range.

Kathryn's pistol of choice was the Walther PPK 7.65. It was a popular service pistol among the SS and Gestapo and the pistol that Kathryn carried during the war. In fact, the Walther was the pistol that Hitler had purportedly shot himself with in the Führer Bunker.

Erika preferred a Beretta Brevettata 7.65. Both guns were semi-automatics. The magazine of the Walther held seven rounds, the Beretta eight.

Kay Carr chose the Smith & Wesson .38 snub-nose revolver and had spent several hours on Thursday and Friday with Kathryn practicing in the basement gun range. Kathryn was skilled with handguns and a good tutor. Kay wasn't yet hitting bulls-eyes at 25 feet, but she had gotten better from one day to the next. Kathryn also showed her how to dissemble and clean the weapon.

After her goodbye to Nick, Erika spent last night at Camp Perry and drove back to Washington early this morning. The three women were now together on the gun range.

The targets were 25-feet away and were a black silhouette of a man from the waist up. Kathryn went first and placed all of her rounds in the heart area of the torso. Kay went next. Some of her shots landed outside the man, but she managed to place two shots on the outer torso. They wouldn't qualify as kill shots but they would without a doubt slow down the opponent.

Erika was in a bad mood after last night. She and Nick kissed goodbye when they returned to the tavern parking lot and she could see the sadness in his face. She picked up her Beretta and purposely missed the target totally with all eight of her rounds.

Kay couldn't help but to rub it in. "I must be wrong. I thought we were supposed to hit the target."

Erika said, "Oh, is that what we're supposed to do? Excuse my error." She loaded another magazine and fired eight rounds between the silhouette's eyes, all in a close pattern. "Is that better, Mrs. Carr?"

"You just can't help yourself from being a bitch, can you?" Kay said.

"No, I like being a bitch. Especially to someone that has no business going on a CIA mission and endangering us all and the mission."

Kathryn stepped in. "Can we get back to business. We have only an hour on the range then Mr. Carr wants us in his office."


**[one hour later]**

Al Hodge and Sheila Reid were already seated in Carr's office when the women came up from the gun range. Three empty chairs were already in place.

"Ladies, this week Al and I have briefed Kathryn and Kay on the mission extensively. Erika, you've been away finishing up the week at the Farm. When we're done here this morning, stay behind and I'll fill you in on the particulars.

43

"Erika needs a place to stay in D.C. I don't want to spend money on the Mayflower if it can be avoided, so Erika will stay with Sheila and Kathryn will move from Sheila's apartment and spend tonight and tomorrow night with Kay and me at our home. I think this is the best solution, since Erika staying with us might be . . . problematic.

"As I've already said, Erika, Kathryn, and Kay are the field team. Erika is team leader. You all know what that means; you have to obey her instructions. Argentina is only two hours ahead of D.C. in time, so there isn't a huge time zone change like there is with a mission in Europe.

"You three ladies will leave Monday morning from the Baltimore airport on a commercial flight. Al will drive you to the airport. I don't want to fly you down on an Air Force plane. The Argentine government monitors who comes and goes on U.S. military aircraft. You'll fly into Buenos Aires, stay there for one night then be met that next morning by an Argentine asset who works for us. He'll be there to help you with whatever you request of him. He is a pilot and speaks English. All of your travels from Buenos Aires will be by car or the asset's small, privately owned airplane that can land in fields or meadows if the need arises."

# Chapter 10

## Baltimore, Maryland
## Monday, 04 August 1947

Erika, Kathryn, and Kay's flight on Pan American flight 212 was scheduled to depart at 9:00 a.m. Al Hodge picked them up at 5:30 that morning for the two-hour drive to Baltimore. The flight on the Boeing 307 Stratoliner would include a brief stop in Miami to disembark and embark new passengers, then a refueling stop in Panama City before continuing on to Buenos Aires.

Luckily the Stratoliner had a small bar area at the front of the cabin, and as soon as the plane reached altitude and the stewardess announced that seat belts could be unbuckled, all three women immediately headed to the bar before it filled up. It would be a long flight. The lumbering Stratoliner cruised at a mere 180 mph, and with the stops in Miami and Panama City, the 5400-mile flight wouldn't get them to Buenos Aires until tomorrow evening. The main advantage of the Stratoliner was its pressurized cabin, allowing it to fly at 20,000 feet, staying above many of the clouds and therefore out of lower rain, unlike other airliners that had to cruise at much lower altitudes so the air was not too thin for the passengers.

The three women sat together around a small, round table. Each ordered a glass of white wine. It was a long journey and none of them wanted to overdo it with alcohol.

"Erika," said Kay, "I think you and I should call a truce for the sake of the assignment. I'm willing if you are."

Kathryn said, "I think that's a very good idea."

"Kay, I've never had anything against you," Erika said. "In fact, I have always liked you, but you shouldn't be on a field mission. I tried to talk you out of it for your own safety. I can't figure out why Leroy asked you to do it. The CIA has plenty of Spanish speakers with some field experience."

"You didn't try to talk me out of it; you tried to scare me away. But I can answer your question about why my husband asked me to be a part of this. He told me he couldn't trust you to give him complete reports. That will be my job."

"So that's it," Erika smiled. "You'll be spying on me and Kathryn."

"No, I will not be spying on you. I hope to work with you. Leroy just wants to make sure he's kept in the loop."

Kathryn had no idea what Kay meant about Erika trying to scare her away, but she sensed things were becoming uneasy again. "Alright, ladies. Erika you are team leader. Kay you are the boss's wife. That puts me in the middle. I don't want to be the referee for your bouts. We need to ring the bell right now. The fight is over."

"Just give me a chance, Erika," Kay said. The words were hard to utter. She hated Erika, but she was doing her best to call a ceasefire because her husband asked for her help.

Kathryn said, "Erika, I agree with Kay. You should give her a chance."

"What if the shit hits the fan, Kathryn, and she has to react like a real field agent for which she's had no training?"

"I can handle myself," Kay injected.

"Let's all hope you don't have to prove that," Erika replied. "Your life, or ours, might depend on it."

"Okay, enough punches have been thrown. Time to shake hands," Kathryn insisted firmly.

Both hesitated but finally Kay offered her hand across the table. Erika looked at Kay's hand, then at Kathryn, who she loved like a sister. Erika slowly reached over, and she and Kay Carr shook hands.

# Chapter 11

## Buenos Aires, Argentina
## Tuesday, 05 August 1947

When the three-woman CIA team arrived in Buenos Aires it was 58° Fahrenheit, not nearly as cold as they expected being that August was the dead of winter in Argentina. Buenos Aires was on the coast and at low altitude; this contributed greatly to the moderate winter climate.

All three women would billet together during their brief stay in Buenos Aires. Since a small suite was less expensive than three single rooms, Sheila Reid had her assistant book one of these small suites at the Alvear Palace Hotel located in an upscale section of Buenos Aires called Recoleta. The hotel was on Avenida Alvear. Opened in the 1930s, the Alvear Palace was considered by most to be one of the top five hotels in Buenos Aires.

It was 11:00 p.m. Buenos Aires time (9:00 p.m. DC. time) when they checked in. They had gotten some sleep on the plane but all three women were tired after the 36-hour journey. Kay called Leroy at home to let him know that they had arrived then they all went to bed, passing on a late dinner. Erika and Kathryn slept together in a queen size bed. Kay used a small Murphy bed that pulled down from the wall. They had to be in the hotel restaurant for breakfast at 8:00 a.m. It was then and there that they were scheduled to meet their Argentinean asset.

## [next morning—06 August]

Erika and Kathryn rose first. Kathryn took a quick shower, then Erika. When Kay got out of bed fifteen minutes later she put on a robe and walked to the bathroom door. Erika and Kathryn shared the mirror doing their makeup. Erika was nude. Kathryn, with more modesty, had a hotel towel wrapped around her.

Erika saw Kay behind them in the mirror and turned around to face her. She smiled. "I'm sorry Kay, am I shocking you?"

Kay promptly walked out.

"Erika! Why did you do that?" Kathryn said with annoyance.

"Sorry, Kathryn. I couldn't help myself."

Erika's lightheartedness quickly left her. Both she and her beloved father had been close to the Führer before and during the war, and she had developed an even closer friendship with Eva Braun. If the rumors were true and they found them in Argentina she didn't know how she would react.

## [breakfast that morning]

Just before eight o'clock, the two Shield Maidens and Kay sat down in a booth at *La Rosa Blanca,* the Alvear's restaurant.

"We might as well order," said Erika.

"Aren't we going to wait for our contact?" Kay asked.

"No, if he's here in the restaurant he'll be watching us until he feels comfortable to approach."

Everyone was hungry. Their last meal was a light lunch on the Stratoliner yesterday afternoon. Kay translated the menu. They all decided on the El Desayuno Americano, which Kay said meant *the American breakfast* and told Erika and Kay that it included ham, scrambled eggs, biscuits with white gravy, and coffee.

The food was delivered and they all dug in. Erika and Kathryn ate in battlefield style, shoveling in the food quickly. Kay ate more slowly; she couldn't take her eyes off her two partners as they ate like wolves—or slobs—whichever description served better. Kay decided on wolves because the analogy best suited these two ominous women.

Kay wasn't halfway through her breakfast (Erika and Kathryn had finished and had ordered some more eggs) when a man carrying a telephone book and a cup of coffee approached their table.

"¿Estás disfrutando Argentina?" he said to the table. *(Are you enjoying Argentina?)*

"Si, la gente es amistosa," Kay replied. *(Yes, the people are friendly.)*

The prearranged code phrases and the telephone book confirmed that he was their contact.

"Siéntate con nosotros, por favor," Kay said. *(Sit with us, please.)*

48

Kay had to do no more translating. The man slid into the booth beside Kay and now spoke in English.

"My name is Carlos Vilas," he told them. "Mister Carr has instructed me to help you while you're in my country. I was told the team leader is a blonde woman." Since Kathryn and Kay were both brunettes, he looked across the booth at Erika.

"My name is Erika Lehmann and beside me is Kathryn Fischer. We will be using our real names. Did Mister Carr tell you why?"

"Yes, he told me you both have Nazi backgrounds and that should aid you on the assignment."

"Beside you is Kay. She is our Spanish translator; no last name is necessary." That Kay was Leroy's wife would never be divulged to anyone. That was Leroy's order and Erika agreed. It could only serve to make it harder for Kathryn and her to protect Kay.

"I understand, of course," Carlos replied.

The waitress appeared and asked the man about his breakfast order. Carlos told her he was just there for his morning coffee. She refilled his cup.

After the waitress walked away, Carlos handed the telephone book to Erika.

"The telephone book is more than just part of my identification. Mister Carr told me there might be some names in the current Buenos Aires telephone book that perhaps you or Kathryn may recognize."

He told Erika and Kathryn the names. Erika was surprised, but in professional form, she didn't display that emotion.

Erika said, "It looks like we'll be staying in Buenos Aires a little longer."

# Chapter 12

**Flashback—Berlin, March 1942**

A cavernous structure on the Unter den Linden, the Prussian State Opera House dated back to the 19th century. Flaunting Italian marble floors and walls, imported teak archways, and glimmering chandeliers, it had served as the main venue for artistic performances since 1933 when, after the infamous Reichstag fire, the Kroll Opera House was converted for Reichstag use. On the walls of the large, L-shaped reception gallery hung Rembrandt's, Cézanne's, and van Gogh's, lately acquired by the Reich in their jaunt across Europe.

The normally quiet gallery was now loud with prattle from the crowded assembling of German elite. A healthy supply of generals, admirals, and top Party officials filled in spaces around tuxedoed industrialists and financiers who bragged and told vulgar jokes while their gaudily bejeweled wives gossiped. The barons and baronesses huddled in cliques, breaking away only briefly to acknowledge another notable, or shake the hand and smile with condescension at one of the capitalists who sought their company. Erika, dressed in a shiny silver gown with her blonde hair piled high, spotted her father talking to Joseph Goebbels, head of the Reich Propaganda Ministry and her father's boss. She accepted a flute of champagne from a SS waiter she noticed was staring at her breasts, then proceeded to walk toward her father.

Goebbels and Erika's father had both been with Hitler since the early days. But in fact, Karl Lehmann predated even Goebbels in the chronology of Hitler's rise to power. Goebbels did not meet the future Führer until late in 1924, after the latter's release from Landsberg prison. At that time, Goebbels' loyalty belonged to another Nazi leader, Gregor Strasser, and it was not until 1926 that Hitler succeeded in convincing Goebbels that he, and not Strasser, was the one true hope for the Fatherland.

But Erika's father had been at Hitler's side even before the Putsch. Before Joseph Goebbels had even heard of the NSDAP or Adolf Hitler, Karl Lehmann was in Munich taking part in the tavern fights with communists or whoever happened to disagree with Hitler's speech that day. Karl Lehmann had been one of the carriers of the famous blood flag on November 9, 1923. He had been there in front of the Feldherrnhalle when government troops opened fire, killing several of his and Hitler's comrades.

And now Goebbels was her father's boss. Despite this, Erika had never detected any animosity toward Goebbels from her father. For several years during the 1930s, her father was a diplomat serving in a foreign country while Goebbels was home in Germany building the world's most impressive propaganda machine. Her father was a fair man who gave credit to Goebbels for his accomplishments. Karl Lehmann was also a soldier, ready to serve where needed, and if his Führer needed him as Goebbels right-hand man that is where he would serve.

Herrs Lehmann and Goebbels were now closely bound in both work and loyalties. Erika had always thought no two men could be more alike in ideology and unlike in appearance than her father and Joseph Goebbels. Her father was over six feet tall, well built and handsome. Goebbels was a foot shorter than Erika's father, a frail one-hundred pounds, and he walked with a limp. But their loyalty to their country and to the man who now symbolized it was complete and unquestionable. Goebbels and Lehmann rose with Adolf Hitler and his movement. They were there in the obscure days of the struggle—old comrades whom the Führer trusted.

Karl Lehmann spotted his daughter as she approached.

"Erika, of course you know Dr. Goebbels."

"Of course," Erika smiled at the diminutive man who was reaching for her hand. "How are you, Herr Doktor?"

"Much better now, Erika," the grinning Goebbels said with a smile. "I always feel younger when I am in your presence." Goebbels offered the comment for protocol's sake, but nonetheless he seemed reluctant to relinquish her hand. Erika was aware of Goebbels' reputation for philandering. A reputation that was justly deserved.

The activity that caught Erika's eye involved a group of uniformed SS men who had entered the great hall and milled around one of the entrances. Others also noticed the activity and those who smoked looked for the nearest place to extinguish their cigarettes. No one smoked in the presence of Adolf Hitler.

As if by instinct, a receiving line quickly formed. At a trot, a plump, heavily bejeweled wife of one of the industrialists rudely bumped past Erika, dragging her husband by the arm and admonishing him to hurry for a better place in line.

Those with daily access to Hitler, and personal friends such as Karl Lehmann, had no need to enter the receiving line. The line was a reward for the loyal German elite lucky enough to be invited to such an affair. For many of them this was a once in a lifetime opportunity. Those who shook the Führer's hand tonight would further enhance their privileged status back home tomorrow.

An SS officer with the rank of colonel entered the room and stood at the head of the line.

"Ladies and Gentlemen," the colonel announced loudly and formally. "Count Galeazzo Ciano, Foreign Minister of Italy, and Countess Ciano."

A polite applause followed as the Italian and his wife entered and walked slowly down the line. The Italians nodded politely and shook hands.

With the Cianos halfway down the receiving line the SS colonel added: "Ladies and Gentlemen, the Führer of Germany, Adolf Hitler."

Upon hearing the words, Erika noticed the attention of everyone in the receiving line turn away from Ciano and his wife. All heads stared at the entry way. Even those in line who were next to shake hands with the Italians could not keep from turning their eyes toward where Hitler was supposed to appear. There was a delay, as if the SS colonel had spoken too soon, but in a moment Adolf Hitler appeared in the doorway.

The applause was much louder and sustained much longer this time. The German guests made no pretense about whom they revered. Accompanying Hitler was his ever-present entourage. Erika spotted Martin Bormann who walked to the side and a step behind Hitler. This made her remember a time at the Berghof when she overheard Heinrich Himmler talking to her father. Himmler had referred sarcastically to Bormann as "the Führer's fat shadow."

Hitler was in uniform. He had not worn civilian clothes in public since the outbreak of the war. The leader of the German Reich wore black pants and a white tunic with the bright red Nazi party arm band. Pinned on Hitler's tunic was the Iron Cross first class he had been awarded for heroic duty as a corporal in the first war. It was the same type of medal Erika's father had been awarded. Hitler's shirt was white, his tie black. Expressionless, Hitler stepped toward the receiving line.

For as long as Erika had known him, Hitler had struggled with his hair. He seemed to have less trouble conquering France than an unruly cowlick that refused to be slicked down like the rest of his black hair. And many times she had noticed Hitler brushing back a wedge of hair from off his forehead. As she watched Hitler now, Erika saw him brush back that same troublesome hair before he began shaking hands.

Hitler worked steadily through the receiving line. He took little interest in the people who kowtowed as he passed. He rarely made eye contact with those whose hands he shook. When he reached the fat lady who had dragged her husband, Erika thought the woman would swoon when Hitler took her hand. Hitler seemed not to notice. When the end of the line was reached and the last hand shaken, Hitler spoke briefly to the Cianos before turning away to whisper something to Bormann and another aide.

Apparently responding to some chore assigned them, Bormann and the aide left the room. The Führer now stood alone in the midst of the crowd, his hands clasped behind his back. As Hitler slowly turned, he spotted Goebbels standing with Karl Lehmann and Erika. Goebbels called on Hitler almost daily with Reich business, but it had been several months since Hitler had seen Karl Lehmann and the drab expression on Hitler's ashen face seemed to change. The eyes brightened a bit. Hitler started toward them so they walked toward him in response.

"Good evening, mein Führer," Goebbels offered his hand.
Hitler nodded at Goebbels and shook his hand, but he quickly turned his attention to Karl Lehmann.

"It is good to see you, Karl." Hitler clasped Lehmann's extended right hand and shook it vigorously.

"Thank you, mein Führer," Lehmann responded. "It is always a pleasure to see you, I assure you."

Hitler turned toward Erika. She had always considered Hitler's piercing blue eyes the outstanding feature of a face quite ordinary. But the eyes—they were so blue they appeared fluorescent. Those eyes now looked into Erika's.

"Hello, Erika."

Hitler clasped Erika's hand in both of his, but before she could return his greeting he looked at Karl Lehmann.

"Karl, your daughter looks more like her mother every time I see her."

"I agree, mein Führer," Karl Lehmann said.

"Thank you, mein Führer," Erika said again. She considered Hitler's comment the most sincere compliment she had received all evening because she knew the man who offered it had no ulterior motives for flattery like Joseph Goebbels.

"Come," Hitler said to Karl Lehmann. "You and your daughter will join me in my box tonight." He offered his arm to Erika.

Operas attended by Hitler started when and only when the Führer decided it was time to start. Sometimes an impatient Hitler would enter his box an hour before the scheduled curtain time. If so, that is when the opera started and the patrons, players, and orchestra knew to be ready. Likewise, if the Führer was busy and running behind, the curtain might go up two hours late. Hitler now nodded to yet another aide who somehow knew this meant curtain time.

With Erika on his arm and Karl Lehmann and the Italian guests of honor alongside, Hitler made his way slowly out of the great hall. As they passed the other guests, some women in the crowd looked on with envy, others with contempt at the young woman on the Führer's arm. *Who is this young girl who receives such favor?*

The same SS colonel who earlier had announced the arrival of the Cianos and Hitler now proclaimed that the performance would begin shortly. The other guests began filing out of the great hall behind Hitler. Each guest took a handful of throat lozenges from one of several crystal bowls placed on marble pedestals by the archways (it was the height of rudeness to cough during a German opera—even one not attended by the Führer).

The Führer Box at the Prussian State Opera House jutted out over the theater's main floor. As in many opera houses, several of these private boxes ringed the perimeter. The occupants of these boxes were the top echelon of the Reich. Joseph Goebbels had a private box as did Herman Göring and Heinrich Himmler, but the Führer Box was specially modified. Larger than the other boxes, it had a separate entrance. The Führer was prone to leave suddenly if the performance, or a visiting luminary sharing his box, bored him.

The opera was Richard Wagner's *Die Walküre*. Well known was Hitler's admiration for the German composer and, although Hitler had seen this opera dozens of times, he never tired of the brooding Germanic gods and Wagner's loud, crashing music. Erika enjoyed *Die Walküre*, although her favorite Wagnerian opera was *Parsifal*. Like Hitler, Erika preferred German opera, which emphasized the story and the orchestra, over Italian, which she felt concentrated too much on the voice of one lead singer and not the music and choreography.

When they reached the Führer Box, Hitler insisted that Erika sit directly on his left. Karl Lehmann sat beside his daughter. Countess Ciano sat on Hitler's right, between the German leader and her husband. Martin Bormann sat toward the back of the box, almost unnoticeable among several SS guards who stood in the shadows.

This was the first opera Erika had ever attended with the Führer. As they waited for the curtain to rise, her father and Hitler briefly recalled a 1934 festival in Bayreuth they both attended along with Richard Wagner's daughter-in-law, Winifred Wagner. The event was a special celebration of the famous German composer's life.

"Those were the days, Karl," said Hitler. Erika felt the words were said with a certain yearning.

"Yes, mein Führer," agreed Karl Lehmann. "Those were the days."

The curtain rose. On stage a wounded Siegmund, pursued by enemies, sought shelter in Sieglinde's forest hut. Erika thought briefly about asking Hitler of Eva Braun's welfare but considered it much too forward. These things were not discussed with Adolf Hitler. Moreover, the thundering orchestra did not lend itself to spectator conversation.

The scene on stage moved to Valhalla, where the god Wotan directed his Valkyrie daughter, Brünhilde, to defend Siegmund against the vengeful Hunding. In the Führer Box, Erika glanced at Hitler and the Cianos. Hitler stared at the stage, a glassed-over look in his eyes. The Cianos seemed bored. Most Italians considered German opera second rate to their own. Mussolini's daughter thought the pounding drums and crashing cymbals of a Wagnerian opera an assault on the senses. Also, the countess was angry that Hitler seemed to take little interest in her and her husband, instead concentrating his attention on the young German woman.

After the final curtain, Hitler drew Karl Lehmann aside and talked briefly as the entourage exited the box. Hitler shook Erika's hand then left with the Cianos and the rest of the human convoy through a special exit. The countess was no doubt glad to be rid of the young German beauty.

Outside, Erika's white fur coat guarded her against the cold Berlin night. The same Wehrmacht sergeant who had earlier driven them to the opera house now held open the back door of the black Mercedes for Karl Lehmann and his daughter. Waiting his turn amid a parade of other chauffeur-driven vehicles, the sergeant guided the car out onto the Unter den Linden.

## Chapter 13

**[Back to Present]**
**Buenos Aires**
**Wednesday, 06 August 1947**

After their initial meeting with Carlos (their Argentinean CIA asset) at breakfast that morning Erika told him their departure from Buenos Aires would be delayed for at least another day.

There were two names in the Buenos Aires telephone book that Erika recognized, one of those two men Kathryn also knew. The third man on the list Erika didn't know but Kathryn did. The fact that their names were in the phone directory was a surprise, but then there had yet to be any organized hunt for former Nazis. Add to that the fact that Peron refused to grant any extradition requests apparently made the men feel safe enough to list their names in the city's telephone book.

Lukas Voight, like Erika's husband, Kai, had been a Skorzeny commando. She knew Lukas and his wife well. They had been friends, going out to dinner together and visiting each other's homes in Berlin regularly.

Ernst Roth had been an Abwehr administrator at the Quenzsee training camp. Erika didn't know him as well as she knew Kai's fellow commando, but she had spoken to Roth if it concerned the business at hand during the four times she was at Quenzsee for various levels of training. Kathryn had also trained at Quenzsee and therefore knew Roth.

The third man, Otto Bergmann, was Gestapo. Kathryn had never worked a case with him during the war but they knew each other from office meetings and passing each other coming and going.

Erika wanted to visit Lukas Voight first. They wasted no time; not even returning to their suite after breakfast. Carlos had a car and knew the city well. He pulled his car up to the hotel's valet station and all three women got in. Erika ordered Kay to sit in the back seat alongside her. Kathryn would ride in the front seat beside the driver.

The car was an American Checker Cab. These taxis had been purchased from the United States before the war and were quite common in Argentina, especially in Buenos Aires.

"Carlos," Kathryn said, "I commend you for this type of car. A taxi is much less conspicuous sitting parked on the street with a driver than a normal sedan."

"It was Mister Carr's idea," Carlos replied. "When he let me know he was sending you, he sent me the funds to buy it. It was built in 1938 and has over 180,000 miles on it. But I took it in for a complete tune-up and new tires. It should do okay for us."

"Kay," Erika said as Carlos pulled out on the Avenida Alvear, "we won't need a Spanish interpreter if we find these men. We'll talk to them in German. You'll stay in the car with Carlos. Carlos will park on the street and wait for Kathryn and me. That's why I have you in the backseat. A parked taxi with a passenger in the back draws no suspicion."

Kay nodded, and was proud of her husband who came up with the taxi cab idea that now seemed very logical. At the same time, she now knew the only reason Erika had brought her along at all today was to serve as a mannequin. If Carlos' taxi was parked on the street without a passenger, others might walk up and want to hire the cab.

Kay's thoughts were confirmed when Erika said to their asset, "Carlos, while you wait for Kathryn and me, no one should approach you for a ride because you have a passenger. If someone does, tell them the lady in the backseat is waiting for two friends for a shopping trip."

"Very good," Carlo responded.

The Buenos Aires telephone book listed Lukas Voight as living on Avenida de Mayo. That avenue included several blocks of apartment buildings. All were whitewashed and indistinguishable aside from their respective addresses printed in large black numbers over the entrance. Finally, Carlos slowed down and parked on the street in front of one.

"This is the address," he said. "They don't include apartment numbers in our city's telephone book, but you can get the apartment number from the mailboxes in the entrance way inside the front door."

Erika and Kathryn got out of the car and went inside. The name 'L. Voight' was on a mailbox, apartment 334. The building had no elevator so they took the stairs. They were forced to wend their way through several children playing on the steps. On the third floor they found apartment 334. Erika knocked on a blue door (each door was a different color).

It took a moment then a pretty blonde about Erika's and Kathryn's age (late twenties) answered the door.

"Hello, Anna," Erika said.

It took the woman a moment, then a scream of joy. "Erika!"

The women hugged and kissed cheeks on the threshold. Anna seemed overcome. All the conversation was in German. "You can't imagine how long it's been since I've seen any old friends. But where are my manners? Come in."

Kathryn had stood back watching the scene.

"Anna, this is my friend, Kathryn."

"Come in, Kathryn," Anna said. "Any friend of Erika's . . . as they say. Lukas is at work, but I'll fix some coffee and we'll do our catching up. Please have a seat. You and Kathryn will stay for dinner, of course."

Erika and Kathryn sat down on the sofa. It was only early afternoon.

"We can't stay that long, Anna, but I would like to take you and Lukas to dinner tonight. What time does he normally get home?"

"Around six o'clock."

"What is Lukas doing for a living?" Erika asked.

"He works at a factory that makes diesel engines for locomotives."

"Sounds like a good job."

"It pays the bills. Erika, I'm pregnant," Anna said with a huge smile.

"That's wonderful, Anna!" Erika hugged her.

"Yes, congratulations," Kathryn added.

"Then dinner it is?" Erika asked.

"That will be wonderful. Lukas will be overjoyed to see Kai."

"It will be just me and Kathryn, I'm afraid. Kai is not here with me."

"Oh?"

"I'll tell you everything tonight. You pick the restaurant."

"There are several German restaurants here in Buenos Aires," said Anna. "One of them in particular Lukas and I especially enjoy. It's called the Landshut Festhalle. If you didn't know better you'd swear you were in Bavaria. I don't know the exact address, but it's near the zoo, and the address is in the telephone directory, of course."

"I'm sure our cab driver will know where it is. It sounds wonderful, Anna. Kathryn and I will meet you there. What time would work best for you and Lukas?"

"Perhaps around 7:30?"

"We'll see you there."

◊ ◊ ◊

The next stop that afternoon was the address listed for Ernst Roth, Erika and Kathryn's former supervisor at Quenzsee. He lived on Calle de Larrea. Here again, a long row of apartment buildings with similar facades lined the street. After four flights of stairs this time, and after knocking several times, there came no answer. For a moment Erika thought about kicking in the door, but this would not fit in with their cover story they would present to Roth, so they left assuming he was probably at work like Lukas Voight. They would call again tomorrow.

Otto Bergman, Kathryn's former Gestapo colleague, Erika did not know at all so Kathryn took the lead. According to the telephone directory, Bergmann lived in a small, modest hotel on the Calle de Austria. From what they had seen so far, both of the Shield Maidens thought it a fitting name for a street in Buenos Aires if it were a name other than Spanish. The number of Germans in this city was substantial.

As with Roth, there was no response after Kathryn knocked several times. Unlike when they got no response to their knocks on Roth's door, this time they decided to enter and search the apartment. Kathryn had brought her Gestapo lock picking kit. She inserted two different shaped, thin metal pins into the door's lock, jimmied them around for a moment while Erika kept a lookout in the hallway. In a moment the door unlocked and the women walked into Bergmann's room.

"Clever, Kathryn, having your Einbruchsset (burglar kit) with you," Erika said.

"I always have it on me in case I lock myself out of my hotel room."

Erika laughed quietly.

The room was a mess. It had been ransacked. Desk and cabinet drawers were open and contents had been thrown on the floor. Erika noticed that the hotel phone cord had been cut. Toppled furniture lay upside down.

They found the corpse of Otto Bergmann in the dry bathtub. His throat had been slit.

Kathryn, the police detective, checked the body for warmth and rigidity.

"There's no water in the tub that might delay a body from cooling." Kathryn bent the joints in the body's fingers. "Rigamortis has started but is minimal. My best estimate is he's been dead less than twelve hours, Erika."

The two women backtracked, wiping away fingerprints from anything they had touched. Kathryn turned the door knob lock from the inside to its locked position and they quickly left the scene, leaving it as they had found it.

# Chapter 14

## Buenos Aires
## Same day—Wednesday, 06 August 1947

This evening Kay was left behind. Erika ordered her not to leave the hotel as she wasn't sure the Buenos Aires streets were safe after dark. Leroy had asked her to protect Kay. She would try. A Spanish translator would not be needed tonight, and Erika knew the safest place for Kay was in the hotel.

"Kay, since it's your job to update Leroy on this mission, call him this evening and tell him Ernst Roth was not at home when we called on him. Also tell him that Kathryn and I are going to dinner with Lukas Voight and his wife tonight. Oh, and one more thing, Otto Bergmann has been murdered."

◊ ◊ ◊

Carlos dropped off Erika and Kathryn at the Landshut Festhalle a few minutes before 7:30 p.m. He would not wait for them. Erika had decided that a taxi waiting for what might turn out to be a long dinner might seem suspicious, as if the riders were either important people or rich. That wasn't a good recipe for remaining inconspicuous. She told Carlos to go home to his family after he pulled up in front of the Festhalle and she would call him tomorrow when he was needed. She and Kathryn would take another taxi back to the hotel.

Erika's husband Kai's old comrade, Lukas Voight, and his wife Anna were already seated when Erika and Kathryn entered the restaurant. Anna spotted them coming through the door. She stood up and waved wildly so they would see her. Erika and Kathryn walked to their table. Lukas stood when they got there.

"Frau Faust," said Lukas (it was Kai's surname), "Anna told me of your visit. I can't tell you how wonderful it is to see you!"

"I share your feelings, Lukas." They exchanged the European kiss on the cheeks. "But no more of this formality. Call me Erika, as you used to do."

"Of course," he said.

Erika and Kathryn sat down at the Voight's table.

"This is my friend, Kathryn," said Erika to Lukas. Anna and Kathryn had met that afternoon. Lukas shook her hand.

The Landshut Festhalle would remind one of Munich's Hofbräuhaus. It was much smaller than the famous Munich beer hall that took up nearly two city blocks. But, like the Hofbräuhaus, the Buenos Aires beer hall had a dome ceiling with German-themed murals, and lots of dark-stained wood highlights. There was a center stage for a German brass band. Although no one was on the stage at the moment, it was obvious that the band was playing that night. Trumpets, trombones, and a tuba lay in open cases. An assembled drum set sat at the back of the platform.

Both Caucasian and Latin Beer Fräuleins waited tables, all wore colorful dirndls.

As they all sat down, Lukas' first question was, "Anna told me Kai is not with you, how is he?" Both Lukas and Anna had learned some basic Spanish, but neither spoke English. The conversation tonight would be in German. This was not unusual in the Festhalle where a major portion of its clientele were Germans who had come to South American after the war for whatever reasons. Some had been innocent civilians who lost their homes in the bombings. Some had fled Germany because their name was on one of the war crimes tribunal lists.

Erika had decided not to tell Lukas that Kai was killed last year; at least, not tonight.

"Kai is still in Germany at the denazification camp in Darmstadt with Otto Skorzeny."

Lukas shook his head. "I knew they were still holding Obersturmbannführer Skorzeny. I didn't know Kai was still being detained."

"As you know," Erika said, "the British and Americans automatically send anyone with the blood tattoo to the camps." Unlike soldiers in the Wehrmacht, Heinrich Himmler required members of the SS to have their blood type tattooed inside their upper left arm.

This allowed the Allies easy identification. "How did you avoid this, Lukas?"

"I didn't. I was at the camp in Garmisch for fourteen months. When Obersturmbannführer Skorzeny was acquitted of war crimes, the Americans let me go. I'm surprised Kai is still being detained. Are you able to communicate with him?"

"No, I haven't heard from Kai in over a year."

"The man who, with his wife, started and owns this beer hall was not SS," Lukas said. "He was a tank driver in the Wehrmacht. He was held for only two weeks. It's that damn Totenkopf (Death's Head) that gave us all in the SS a stigma we'll have to live with for the rest of our lives. SS like Kai and me, who were Liebstandarte-SS, were just soldiers. It's the Totenkopf-SS that ran the concentration camps where the abuses happened. The dirty bastards."

Anna was glad the Beer Fräulein showed up for their drinks order. She had heard her husband rant about the Totenkopf often and it had ruined other dinners. They gave the waitress their beer order—a large pitcher of dark Warsteiner from Bavaria.

For Erika, she was glad she had decided to not tell Lukas about Kai's death. The two men were friends and comrades-in-arms. It would have served to only upset him further, and she and Kathryn were visiting the three men in the telephone book on a mission. Otto Bergmann was now out of the picture. What did the other two know, if anything, about the rumors of Adolf Hitler not dying in the bunker?

The waitress was a buxom blonde who spoke German with an Austrian accent.

"I wonder where she comes from in Austria?" Erika asked after she walked away.

"She's from Linz," Anna replied. "Her name is Crimhild."

"I'm quite surprised Warsteiner is available," Kathryn commented. "I have to assume the brewery escaped the bombs."

Lukas said, "The beer hall owner told us the Warsteiner brewery suffered minor damage, but was repaired quickly." He filled all their steins, leaving plenty of foam as most Germans prefer.

"I'm surprised a Wehrmacht tank driver could afford a place like this," Kathryn said. "It's beautiful. Anna told us this afternoon that we would feel like we're back in the Fatherland."

"His wife's parents died in the Hamburg bombings," Lukas responded. "They were quite wealthy. She was an only child and inherited everything. If we're ready to order we don't need menus. Anna and I know the menu by heart. There are not that many choices. Is everyone open to sausages? They offer a family-size plate of sausages with Bratwurst, Knockwurst, and Mettwurst. It comes with Blaukraut and fried apples. Anna and I think it's very good."

Erika and Kathryn agreed that it sounded delicious. Lukas managed to get Crimhild's attention in the busy beer hall and ordered the meal and another pitcher of Warsteiner Dunkel.

Lukas turned his attention to Kathryn. "So you are Erika's friend. You sound like a Berliner."

"Yes, both my sister and I are from Berlin. She died during the war."

"I'm very sorry to hear that," Lukas said sincerely. "How did you escape the Russians?"

"I didn't. I was captured but managed to escape when I ducked into the trees during a forced march to the Elbe. There was a line of us over a mile long. Luckily for me the Soviets could not keep their eyes on all of us every minute. A few others also managed to make it into the forest."

Kathryn had indeed been captured by the Red Army, but the escape story was a fabrication. Erika had rescued her. Kai had never revealed to any of his comrades what his wife really did during the war. That information was top secret. Otto Skorzeny eventually found out that Erika was a spy, but that wasn't until late in the war. Erika was certain that Lukas knew nothing about her service for Abwehr.

"Are you a war widow, Kathryn?" Anna asked. "Like so many German women."

"No, I was in the Gestapo."

Anna's jaw dropped and Lukas stared at her.

"Kathryn was a police detective in Berlin," Erika added for clarification. "Her only duties concerned investigating local civil crimes. She had nothing to do with the abuses attributed to the Gestapo, but she bares that cross, just like you do, Lukas, as former SS."

Crimhild delivered the food and another pitcher of beer.

"I was unaware the Gestapo had female detectives," Lukas said as everyone stabbed sausages from the common plate and scooped up their cabbage and fried apples.

"I was an officer," Kathryn replied.

"She's being modest," Erika interjected. "Kathryn was a Kriminalkommissar."

"You were a major?" Lukas seemed surprised.

Kathryn nodded her head as she cut into a Knockwurst.

"That impressive," he said.

"Lukas, I also have to tell you something about what I did during the war," Erika confessed. "I was a spy for Admiral Canaris. I had missions in Spain, England, and America during the war. I know Kai never mentioned this to you."

The dinner was becoming one big surprise after the other for Lukas and Anna Voight.

"A spy for Abwehr?" Lukas reacted. His tone indicated it was more of an exclamation that a question. "During the war, most of us heard rumors about a female Abwehr uber spy codenamed *Lorelei.* Was she real? Did you ever meet her?"

Kathryn stepped in. "Untersturmführer Voight, you're sitting across the table from *Lorelei."*

◊ ◊ ◊

After the initial shock of both Erika's and Kathryn's truthful revelations wore off from Lukas and Anna Voight, Erika continued. "Kathryn is on wanted lists in Germany, as are all the members of the Gestapo, especially officers. My name is on wanted lists in the United States." Both claims were true, but because of Leroy Carr and the CIA, the United States protected them both. Erika could not, of course, reveal that she and Kathryn both now worked for the CIA. Now the cover story lies would begin. This was the dirtiest part of being a spy in Erika's opinion, the necessity to lie to friends and family.

"Because of our backgrounds during the war," Erika said, "Kathryn and I came to South America for the same reason you did—to hopefully build a new life. The Odessa helped us get here."

The Odessa was an organization of Nazis and Nazi sympathizers who aided SS members and other wanted Nazis to flee to South America. Most ended up in Argentina, but there were a substantial number of former Nazis in Paraguay. Like Argentina, Paraguay's leaders were affable to fascists and that country also refused extradition requests.

Lukas nodded. "Yes, the Odessa also helped me and Anna."

Erika would like to know more about Odessa, but that was not her mission.

"Lukas," Erika said. "Both Kathryn and I have heard rumors that the Führer did not die in the bunker below the Reichstag. Have you heard these rumors?"

"Yes."

Erika continued, "My father was a close friend to the Führer and Eva Braun was a friend of mine (this was true).

"I didn't know about you and Fräulein Braun; few of us even knew about her at all during the war. Of course, we all knew of Karl Lehmann of the Propaganda Ministry, and we knew he was an old colleague of the Führer since the early days in the 1920s."

"That's right," Erika said. "My father and the Führer were close friends. If the Führer and Eva are indeed alive and here in South America, I'd like to visit them. Do you have any information about any of the rumors? I'm Eva's friend, an acquaintance of the Führer, and I'm asking you as Kai's wife and a loyal Party member. I'm sure the Führer and Eva would welcome my visit."

"Erika, I have no direct knowledge about any of the rumors," Lukas conceded. "But I know someone who might be able to help you. He lives here in Buenos Aires. He was Gestapo. His name is Otto Bergmann."

That was the end of the Hitler conversation. Erika didn't tell Lukas that she and Kathryn had found Bergmann murdered in his apartment earlier that day.

The rest of their time at the Festhalle was spent on finishing the meal, sharing a third pitcher of beer, and small talk about old, happier days in the Third Reich during a time when they were all still true believers.

# Chapter 15

**Buenos Aires**
**Next day—Thursday, 07 August 1947**

Erika and Kathryn had not left the Landshut Festhalle until 11:00 last night. After everyone finished dinner, both found themselves enjoying the time spent with Lukas and Anna, former comrades of the cause. Two more pitchers of beer were ordered, making a total of five. This amounted to over a pitcher apiece.

This morning neither Erika nor Kathryn arose from bed with a headache. Pure German beer did not cause next morning headaches for most people because of the Reinheitsgetbot, the German beer purity laws dating back to 1516. Yet, even though the Reinheitsgebot saved them from a harsh hangover, both women were a little sluggish this morning, as would be expected after consuming an ample amount of any kind of alcohol.

After all three women were up and dressed, Erika briefed Kay about the dinner with Lukas Voight. There wasn't much to report. Kay called Leroy to tell him that Lukas had heard the rumors swirling about Hitler escaping the bunker and making his way to Argentina, but Voight considered them no more that that—rumors, and he knew nothing more.

When Kay got off the telephone, the plan for today was discussed.

Kathryn, the former police detective who had investigated murders for the Gestapo, spoke first. "We need to find out who killed Otto Bergmann, or at least if there are any suspects. If that's not possible, we at least need to know the motive behind his murder. He was a former comrade of mine so it shouldn't be suspicious to the police for me to inquire. I'll go to the precinct that covers the area where Bergmann lived and see what I can find out."

"Good," said Erika.

"I'll need Kay as a translator."

Both Erika and Kathryn looked at Kay. A poker face was Kay's reaction. She refused to let the other two women, especially Erika, sense her nervousness.

"Fine," Erika said. "You can have Carlos and his taxi today. I'll hire another cab and see if I can find Ernst Roth."

◊ ◊ ◊

Kathryn and Kay walked through the front door of the Recinto Veinte (20th precinct) police building at 11:00 a.m. This was the precinct whose jurisdiction included the Calle de Austria area where Otto Bergmann lived. They reported to the front desk sergeant.

"Sir, I'd like to report a missing person," Kathryn told him.

"No entiendo Inglés," the sergeant said gruffly (I don't understand English).

Kay translated to Spanish. The policeman handed her a form to fill out. Someone stood behind the two women so the sergeant told them move to the side while they filled out the form. Kay did the writing in Spanish, asking Kathryn how she should respond to each question. She filled in Kathryn's real name as Kathryn instructed her to do and the missing person name Otto Bergmann.

"There is a question here about your relationship to the missing person," Kay whispered to Kathryn.

"Write that I'm an old friend of Otto and that we were both Gestapo police detectives in Berlin during the war."

Kay was taken aback. "You're sure you want me to write that?"

"I'm sure. It's the only way we'll get any information."

"That, or prison," Kay replied.

"Not in this country, Kay. Just please write what I ask you to write."

When the form was filled out and the other person had left, Kay handed the paperwork to Kathryn. She stepped back in front of the sergeant and handed it to him. He read it quickly, then paused and looked up at her.

"Gestapo?" he asked. Kay didn't have to translate.

"Si," Kathryn answered on her own.

The sergeant summoned another police officer who led the women to an interrogation room where they sat by themselves for nearly an hour.

"What's going on, Kathryn?" Kay asked at one point.

"Nothing to be concerned about, Kay. Just relax."

Eventually, two men entered the room and closed the door behind them.

One of them sat down across the table.

"I'm Capitán Juan Zapatero." He did not bother to identify the lower ranking policeman who stood by the door holding a folder.

"I speak some English," he said in English, "but it is not well. A translator you have I was told. Who is who?"

"I'm Kathryn Fischer and this is my translator Kay Becker. She's an American here in Buenos Aires visiting some Argentinean friends. She studied Spanish in college and spent a semester in this country as an exchange student. She made friends during that time. I met Kay in a cantina here in your city and asked her if she would translate for me today." (Becker was Kay's maiden name and the name on her forged passport).

"'Becker' is a German name, but she's American. It doesn't bother her that you were Gestapo?"

"No, Kay has had bad experience with Jews in the United States."

Kay almost choked on the lie but held herself steady.

"I see," the captain turned to Kay and asked. "So you don't admire Jews?"

"There are some good Jews, but many problem ones," Kay tried to keep the cover even though her own words made her nauseas. "My German roots go back centuries. We have many relatives in Germany. Many in my immediate family in the United States were members of the German-American Bund before the war."

The German-American Bund was a legal organization in America in the 1930s made up of Americans who supported Hitler and Nazi ideals. It was outlawed after the U.S. entered the war after Pearl Harbor.

Kathryn had to admire Kay's creativity. Leroy's wife had come up with that explanation off the cuff.

"Yes, Jews can be a problem," Zapatero agreed. "We have very few here in Argentina because we discourage their entry into our country. The Americans can learn something from us."

Kay nodded her head. "Indeed."

"I'm not familiar with that last word."

"En efecto," Kay said.

He nodded and said, "I will speak Spanish now so I make no mistakes." Kay translated from here on out.

"Before I continue, I'd like to see your passports," Zapatero said.

Both handed them over and he confirmed the names. Kathryn Fisher had a Swiss passport, which did not surprise Zapatero. He had seen many passports of former Gestapo and SS issued from Switzerland or Italy, and the American passport confirmed Kay Becker's name.

"I assume Odessa made this Swiss passport for you," he stated to Kathryn.

"Yes."

"So tell me why you are looking for Otto Bergmann. I read your missing persons report. What exactly was your relationship with him? You claim Bergmann was in the Gestapo. We did not know this. Give details."

Kathryn began, "During the war, Otto and I both served as detectives at 8 Prinzalbrechtstrasse, Himmler's headquarters in Berlin (this was true). Both of us investigated civil crimes: robbery, burglary, rape, and murder."

Zapatero stopped her right there. "You served as a homicide detective?"

"That's right."

The captain flagged over the silent man by the door who held a folder, took it from him, and tossed it across the desk to Kathryn.

"Your friend is not missing," Zapatero told her. "He's in the morgue. Someone murdered him. At this point, we're considering it a run of the mill burglary of his apartment that he stumbled in on. In that folder is the current case report. When you mentioned Bergmann was Gestapo, this perked my interest. In the last six weeks four other former Gestapo members have been murdered here in Buenos Aires along with two former SS members."

"Do you think these killings are Jewish reprisals?" Kathryn asked.

"That would be impossible to comment on from what we know now. From putting together the few clues we have, we think they were silenced for some information they possessed. All of the victims apartments were ransacked but nothing of value was taken as far as we know after questioning wives, sweethearts, what have you—people who lived with or knew the victim well. It leads us to believe the killer was looking for something specific. Unfortunately, on Bergmann's part, it appears he had no close relationships so our information on his case is sketchy."

"Any fingerprints?" Kathryn asked.

"Yes, some, but none we can identify. If the killer or killers committed previous felonies, they didn't do it in Argentina. In Bergmann's case, no fingerprints were found, not even his. The place had been sanitized. (A common police euphemism for no evidence left behind.)

Kathryn knew that she and Erika, as they wiped away their fingerprints after finding Bergmann's body, also did away with the killer's prints.

# Chapter 16

**Buenos Aires**
**Same day—Thursday, 07 August 1947**

While Kathryn and Kay were at the police station, Erika was out looking for Ernst Roth. She again knocked on his apartment door. Again there was no answer. She wondered if Roth, like Bergmann, had also been murdered. She found the building superintendent and told him she was an old friend looking for Roth. The man said he wasn't sure where Roth worked, but he normally returned to his apartment between 6:00 and 6:30 in the evening.

Instead of returning to the hotel, Erika dismissed the rented taxi and bought a choripán from a street vendor. She had never had one, but the aroma tempted her. The choripán was a popular street food in Argentina. It consisted of a bread roll stuffed with grilled sausage topped with garlic and parsley salsa.

After she finished the choripán she settled into a small café a half block down and across the street from the apartment building on the Calle de Larrea. She picked a small table by the window for the long wait and ordered coffee. If Roth didn't show, she would return to the hotel and bring back Kathryn's burglar kit and check his apartment. However, just after six o'clock a city bus stopped on the far corner of the street and Ernst Roth, one of Erika and Kathryn's former Abwehr training directors, stepped off the bus. Even though he now wore eyeglasses and sported a goatee, Erika knew it was him. She waited until he walked up the sidewalk steps and disappeared through his apartment building door.

Erika paid her bill, stepped out of the café, and crossed the street. The mild winter weather of the past two days had now turned cold and blustery. She passed the street vendor who was packing up his few remaining choripáns and heading home.

She walked up the apartment building stairs and knocked on Ernst Roth's door. No answer. She knocked again. The third time Erika knocked, she said in German, "Herr Roth, it is Lorelei." It was the only name he would know her by. It took a delay but finally Erika heard numerous locks being unbolted and the door finally open, at least as far as the door chain would allow. Roth peaked around the door.

"Lorelei," Roth kept his voice low but it was easy to tell he was flabbergasted.

"Yes, Herr Roth, it's me."

"What do you want?"

"Just to see an old friend. I saw your name in the phone book. Róta came here with me but she's back at our hotel." *Róta* was Kathryn's codename at Quenzsee.

"Róta is here, too? Why are you in Argentina?"

"Same reason as you, I suppose," Erika replied. "May I come in?"

Roth studied her for a long moment but eventually shut the door, slid off the chain and reopened it. "Come in."

As soon as Erika entered she could tell right away that Roth was packing to leave. An open trunk and two suitcases were spread out in the living room already half full of his belongings. She didn't comment.

"So how have you been, Herr Roth?" Erika said pleasantly.

"Things have been going fine until the last month or two when some of our former Party comrades have died under mysterious circumstances. My biggest mistake was allowing my name to be listed in the telephone directory. I thought I was safe at the time but I now believe that might not be true."

"Why do you think that?"

"Five or six former members of the Gestapo and SS have been killed recently here in Buenos Aires. No former Abwehr have been targeted—so far. I took part in none of the war crimes and was never charged with any misconduct by the Allies so I thought I was safe. This might not be the case so I'm being cautious and moving to a different location. I advise you and Róta to be cautious, as well."

"I had no idea," she said truthfully. Erika had not yet spoken with Kathryn since they split up that morning.

"Herr Roth, I know Róta would enjoy seeing you. We are staying at the Alvear Palace Hotel. Would you be agreeable to meeting us in the hotel bar later this evening? Perhaps around ten o'clock?"

**[later that evening]**

"Do you think Roth will show up?" Kathryn asked Erika as they sat in a booth in the hotel bar.

"I think so. At first he seemed as if he thought I might be there to do him harm, but he's wily and knows if I was sent there to kill him I would have done it in his apartment and not some public place like a hotel bar."

Kay was ordered to remain in the hotel room. Having her along would serve only the need to do further explaining to Roth. Kathryn had briefed Erika about the information she had garnered from her visit to the police station. Erika now knew Roth was right about other members of the Gestapo and SS being killed recently in Buenos Aires—not just Bergmann.

"Who could be killing these men?" Kathryn asked softly, almost as if she were asking herself, not Erika.

Her partner answered, "My visit with him was brief. We'll see if there is anything else he knows, or at least suspects."

It was nearly 10:30, a half hour past the agreed upon meeting time when Ernst Roth walked into the Alvear Hotel bar. He stopped and looked around. Neither Erika nor Kathryn was surprised by his tardiness. They knew he had probably staked out the hotel until he felt comfortable.

Erika spotted him and waved. Roth walked to their booth and sat down beside Erika.

"What are you drinking, Herr Roth?" Erika asked. Both she and Kathryn had a shot of Jägermeister with a beer chaser.

"What you're having looks fine," Roth said.

The waitress appeared quickly, and he placed his drink order.

Roth looked across the table at Kathryn. "Róta, it is very good to see you again. We lost track of you early in the war."

"Admiral Canaris sent me on a deep cover, long-term assignment," Kathryn replied. She didn't mention that that assignment was to infiltrate the Gestapo. That might further spook Roth.

"How is your sister?" Kathryn and her sister, Stephanie, went through Abwehr training together.

"My sister died during the war."

"Very bravely," Erika added. "She died a hero."

"I'm sorry to hear of her death," Roth said. "So many died."

The waitress delivered Roth's Jägermeister and beer. He downed the schnapps in one gulp and ordered another before she walked away.

For a short time they shared a few laughs about the old training days at Quenzsee, then Erika got down to business. Everything was spoken in German.

"Herr Roth, you told me at your apartment that some former Gestapo and SS have been murdered in this city recently. Do you have any idea why? Argentina is a country that has welcomed those who served the Reich." No need to tell him that Kathryn had confirmed the information about the other deaths.

"Do you think there could be Jewish reprisals?" Kathryn asked.

"No, I would doubt that," said Roth. He paused as he downed another Jägermeister and chased it with an ample swig of beer. "The European Jews, what is left of them, are penniless and in disarray. You've probably heard the news reports that a nation state is planned for the Jews in what is now Palestine, but that hasn't happened yet and most European Jews now spend their days wandering aimlessly around Europe and the Mediterranean. The only Jews left with any money are the American Jews and they're not going to get involved in reprisals. Their only interest is fattening their bank accounts."

Kathryn continued. "What about the rumors that the Führer did not die in the Reichstag bunker but is now in Argentina? I'm sure you've heard the rumors, Herr Roth."

"Of course I have heard the rumors and that leads me to my theory. Stalin has never believed that the Führer died as reported by German radio. He told Truman and Churchill this at the Potsdam conference after the war. I believe the killings of our former countrymen have been at the hands of Soviet agents sent here to search for the Führer."

"What leads you to believe that?" Erika asked.

"The rumors about the Führer surviving might be true," Roth stated. "Two of our U-boats didn't surrender to the Allies until months after the war—U-530 and U-977. Both submarines were reported spotted off the coast of Patagonia in southern Argentina in July of 1945, two months after the Führer's reported death. There are witnesses who maintain that U-530 dropped off people near Puerto San Julián, including a man and women who resembled the Führer and Eva Braun. These witnesses claim the Führer had shaved off his moustache and Eva Braun had changed her hair color. The witnesses are solid people, not crackpots, and seem sincere in their testimony."

◊ ◊ ◊

Ernst Roth left a few minutes before 1:00 a.m., wishing them both well. Erika and Kathryn returned the same wish to him. Both of them liked Roth. He had been a tough but fair taskmaster at Quenzsee.

The hotel bar stayed open until 2:00 a.m. so Erika and Kathryn stayed behind to talk after Roth left.

"Erika, do you think there is any possibility that Hitler is still alive?"

"I don't know, Kathryn. The important thing right now is that apparently the Russians believe it if Herr Roth's theory is correct."

"It's too bad Zhanna disappeared," Kathryn stated. "If the Russians are involved, we could use her on this mission."

Erika paused for a moment before she said, "Kathryn, I know where Zhanna is hiding."

"What? How do you know?"

"Remember Leroy giving me the month of May to visit Ada in London?"

"Yes. I remember."

"Zhanna contacted me."

"So you're telling me Zhanna is in London?"

"No. In April, Zhanna called my grandmother in London and asked for me. My grandmother remembered Zhanna because the three of us visited my grandmother's house in Kensington. You remember."

"Yes, I remember, of course."

Because my grandmother knew Zhanna was our comrade, she told Zhanna that I wasn't there but that she was expecting me in May. Zhanna called again in May when I was there with Ada."

"So where is she?"

"She's somewhere in Guatemala. When she hung up I called the operator and found out the call came from Puerto Barrios. It's a city on the east coast of that country. I don't know exactly where she is but I'm guessing she is in or somewhere near that city."

"Why did she call you?"

"She asked if the CIA was hunting her and did they have any leads."

"What did you tell her?"

"The truth. That Leroy had notified CIA people around the globe to keep an eye out for her but he had not yet committed a team specifically tasked to find her."

"Withholding the fact from Leroy that she contacted you, not to mention giving her that information, can get you in big trouble, Erika."

"She's our friend, Kathryn. All of us have guarded each other's backs on two missions."

Kathryn nodded. "True. So what's on your mind?"

"We must find Zhanna. Our biggest problem is that in order to find her we'll have to take Kay with us."

# Chapter 17

**Buenos Aires**
**Next day—Friday, 08 August 1947**

Despite the late evening last night, Erika and Kathryn rose early. At 6:00 a.m. Kathryn shook Kay's shoulder.

"Wake up, Kay," Kathryn said. "We have work in front of us."

Kay sat up on the edge of the bed, still drowsy.

"Get dressed," Erika told her impatiently.

"What's going on?" Kay asked.

"None of your business right now," Erika groused.

Kathryn stepped in. Despite the truce declared on the plane ride from Washington, the friction between Erika and Kay was still in the air and Kathryn was growing weary of it. "We're going on a trip, Kay."

"Where to?" Kay asked.

"Guatemala."

"Guatemala? Why?"

"We'll explain all that when we get there," Kathryn answered.

"I should call Leroy, that's my job."

"No time for that now," Erika cut in. "Besides, our room telephone is out of order." (Erika had sliced the room phone line.)


**[two hours later]**
From the Buenos Aires airport, Erika called Carlos and informed him they wouldn't need his services for a few days. No explanation was given. Nothing about a trip was mentioned. Erika told him she or Kathryn would call him when they next needed him.

It would be a long and arduous journey. They were growing thin on money, and because they were going rogue, they could not charter a plane and charge it to the U.S. government. They would have to take a commercial flight to Guatemala City which was nearly 4000 air miles, or about 20 hours in the air, from Buenos Aires. Then it would be a bus journey of about six hours from Guatemala City to Puerto

Barrios on the east coast. Many of the bus miles would be on narrow, twisting, mountain dirt roads during Guatemala's rainy season.

Looking on the bright side, Guatemala was in the Northern Hemisphere so once again summertime. In Central America about 1000 miles north of the equator, Guatemala's average August temperatures usually hovered around 70 degrees Fahrenheit. They would leave winter behind in Argentina, at least for a while.

As they boarded the DC-3 in Buenos Aires, the only thought in Kay's mind was something was not right. She felt like she was Erika Lehmann's prisoner. Kay knew she had to call her husband. Even though she didn't really know what was happening, Leroy should at least know that they were leaving Argentina.

**[later that morning—Washington. D.C]**
Sheila Reid buzzed Leroy Carr.

"Carlos Vilas is on the phone from Buenos Aires," Sheila told him.

"Put it through." Carr picked up his desk telephone. "Carlos, how are things going down there?"

*"Mister Carr, I just thought I should update you. Erika, your team leader, called me today and told me the three ladies would not require my services for awhile. She didn't mention how long this would be. This struck me as curious, so I tried calling them back at the hotel a half hour ago. They have checked out."*

# Chapter 18

## Guatemala City, Guatemala
## Next day—Saturday, 09 August 1947

The customs official at the Guatemala City airport found their handguns when he opened the women's suitcases.

"Why do you have guns," he asked in Spanish. Kay translated.

"Tell him it's none of his business," Erika said to Kay.

Kay amended Erika's response. "We are three lone women in a strange country."

He shrugged and passed them on through. There were no restrictions against handguns in luggage.

Erika knew Leroy Carr could track the team to Guatemala City. All three women had to show their passports to buy a plane ticket in Buenos Aires and then produce them again to get through customs at the Guatemala City airport. But she knew it would take at least a day for the CIA to uncover this information so they were safe for tonight. Tomorrow they would leave Guatemala City for Puerto Barrios.

They rented a room at a downtown fleabag hotel.

The room was on the second floor and they had to step around a passed out drunk on the stairs. The room was filthy, and the common toilet facilities were located at the end of the hall.

Kay grimaced when she entered the room but quickly wiped the expression from her face and made no comment. The bed was a double bed with rumpled sheets that looked like they hadn't been washed in awhile. The only other place to sleep was a worn sofa. The remainder of the furniture consisted of a wooden chair in dire need of varnish. As far as décor, that was it. Not even a cheap print for a wall. The only thing hanging was a corner spider web complete with spider and fly shells the resident of the web had already feasted upon.

"I'll sleep on the sofa," Erika said. "Kay, you and Kathryn can have the bed." Kay assumed Erika thought she was making a nice gesture, but from the looks of the bed that was debatable in her mind.

Kathryn sensed Kay's misgivings.

82

"Kay, now you see why a spy's life is not as glamorous as in the movies. To remain under the radar we sometimes stay in places like this."

By the time they settled in, it was three o'clock in the afternoon.

Kay said to both Erika and Kathryn, "You told me when we got to Guatemala you'd tell me what we're doing here."

"Have a seat, Kay," Erika said. Kay sat on the wood chair.

"Kathryn and I believe there might be some truth to Ernst Roth's theory that the Soviets are also seeking Adolf Hitler. We've come here to find someone who can help us. I know your husband must be worried since you didn't make your daily contact with him yesterday or today. Tomorrow morning I'll let you call him before we leave this city. For now, that's all you need to know."


**[Same day, 4:00 p.m.—CIA Headquarters on E Street, Washington, D.C.]**

Leroy Carr didn't sleep last night after not receiving his daily phone call from Kay, and after learning from Carlos that the team had checked out of their hotel. Early this morning he contacted Carlos and ordered him to check the Buenos Aires airport, train, and bus stations for records of tickets purchased. Carlos worked efficiently and just a few minutes ago had called back to tell Carr that the three women had purchased airline tickets to Guatemala City. Carr immediately summoned Al Hodge to his office.

"Al," Carr said before Hodge had a chance to sit down. "Erika and Kathryn have gone rogue and taken the team to Guatemala to find Zhanna Rogova!"

"What!!! How do you know that?"

"Carlos Vilas just called to tell me they purchased airline tickets to Guatemala City yesterday. You remember Zhanna's Guatemalans who worked with her at the cabin in Maryland where she held Erika captive. Zhanna got them from some former colleague of hers when she was with the Russian SMERSH. We know the man is somewhere in Guatemala. One plus one always equals two, Al. I should have thought of Guatemala as soon as Zhanna disappeared. That's got to be where Zhanna is hiding and Erika knows it."

"Why would Lehmann decide she wants to find Rogova in the middle of a mission in South America?"

"I don't know, but we're going to find out. Pack your bags, Al. We're going to Guatemala."

"We? Do you think Hillenkoetter will let you, his deputy director, go into the field in Guatemala? There's a lot of guerilla warfare that has flared up recently between the nationalists and the communists. It's not a safe country." (Rear Admiral Roscoe H. Hillenkoetter was the current CIA director. He was the third director Carr and Hodge had worked under in just over a year.)

"I don't give a damn." Carr was obviously highly agitated. "These directors have been coming and going through a revolving door since you and I started here. If Hillenkoetter won't let me go I'll quit the CIA and go on my own. I can always go back to practicing law. We're talking about Kay, Al."

Hodge nodded. "I'll be ready."

# Chapter 19

## Guatemala City, Republic of Guatemala
## Next day—Sunday, 10 August 1947

The only bus departing for the east coast of Guatemala had a 10:15 a.m. departure time. At 8:30 that morning, a half hour before they would leave the hotel for the bus depot, Erika told Kay she could call her husband. Their sleazy hotel room didn't have a telephone so Kay had to call from a phone booth across the street. Erika and Kathryn were by her side when she got Leroy on the phone.

The Carrs' phone at their Annapolis home rang. Kay heard Leroy say hello.

"Leroy, it me."

*"Kay! Are you okay?"* his nerves had him shouting into the phone even though the connection was good.

"I'm okay, we're in Guatemala."

Erika knew Carr could easily find out the country where the phone call had originated; consequently, it was useless to order Kay to not divulge their location.

*"I know that,"* Carr said. *"We traced your plane tickets. Where are Erika and Kathryn?"*

"They're standing beside me."

*"I'm getting you out of there, Kay. Put Erika on the phone."*

"He wants to talk to you," Kay said to Erika. Erika took the phone.

"Hello, Leroy."

*"I know why you're in Guatemala. You're trying to find Zhanna, right?"*

"That's right."

*"Listen to me very carefully, Erika. If anything happens to Kay I'll spend every waking moment of my life, and use every resource I have at the agency to track you down. Then I'll turn you over to the Justice Department faster than you can say 'Sieg Heil.' You'll be tried for your crimes during the war. That will lead to life imprisonment at the least, and hopefully execution, which is what I'll recommend. I want you to put Kay on the first plane back to the States. Is that clear?"*

85

"Sending Kay back to you sounds like a good deal, Leroy. She shouldn't have been sent along in the first place. She's too weak. We can find another Spanish interpreter."

*"Put Kay back on the phone. Now!"*

Erika had made sure Kay had heard her comment about her being weak. She handed Kay the telephone. "Your husband is worried about you so you're going home where you can curl up in bed and be safe."

Kay glared at Erika and yanked the phone out of her hand. "Yes, Leroy."

*"Erika will get you on the first available flight back to the States. It doesn't matter what city. If it's not D.C., I'll have men and a plane there waiting to pick you up. Just give me a call from the airport when you know your arrival city."*

Kay paused and again gave Erika an angry stare. "I'm not leaving, Leroy. I'm staying to complete the mission. I'm sorry, darling."

Erika's manipulation had worked. She didn't want Kay along in the first place, but now it was too far into the game to search for another translator, a stranger she didn't know or trust. Another reason she allowed Kay to call Leroy was that she had done her research and knew that bus tickets in Guatemala could be purchased with cash without using a name. She knew the trail for Carr would dry up in Guatemala City.

◊ ◊ ◊

Carr didn't bother attempting to get CIA Director Hillenkoetter's permission for his trip to Guatemala. Carr knew that even if Hillenkoetter agreed to sign off on the mission, it might take days. Carr wasn't about to waste that much time.

Two hours after Kay's phone call, Carr and Al Hodge boarded an Air Force version of the DC-3 at Andrews Air Force Base. Carr ordered Major Sheila Reid, one of the four Shield Maidens, to stay in Washington. Sheila's left shoulder was still weak from a deep stab wound she suffered on the last Shield Maiden mission, plus he needed someone qualified to run his office in his absence. He also didn't take along a team. Putting a team together would delay their departure and alert Hillenkoetter. Carr knew the CIA already had Spanish speaking agents in Guatemala that he could call upon.

"So, is this finally the end for Lehmann?" Hodge asked after they settled into their seats.

"Yes," said Carr. "You were right all along, Al. I should have turned her over to the Justice Department after the war. I put up with the improvising and straying from her orders in the past because she produced results, but she's gone way over the line this time. When we find her she'll stay in cuffs until we get her back to the States where she'll pay the fiddler."

◊ ◊ ◊

At the same time, Erika, Kathryn, and Kay were on a bus that had just pulled out of the depot in Guatemala City—final destination, Puerto Barrios.

# Chapter 20

**Guatemala**
**Next day—Monday, 11 August 1947**

The bus trip would take around six hours.

The distance from Guatemala City to Puerto Barrios was only 200 miles, yet because of poor road conditions, many of which were narrow dirt roads wending their way through sharp, hair-pin mountain turns, the bus could average only about 30 miles an hour—35 at best.

Erika, Kathryn, and Kay were the only Caucasians onboard the rusty, rickety, and crowded bus. The other passengers were either native Central American Guatemalans or Mestizo, the two groups that made up over 80% of the Guatemalan population.

"Are you ready to tell me now who we're trying to find?" Kay asked Erika. She and Erika sat beside each other with Kay pinned into the window seat; Kathryn sat in the seat in front of Erika.

"We're searching for a woman named Zhanna Rogova," Erika answered. "Has your husband ever mentioned her to you?"

"No."

"Good."

Kay commented, "That name sounds Russian or Ukrainian."

"She's Russian."

"You know I don't speak Russian, right?"

"Besides Russian, Zhanna speaks English, but if we need Russian I speak it," Erika replied. "We just need you for Spanish, that's all."

The bus was only an hour out of Guatemala City when an incident occurred. In a mountainous area near the Sanarate region, a road block stopped the bus. Two armed partisans entered the bus door to the right of the driver. One stayed outside. Everyone was ordered to exit the bus. The partisans went down the line demanding to see identification. When they got to Erika, Kathryn, and Kay, they produced the identification papers Erika had told them to use for this trip. It identified them as American Red Cross workers. Their other numerous I.D.s, all supplied by Leroy Carr and the CIA were hidden in a false bottom to a large jar of cold cream in their luggage. This time, luggage was never opened. The partisans identified who they were looking for and shoved him roughly from the line up.

Everyone else was ordered back onboard. As the bus pulled away, the CIA team, and the other passengers, watched the man being forced to his knees just before a partisan shot him in the back of the head.

Luckily there were no more incidents and the bus pulled into the Puerto Barrios depot at 5:30 after a bone-jarring seven-hour journey made longer than it should have been by the unpleasant episode in the Sanarate district. Kay was greatly shocked from what happened and still was not fully recovered.

"Pull yourself together, Kay," Kathryn said when they stepped off the bus. "We have work ahead of us."

Puerto Barrios was a medium-sized city on the eastern coast. At the bus depot they hired a taxi.

"Kay, tell the driver we don't want the finest hotel, but a good one—something decent with a bathroom in the room," Erika said. "We can stay in a better place here without being suspicious because we are now American Red Cross workers. Guatemalans think all Americans are rich. American Red Cross workers would not have the money to stay in a luxury hotel, but it would raise more suspicion if we stayed in a shabby place."

Kay translated and the driver delivered them to a hotel called El Hotel de la Fuente located on 15 Calle.

The hotel was many steps up from the flea bag were they had stayed at in Guatemala City. In the lobby was a marble fountain (therefore the hotel's name: Fuente). Although the room was not as luxurious as the Alvear in Buenos Aires, it was clean and there were three beds—two twins and a rollaway that was bought up promptly by a bellman. No one would have to sleep on a sofa.

It was 6:30 by the time they were situated in the room. All of the women were starving.

"Tomorrow we start the hunt for Zhanna," Erika told Kathryn and Kay. "Now we find some dinner."

The hotel had a small café, but it only served breakfast and lunch. Just a half block down was a large, popular cantina.

◊ ◊ ◊

The U.S. Air Force plane carrying Leroy Carr and Al Hodge landed in Guatemala City later that evening after a ten-hour flight from Washington.

# Chapter 21

## Puerto Barrios, Guatemala
## Next day—Tuesday, 12 August 1947

Erika, Kathryn, and Kay had a hearty dinner the night before so breakfast in the Hotel de la Fuente was a light one—just coffee, a piece of fruit, and a piece of bread that was curiously called a croissant but was denser than the French version. It reminded Erika more of an English scone than the light, flaky croissant. After breakfast they returned to their room. They spoke in English so Kay could understand.

"Fill me in, Erika," Kathryn said. "What makes you think that Zhanna is somewhere around here?"

"You remember when Zhanna captured me and held me in the cabin in Maryland."

"How could I forget?" Kathryn responded.

"Her team was made up of Guatemalans."

"Yes, I remember that."

"And during our last mission, Zhanna told me she called an old SMERSH colleague named Demetri who was now in Guatemala. From him she learned the truth about Grusha, an enemy on a former mission."

"Okay, I see where you're going." Kathryn said. "We need to find this 'Demetri.'"

"Exactly. I told you Zhanna called me in May when I was in London with Ada. She asked if Carr had any leads to her whereabouts. I traced the phone call and it came from somewhere around here—it came from a telephone booth in Puerto Barrios.

"So this is something else you didn't tell my husband," Kay interjected. "I can see why he needs to keep a close eye on you."

Erika ignored her.

"Do you know anything about this Demetri?" Kathryn asked.

"Only that he was a former member of SMERSH with Zhanna and is now involved in the drug trade. The thugs he sent to help Zhanna in Maryland were drug traffickers on his payroll."

"My husband will track the phone call I made to him yesterday. He'll know we're in Guatemala," she said to Erika.

"He'll know the phone call came from Guatemala City and that's all, Kay. I bought our bus tickets with cash. No names were required. Leroy's trail will end in Guatemala City. So don't get your hopes up."

**[same time—Guatemala City]**

Leroy Carr and Al Hodge had spent the night in a cheap hotel near the airport. They had skipped breakfast in order to not waste time. Currently, they both stood in front of the hotel waiting to be picked up by one of the CIA's Guatemalan assets.

"How in the heck are we going to find Kay, Leroy?" Hodge asked. "You know how cagey Lehmann is. She wouldn't have let Kay make that phone call if she knew that would make it easy to find her. She has to have something else up her sleeve."

"First thing we have to do is find out where they stayed here overnight." Carr said. "Their plane landed two days ago and Kay made the phone call yesterday morning. That probably means Lehmann is taking them somewhere else, but they would have to have spent at least one night here. We'll find the hotel and see if we can get any information from the staff."

**[that afternoon—Puerto Barrios]**

Taking advantage of Guatemalan businesses lack of interest in proper identification as long as you had cash, Kathryn made up a name on the spot that was not on any of her phony I.D.s supplied by the CIA and rented a car, an old Citroën sedan. Kay, of course, had to translate. Kathryn drove with Kay sitting shotgun with a city map in Spanish. Erika took to the back seat. The women made their way to the seediest area of Puerto Barrios. The drug dealers were easy to find, many stood on the streets like prostitutes making transactions in the open with obviously little concern about the law. Erika and Kathryn assumed that the local police had given up on the area or had been paid off.

They stopped in front of one of the dealers, a boy who couldn't have been more than sixteen years old. He approached the car.

"I'm out of everything but heroin and cocaine," he said. Kay translated.

"Tell him we have a message for Demetri and want to know where to find him," Erika told Kay.

Kay said the words in Spanish and the boy looked at her dumbly before speaking.

"He doesn't know a Demetri," Kay told the other two women.

They drove off. After repeating the process with three more dealers on other street corners who also knew nothing, Katherine pulled over in front of another dealer. This man looked to be about 30 years old and was selling drugs to a boy who looked to be around 11 or 12. The boy walked off with his drugs as Katherine stopped. When Kay asked the dealer about Demetri he hesitated. Erika spotted the look of fear in his eyes.

"Kay, stay in the car," Erika said. "Let's go Kathryn."

Kathryn knew what to do. They got out of the car, drew their guns, and forced the dealer into the car. He tried to fight but Kathryn hit him behind the ear with the butt of her gun before Erika roughly threw him into the back seat and entered beside him. Kathryn quickly jumped behind the wheel and drove off.

There were more horse-drawn carts on the streets of Puerto Barrios than automobiles so the going was slow. Erika put her gun to the man's temple.

"Tell us what you know about Demetri," she said sternly. Kay did the translating.

"I know nothing!" He stammered out the words even though he could barely move his jaw from where Kathryn had struck him. "I think my jaw might be broken!"

"That's the least of your worries if you don't tell us about Demetri," Erika shouted fiercely.

"I know nothing about a Demetri!"

"You're lying! When I mentioned the name to you on the street, you paused and I could see the fear in your eyes. Erika pulled out her knife that was strapped to her lower leg and stabbed the man's foot through his shoe. She knew the blood would collect in the shoe and not leave blood stains in the car.

Kay gasped as the man screamed in agony. "I have never seen him," he moaned in pain. "I only know that he is called El Búho and that I pick up my drugs in a cantina from men who work for a man named Señor Munoz. He owns the cantina and works for El Búho (the owl)."

"What's the name of this cantina and where is it?"

"Dama Azul. It's on 3 Avenida near 5 Calle, not far from the docks. I swear to the Virgin that's all I know. Now let me go now, please!"

Erika searched his pants pockets and took a considerable amount of money the man had earned from his drug sales, and then she cut off the bag looped to his belt that held the drugs. She opened his door and kicked him out onto the street without Kathryn slowing down. The car was moving at barely 10 mph but still the man thumped heavily onto the gravel road and rolled several times. Even Kay got some satisfaction from what Erika did to the lowlife who sold drugs to children.

"Kay," Erika said. "Check the map and tell Kathryn how to get to that bar. Did you hear the address?"

"Yes, I heard it." Kay unfolded more of the map.

"What about the guy's drugs?" Kay asked. "What are you going to do with them?"

Kathryn interrupted. "There's one, Erika." She pulled the car over; Erika got out and threw the bag of drugs down a curb rain gutter into the sewer.

# Chapter 22

## Puerto Barrios
## Same day—Tuesday, 12 August 1947

Puerto Barrios, on the eastern coast of Guatemala, was located on the shores of Bahia (Bay) de Amatique in the Gulf of Honduras. The Dama Azul cantina (Blue Lady) sat just two blocks from the shipping docks.

When Erika, Kathryn, and Kay walked into the bar they all immediately saw a naked woman dancing to no music on a small stage in the middle of the crowded room. "This isn't a cantina; it's a striptease club," Kay said.

A burly doorman stopped them.

"No prostitutes allowed," the man said sternly in Spanish. "It takes business away from the girls who work here."

"We're not prostitutes," Kay told him. "We are here to see Señor Munoz."

Kay couldn't tell from the man's shady look what he was thinking. Erika hadn't understood all of the conversation, but when the bouncer hesitated she handed him a 50 quetzal note from some of the money she had taken from the drug dealer. He took the money and told them to wait at the bar.

The three women wended their way around tables of half-drunken, nefarious looking men. Before reaching the bar, one of the seated men grabbed Kathryn around the waist and pulled her onto his lap. He and his partners laughed loudly until Kathryn drew her knife and placed it to the man's neck.

Kathryn glared cruelly. "Touch me again, you pig, and I'll open your throat!"

The man didn't understand the English words but the knife translated. He released her. Erika had her hand on the gun concealed under a light sweater in case Kathryn needed backup, but it proved unnecessary. Drunks at surrounding tables laughed hysterically. No one came to the man's defense or seemed the least bit surprised at what had just happened.

There were plenty of open seats at the bar since most of the men sat at tables watching the naked dancer. The women picked three stools. The bartender was a female with the top of her dress pulled down enough to expose her breasts.

"Order all of us a beer, Kay." Erika said. "It doesn't matter the brand. Hopefully we won't have to sit here for long."

Erika was right. They had taken only a couple sips of their beers when a man (not the bouncer) approached them.

"I'm told you want to see Señor Munoz. Why?"

After Kay translated his words, Erika told Kay to tell him they have something of interest to Munoz. The man studied them for a long moment then said, "Follow me."

He led them from the bar and through a room in the back where a high stakes card game was being played between six men at a table. Before opening another door, the body guard frisked them and confiscated their weapons. He opened the door and motioned them to enter. The room was an office. Inside, a middle-aged, bald-headed man with a black moustache sat behind a desk. He was wearing an expensive suit. Two more bodyguards stood next to the desk.

Señor Munoz looked up from a ledger he had been writing in and asked them, "I'm Munoz. Who are you and what do you want?"

Erika did the talking with Kay translating

"We are friends of a friend of El Búho," Erika answered. "We are looking for that friend and think El Búho might be able to help us."

The man studied them for several seconds. "Asking to see El Búho can many times be a bad idea. It might affect your health."

"Just put us in touch with El Búho." Erika demanded. "He'll want to see us. If you don't, it is you whose health might be affected."

Munoz didn't appreciate the threat, yet he feared more the backlash from El Búho if he were to make a mistake. He gave his men an order. They handcuffed the three women, blindfolded them, and took them to a dark room where they forced the women down onto chairs. The room smelled of ammonia and detergent. Although they could not see, all of them assumed it was a cleaning closet.

Kay was now having great doubts about her decision to not let Erika send her home. "What's going on, Erika?" she asked in the darkness.

"Don't be concerned, Kay. Kathryn and I knew we'd probably have to go through this. This is the way amateurs like Munoz handle these things. He's scared to death of El Búho. He'll contact him before he dare do anything to us. We'll be taken to him, eventually."

This did little to calm Kay's nerves. "I have to pee."

# Chapter 23

## Puerto Barrios, Guatemala
## Wednesday, 13 August 1947

Around midnight, one of Munoz's bodyguards at the Dama Azul let the women use the toilet, much to Kay's relief. Munoz had had second thoughts about the way he treated the women in case what they claimed was true—that they were friends of a friend of El Búho. The last thing Munoz wanted to do is anger The Owl. He instructed his men to un-cuff the women and remove the blindfolds. They were still held in the cleaning closet but a weak light was turned on.

A couple of hours later, around two or two-thirty in the morning, three men who the women had not seen, entered the closet and escorted them to a cargo van parked in an alley next to the Dama Azul. Outside, the rain poured. Luckily it took only a few seconds until they were loaded into the van where they had to sit on the floor as the journey began. One of the men placed hangman hoods over the women's heads so they could not see where they were going.

Approximately an hour later the van stopped, the women were unloaded and taken into a building to a room where the hoods were taken off and the door behind them closed.

They were in an elegant room of rustic hardwood floors and ceiling. The walls were stucco where many expensive-looking paintings hung. On shiny mahogany shelves and tables stood antique porcelain vases, fragile china dolls, and handmade blown glass figurines. There were no windows.

"What's going to happen now?' Kay asked.

"There will be guards outside the door, but that's okay. We don't want to escape. We accomplished what we wanted. We'll sit here for a while and either the man we want to see or one of his top lieutenants will enter the room," Erika answered. "Or maybe the guards will take us somewhere else."

"That answer leaves it pretty much up in the air, Erika," Kay said.

Erika shrugged. Kathryn said, "She's right, Kay. Since the room has no windows, I'm guessing either the man we're here to see, or one of his top aides, will come to us."

For the next three hours, the women either sat on luxurious sofas and chairs, or walked around the room looking at paintings and the other decorations. Rain still pelted the roof. The marble fire place was unlit, of course, as it was summer in the Northern Hemisphere. A grandfather clock stood against a wall ticking life away.

At 6:30 a.m., a guard opened the door and a man entered. His gray hair and features gave away that he was probably in his mid-sixties.

"Good morning to you," he said in Spanish. "My name is Diego. What are your names?"

Kay translated. Erika and Kathryn told the man their real names. Kay identified herself as Kay Becker. When the man saw Kay translating, he asked Kay, "What language do the other two speak?"

"Inglés," Kay told him.

The man was obviously Latin but switched to acceptable English; although, with a heavy Guatemalan accent which in ways sounded similar to a Mexican accent but at the same time different with a Mayan influence. "I've been told you want to see El Búho," he said. "May I ask why? I understand it has to do with a friend of El Búho. I must warn you that if you are lying, things will work out badly for you. What is this friend's name?"

"Zhanna Rogova," Erika answered.

The man didn't respond and looked them over for a long moment. He turned and walked out of the room. A half hour later the door opened and a guard told them in Spanish to follow him.


**[same morning, Guatemala City]**

It took Leroy Carr and Al Hodge a day and a half of combing the city's hotels, but they eventually found the flea bag hotel that the female CIA team stayed in two nights ago. Before they left Washington, Carr had ordered one of the CIA's assets who lives in Guatemala City to be their driver and translator. When they finally located the correct hotel, the unkempt man behind the hotel's desk could give them no information other than to confirm a room had been paid for by a woman named Kathryn Fischer.

"This is textbook Lehmann," said Hodge. "She stays in a flea bag one day and the next night she's in an expensive hotel."

"I know that, Al," Carr said with irritation.

"I guess the only thing we can do now is check with the local train and bus stations," Hodge added.

"That's right," Carr said with uncharacteristic distress in his voice. "Our problem is that Erika would not have had Kathryn rent the room under her real name if they were staying in this city for more than a night. It's going to be tough to track them. The train and bus stations in this country do not ask for I.D. if the ticket is purchased with cash. You can bet Erika knew that before she let Kay call me."

# Chapter 24

**Puerto Barrios**
**Same day—Wednesday, 13 August 1947**

Inside a dining room with a sliding wooden door, the women were told where to sit at the end of a long, red linen-covered table. The heavy wooden chairs were padded with red upholstery that matched the table cloth. The armed guard remained in the room, stationing himself in front of the door. A maid brought them coffee, poured each of them a cup and left the decanter on the table. Kay said, "Gracias." The woman left the room without speaking. They sat drinking coffee for about fifteen minutes when a man of about fifty years entered. He looked to be around 5'10". He carried a few extra pounds but it was obvious he was powerfully built. His face was clean-shaven, his hair dark with heavy eyebrows. He wore a white long-sleeved shirt, buttoned to the collar, and black dress pants. Without looking at the women, he moved to the other end of the long table and sat down.

He ignored his guests as he drank coffee from a small, clear glass and read a newspaper. In ten minutes the same maid reentered the room with a teenage girl pushing a cart. The maids first served the man then the young girl rolled the cart to the women's end of the table where the older maid served them. Breakfast consisted of black beans, fried plantain slices, fresh cheese, scrambled eggs, fruit and tortillas. Kay, who had studied in Mexico City, noticed that the Guatemalan version of tortillas were smaller but thicker than the ones she had eaten in Mexico. While the man sat ignoring them, the three women tucked in to their breakfast. Their last meal was breakfast the previous day. Like Kay had seen before, Erika and Kathryn shoveled the food into their mouths. Kay was hungry herself, and ate earnestly, but couldn't keep herself from watching the other two women eat.

Erika noticed Kay watching her and Kathryn. "What's so interesting, Kay?"

Kay replied, "You two eat like starving hobos."

The man overheard them and finally spoke. "I see you all speak English." His English was acceptable, but with a heavy Russian accent.

"Yes," Erika replied.

"Good, I can speak Spanish but my English is better. If you don't know what you're eating that is the most popular breakfast here in Guatemala."

"It's delicious," Kathryn commented.

The man looked at her. "You sound German."

Unlike Erika, who could speak English with both a British and American accent, a slight German accent still lingered within Kathryn's English.

"I *am* German," Kathryn confirmed. "My name is Kathryn Fischer. You have to be El Búho."

"That name is a creation of some of the people who work for me. I might have picked another name, but sometimes a nickname can be of service so I let it be."

"Especially if it strikes fear," Erika added.

El Búho took a bite of his fried plantain before looking up at Erika. "I know who you are. You have to be Erika. Zhanna told me about you. You're right according to what you told Señor Munoz about being a friend of a friend of mine. Wisely, you didn't mention Zhanna's name or you wouldn't be alive to eat that breakfast. Zhanna has in the past also mentioned you, Señorita Fischer. Who is this translator?"

"My name is Kay Becker."

"Do you also work for the CIA?"

Kay hesitated, not knowing what to answer. Erika stepped in for Kay.

"Yes, Kay is CIA like us, as I'm sure you know."

"Yes, I know you and Señorita Fischer are CIA," said El Búho. "So certainly I suspect the same for Señorita Becker (Kay had left her wedding ring at home per her husband's advice so the man assumed she was unmarried). I appreciate you not thinking I'm a fool. Finish your breakfast ladies then we'll talk."

◊ ◊ ◊

By the end of breakfast, the Guatemalan rainy season finally took a nap and El Búho took the three women outside. They were on an expansive ranch outside Puerto Barrios. El Búho told them the ranch covered 400 acres. The main compound, about seven acres, included a large barn and several outbuildings that were encircled by ten-foot high stone walls patrolled by armed guards and their leashed Doberman Pinschers. Two of the armed guards (sans dogs) followed El Búho at all times when outdoors. They strolled on a winding flagstone walkway that kept them from slogging in the mud as El Búho led them to his barn. Stalls in the barn housed several exquisite looking horses, among them a couple of sleek thoroughbreds; a mighty, pure white Andalusian; and two lustrous, brown quarter horses. Three grooms scrambled about to look busy when El Búho entered the stables.

The former SMERSH colleague of Zhanna Rogova introduced the women to each of the horses. When finished he said, "The grooms speak no English. What is it you ask of me?"

"We want to find Zhanna," Erika answered. "I know you must be protecting her."

"For what reason do you want to see her?" he said as he petted the last horse.

"We need her help on a mission we have in South America—Argentina to be exact."

"What mission is that?"

"With due respect, I cannot tell you, sir."

He gazed at Erika for a long moment. "You do know that Zhanna is a dear friend of mine. Both of us suffered much during the war. I will let nothing happen to her that's in my power to prevent."

"I'm also her friend and feel the same way."

The Russian returned to petting the horse and didn't speak for at least two minutes. The women waited.

"Zhanna is not on my ranch," he finally said. "I will contact her to see if she wants to see you. Until I know her answer, all of you will stay here on my Hacienda. You have willingly placed yourselves in danger. For this reason I will contact Zhanna. If she doesn't want to see you, it is then that I will decide your fate."

**[same day—Guatemala City]**

Leroy Carr and Al Hodge had uncovered nothing new since finding the hotel that Erika's team had stayed in for one night in Guatemala City. Both the ticket counters at the train and bus stations had no names recorded that were either the women's correct names or one of their aliases.

"She paid with cash, Al, I expected as much." Carr said to Hodge. "Damn it, this should have been a simple intelligence gathering mission with practically no risk or I would have never sent Kay."

"Nothing ever goes like it should if Lehmann is involved," Hodge replied. "I'm so sick of dealing with that broad I get nauseous when I hear she's been selected for a mission."

"Well," said Carr. "You won't have to worry about that again, Al. Erika has burned her last bridge with me."

# Chapter 25

## El Búho's Compound outside Puerto Barrios, Guatemala
## Next day—Thursday, 14 August 1947

After spending last night at El Búho's Hacienda, and having another breakfast (this time without The Owl at the other end of the table), a guard ordered the three women to follow him. He drove them outside the compound gates which encircled only seven acres of the 400-acre property.

Ten minutes later he stopped in front of an airplane hangar. At the end of a gravel runway a twin-engine Cessna T-50 sat with both engines running. The women were escorted to the plane and entered through a side door in the fuselage. Inside were four chairs behind the pilot's and co-pilot's seats. The rest of the area behind the seats was for cargo. Although empty now, Erika felt sure the cargo area had seen its share of illegal drugs.

El Búho sat in the co-pilot's seat. The pilot was a Caucasian woman in her thirties who was not introduced by name. El Búho turned to the CIA team and told them to sit down.

"I spoke with Zhanna last night," El Búho told them. "She is not in this country, but not far away in Honduras. It's only an hour-and-a-half flight to where she stays. She has agreed to see Erika. You other two will remain on the airplane. Never forget, Erika, that Zhanna is under my protection. If you have come to do her harm in any way, you and your comrades will not see another day."

The female pilot handled the takeoff then El Búho took the controls. Apparently he was learning to fly. Erika heard the woman flyer give her co-pilot instructions in Russian.

"My friend next to me was a bomber pilot for the Soviet 587th Bomber Aviation Regiment during the war," El Búho explained to his passengers. "That Regiment was made up of many female pilots and they proudly earned the nickname 'Night Witches' given them by the Germans for the havoc they wreaked on the Nazi forces invading our country."

"I have heard of them," Erika said to El Búho. "In Germany, our troops called them the *Nachthexen,* the German word for Night Witch. Does she speak English?"

"No," he said. "And if she did, she wouldn't want a conversation with a Nazi."

"That's a *former* Nazi," Erika emphasized.

"There are no *former* Nazis. Not in her mind or in mine," he said. "Once a baptized Catholic, always a Catholic despite if one chooses another faith later in life. The same holds true for Nazis who have opened their wrists and taken the blood oath to Hitler, as you have. In fact, you have done both. You're a baptized Catholic and a blood oath Nazi. This makes you a mockery, does it not?"

Erika didn't answer; instead, she turned her head and looked out the window. Zhanna had certainly told this man much about her. For the rest of the flight she remained silent.

Kathryn was also Catholic and had taken the blood oath but only because she had to when she infiltrated the Gestapo. Her blood oath was a farce. Erika's was sincere when, before the war, she pricked her wrist and shared blood with a young girl in the BDM, the girl's branch of the Hitler Youth.

## [Honduras, South America]

El Búho had been correct about the flying time. About an hour-and-a-half after taking off from his private landing strip, the T-50 set down on a brick runway in Honduras, just outside Santa Bárbara. A car and driver waited. Two men carrying sawed-off shotguns got aboard the plane before El Búho and Erika disembarked and walked to the car. The 'Night Witch' pilot stayed on board with Kathryn and Kay, as did the two sinister looking Latin guards.

After a thirty-minute drive, the sedan containing the former Nazi spy and former Russian Secret Police colonel pulled into a drive that led to a church named Sangre de Cristo (Blood of Christ). Behind the church stood a rectory for the priests and a separate convent for the sisters. The driver stopped in front of the convent, the Cloister of Saint

Flora and Mary. The driver got out and took Erika into the chapel. El Búho walked a different direction.

Erika didn't know how long her wait would be so she lit candles for her deceased parents and husband. A couple of nuns kneeled in the front pew. Erika sat down in the rear pew, dropped the kneeler, and crossed herself.

◊ ◊ ◊

Twenty minutes later, the Mother Superior entered the chapel and tapped Erika on the shoulder while she was still praying.

"After prayer, please come with me," the nun said quietly. She spoke in very broken English, but Erika understood.

Erika finished, crossed herself again, and rose from the kneeler.

She followed the elderly nun through the convent until they came to a heavy wooden door. The nun did not knock. She opened the door and on her cot sat Zhanna Rogova in a nun's cell that was just as small and spartan as a prison cell. Besides the narrow bed, the only items in the tiny room were a crucifix, a small painting of Jesus, and a candle on a small stand that was not lit. The walls were egg-shell stucco and the floor concrete, the ceiling rustic wood with exposed rafters. A trunk sat in a corner. There was not a window. The former top assassin for the Soviet Union wore a simple, brown peasant dress.

"My child," said the Mother Superior to Zhanna. "The visitor you agreed to see is here."

Erika entered the cell; the old nun stepped out and closed the door behind her.

"Hello, Zhanna," Erika said.

Zhanna looked up. "Hello, Erika."

# Chapter 26

## Saint Flora and Mary Convent, outside Santa Bárbara, Honduras
## Same day—Thursday, 14 August 1947

Although a cloister bedroom might remind one of a prison cell, the sisters were free to come and go around the parish grounds, and they could leave the grounds for excursions to town or leave on trips to visit family anytime they wished. The only condition asked of them if they left the parish grounds was to inform the Mother Superior of where they were going.

Erika and Zhanna took a walk around the parish grounds. Several vegetable gardens helped supplement the food pantries in both the convent and the rectory. The nuns also maintained a beautiful red rose garden. Erika could smell the sweet fragrance as they passed by. The priests and brothers maintained several beehives. The honey was sold in the parish gift shop and at stores in nearby Santa Bárbara. Apparently many of the bees had made the break from the hives as they were quite thick on the roses.

"They release some of the bees so they can pollinate the roses," Zhanna told Erika.

They walked in silence for a moment. A group of three nuns in black habits passed on the perpendicular walk in front of them. The brides of Christ smiled and nodded to Zhanna.

"Are you happy here, Zhanna?"

"I think I am. It's peaceful. I've been helping the sisters tend the gardens. I've even considered beginning catechism so I can be baptized. I am searching for your Valhalla, Erika—your Christian Heaven. I'm sure that must sound very funny to you. You know some of the things I've done in the past."

"I don't think it's funny at all, Zhanna. How do you think I feel about myself? You know a lot about my past. They had me wait in the chapel until they took me to your room. I knelt and prayed. I felt like a hypocrite—as if I've failed God."

Again, more walking in silence.

"So why are you here, my friend?" Zhanna asked.

"I was going to ask for your help on a mission in Argentina, but forget about that. If you are at peace here I want you to stay."

"What is the mission?"

"Never mind that. It was wrong of me to come here, Zhanna."

"What would Mr. Carr think about you finding me? You know I deserted the CIA."

"He has no idea where we are. Then after the mission you would return to the protection of your friend, El Búho."

"Demetri is his name. We went through the worst sort of hell together during the war. Both of us nearly starved in Stalingrad. Toward the end of the war we were both transferred to SMERSH. For a while he was my supervisor there. The priests here don't know who I am. Demetri told them I am his niece and fleeing from a husband who constantly abused me."

Erika had to smile. "That's heavy on imagination. I would feel sorry for any man who attempted to abuse Zhanna Rogova."

Even Zhanna grinned. "Still, Demetri gives the church a generous monthly donation for housing me."

"It's apparent that your former comrade values you highly, but he is now in a very dangerous and unsavory business. Stay here at the convent, Zhanna. Take your catechism if that's what you decide to do. You'll never be found here by the CIA or the NKVD. Your friend is clever. (Not only was Zhanna wanted by the CIA, but also by the Soviet NKVD, the Russian intelligence service.) I'll say goodbye now, Zhanna. I'm happy I got to see you."

The two women hugged and kissed on both cheeks in European fashion. Zhanna watched Erika walk away.

Erika returned to the sedan and the driver took her to the waiting airplane. The two armed guards sat behind Kathryn and Kay. Erika had expected El Búho to be already on board but he was not. The sedan drove away.

"Kay, ask those guards when will El Búho be here?" Erika said.

After a brief conversation in Spanish, Kay turned back around and told Erika and Kathryn. "The one that did the talking said El Búho would be here when he wants to be here. That we will shut up and wait."

"Mr. Personality," Kathryn said sardonically.

The wait ended up being thirty minutes. Finally, the sedan returned and El Búho stepped out from the back seat followed shortly by Zhanna Rogova. Zhanna climbed the four stairs and entered the large Cessna T-50. The peasant dress was gone, replaced by dark green slacks and a gray blouse she retrieved from her trunk. The former Russian assassin immediately spotted Kathryn and said hello.

"What are you doing here, Zhanna?" Erika asked. "I hope it's just to say goodbye."

Zhanna didn't answer. El Búho entered next and told his men to fetch Zhanna's luggage from the trunk of the car. They hustled off and Zhanna took one of the seats they vacated.

Zhanna knew Erika spoke Russian. "I'm going with you on the mission," Zhanna said in her native tongue. "Who is this other woman?"

The name she is using is Kay Becker," Erika answered in Russian. "She's our Spanish translator."

"She doesn't look Latin. Is she CIA?"

"Yes, sort of. Actually she is Leroy Carr's wife. Leroy stuck us with her. She's a civilian and unqualified."

Zhanna stared at the back of Kay's head.

Now it was Kay's turn. "Who is the Russian?" She asked Kathryn in English.

"The person we left Buenos Aires to find."

"When are you going to let me call my husband?" The irritation in Kay's voice was obvious.

Erika overheard. "I doubt that he's in Washington, Kay," she said, not really answering the question.

"I can call Sheila."

"I will call Sheila myself when the time is right."

After the guards brought Zhanna's luggage onboard, they stepped off and El Búho came aboard.

"I have ongoing business back in Guatemala and cannot fly you to Argentina from here. I need to return home. Then I will have my pilot fly you to wherever you want to go."

El Búho climbed into his co-pilot seat. The Night Witch fired the engines and within twenty minutes they were in the air and on their way back to Puerto Barrios.


## [Guatemala City]

Since the train and bus ticket sellers in Guatemala required no identification if tickets were purchased with cash (I.D. was required only when using a bank check or money order), Carr and Hodge had spent the past two days combing through the travel logs that train engineers and bus drivers were required by the government to log after a trip.

Finally, after reading through logs to the point where their eyes were swimming, Al Hodge came across one of interest. After reading it he said, "Check this one out, Leroy."

Carr snatched it out of Hodge's hand. It was a report from a bus driver whose bus was stopped by partisans and a revolutionary was taken off the bus and shot. All the passengers had been ordered off the bus and the driver was asked for descriptions of all his passengers. In one sentence of the transcript the driver was recorded as saying there were three Caucasian Red Cross nurses among the passengers—two brunettes and a third with bright blonde hair. The final destination was Puerto Barrios.

## Chapter 27

**Puerto Barrios, Guatemala**
**Next day—Friday, 15 August 1947**

After a short hiatus, the Guatemalan rainy season returned. The gray Cessna T-50, piloted by the Soviet Night Witch, took off with cockpit wipers on full. Onboard now were three Shield Maidens instead of just two—Erika, Kathryn, and Zhanna—along with Kay. Once they got back to Buenos Aires, they knew they could no longer use Carr's CIA asset in Buenos Aires as Carlos would immediately notify Carr's office when the women resurfaced. El Búho told Zhanna he would have two of his associates in Buenos Aires meet their plane, supply vehicles, and transport them wherever they needed to go.

All of this was discussed at breakfast earlier that morning.

When the meal finished, Zhanna thanked her former war comrade in Russian. "Spacibo, Demetri." She walked over to him and kissed him on the cheek.

◊ ◊ ◊

The airplane carrying Leroy Carr and Al Hodge touched down in Puerto Barrios on the town's public runway thirty minutes after the T-50 took off from El Búho's private air strip. Before they left Guatemala City, Carr contacted Sheila Reid and put her to work trying to gather information on any Russians in the Puerto Barrios area. Carr had to conclude that the person helping Zhanna hide was some old friend or former colleague.

"I think I'm losing my touch, Al," Leroy said as they disembarked. "I should have figured out a Guatemalan connection to Zhanna as soon as she disappeared seven months ago."

"Don't blame yourself, Leroy. It should have occurred to me, too, after the incident in Maryland when Zhanna captured Erika with the help of those Guatemalan thugs."

"Let's get to the nearest phone and call Sheila," Carr said. "Hopefully she has discovered something."

Hodge had never seen his friend this jittery. "Sheila has had only overnight, Leroy."

Carr and Hodge found a Puerto Barrios hotel as quickly as they could. This ended up being the Hotel Pescador near the bay. Before the bellman had had time to drop their luggage in the room, Carr placed a phone call to Sheila Reid in Washington.

"Anything yet, Sheila?"

Sheila was the fourth Shield Maiden, but like Carr, she felt her comrades might be in danger and was doing what she could to find a clue to their whereabouts. *"Nothing yet, Leroy,"* the Army major said from the other end. *"I have our best people on this and I'm hoping we'll have something that might help you soon. Call me back this afternoon."*

### [5:00 p.m. Puerto Barrios time]

Leroy Carr placed the call.

*"I might have something for you now, Leroy"* said Sheila from D.C. *"I got this from the State Department. A Soviet Army colonel during the war named Demetri Mikhailov is now a major drug kingpin who operates from a highly guarded compound just outside Puerto Barrios. I did some checking and found a connection. Zhanna served under him for a time during the war."*

◊ ◊ ◊

Sheila Reid discovered the location of Demetri Mikhailov's compound from State Department records, so Carr and Hodge were not forced to go through the process of intimidating various drug dealers to find El Búho, like Erika and Kathryn had had to do.

The rain had again taken a breather a couple of hours ago. At eight o'clock that evening, when the summer sun had not yet fallen, Leroy Carr and Al Hodge, along with their driver, pulled up to the guard shack at the main entrance to El Búho's compound.

Carr produced his CIA picture I.D. "We're here to see Demetri Mikhailov," Carr told the guard standing beside the car. The driver translated. The guard was surprised and seemed unsure of what to do.

113

Few people knew The Owl's real name, and the CIA identification gave him pause.

Finally, the guard decided it was in his best interest to let El Búho know about these men at the gate. With the iron gate still closed, the man returned to the guard shack. Carr and Hodge saw him on the phone. It took about five minutes, but the gate opened. A different guard appeared and instructed Carr's driver to follow him. This new guard mounted a Vespa scooter and led the car down the gravel road toward the hacienda, which was not visible from the main gate.

Two guards armed with shotguns waited in front of the hacienda when the scooter and the car arrived. The scooter drove off, apparently to return to the guard shack. Car windows were rolled down because of the summer heat and humidity. The two armed guards demanded Carr and Hodge turn over their identification, which they did. One guard took the CIA I.D.s into the large residence while the other guard remained with the car, pointed his shotgun at the passengers and ordered them in Spanish to stay in the car. Their driver translated.

The wait in the sedan was a long one, nearly thirty minutes. Finally, the guard that had entered the hacienda returned and told Carr and Hodge to follow him. He informed the CIA duo that their driver would remain in the car, as El Búho spoke English.

They followed the guard into the hacienda and through a large atrium and a piano room, emerged into an open-air courtyard of flowers and two rock fountains. After passing through the courtyard they entered a study. Demetri Mikhailov sat on a sofa with Carr's and Hodge's I.D.s on a shiny mahogany coffee table in front of him. He rose when the guard and CIA men entered the room.

"Hello, welcome to my home, gentlemen," greeted Mikhailov in satisfactory English but with a heavy Russian accent. "Please, have a seat." They did not shake hands. He pointed to two leather-upholstered arm chairs on the opposite side of the table from his sofa. All three men sat down.

"I'm honored that two such high-ranking men in the new American CIA have graced my home. As allies during the war, I'm pleased to see you. May I offer you a drink, or something to eat, perhaps? I enjoy the new American food called pizza, or at least it is new to me. I can have my chef make one if you have the time."

"No thank you," said Carr.

"Then you will have a drink with me." Mikhailov rose, walked to a table near the window, and brought back three glasses and a bottle of Scotch. "This is Edradour," he said as he poured each of them a snifter. "It is the smallest distillery in Scotland. They produce only ten barrels a week. I have it shipped to me by airplane."

He scooted the glasses across the table. Carr and Hodge picked them up and took a sip.

"Good stuff," said Hodge.

Carr cut to the chase. "Colonel, we suspect you have been protecting Zhanna Rogova. Where is she?"

"Zhanna? I have not seen Zhanna since shortly after the war when the Politburo disbanded SMERSH." Mikhailov knew he couldn't lie about knowing Zhanna, as it was on record that they had worked together during the war. The CIA would know that. "What makes you think she has been under my protection?" The Russian took another sip of his Scotch.

"That's confidential, but we have our reasons for such suspicions," Carr answered. "I also suspect that if Zhanna is not here, then three other women recently showed up at your door asking about her."

"Three women have not called on me. I would remember that."

"I noticed there is a runway outside your compound walls, but no airplane sits there and it is not in the hangar. The hangar door was open."

"I flew some business associates to Columbia. Anything else, Deputy Director Carr?"

The two men stared at each other.

"I have ways of making your dirty business hard for you," Carr threatened.

"Yes, but you won't do such a thing. I also have suspicions. I suspect for some reason you are here without your agency's approval. You forget yourself Mr. Carr. I was a high-ranking officer in the Soviet intelligence network. I know how things work. The CIA would never let its second in command go on a field mission; especially, not to

115

Guatemala with all the unrest. You're priority is not to find Zhanna. You're here to find the three women you *think* called on me, or at least one of them. Am I correct?"

# Chapter 28

## Buenos Aires, Argentina
## Next day—Saturday, 16 August 1947

The Soviet Night Witch first flew the T-50 to Lima, Peru for a refueling stop. It was a lengthy layover of nearly four hours. The Russian pilot checked both engines and both needed oil. This, along with refueling, contributed to the long layover as the airport personnel were not efficient.

The aircraft touched down in Buenos Aires in the early morning hours of the day after it took off from Guatemala. The skies were clear but the temperatures had dropped about twenty degrees from when they had left Guatemala. It was currently 53° Fahrenheit. As El Búho had promised, a man was waiting for them when the T-50 sat down. He drove the Shield Maidens (now three) and Kay to a private residence located in the outskirts of the city. No one was there. They had the small house to themselves. The man gave them a phone number where he could be reached and told them to call when they needed him for transportation. In the meantime, the Night Witch waited for refueling then took to the air for the journey back to Puerto Barrios. The three had never learned her name.

**[that afternoon]**
Demetri Mikhailov had told Zhanna he would arrange for a place where she and her comrades could stay while in Buenos Aires. The small house, located just outside the city limits of Buenos Aires, had one bedroom and a kitchen with a gas stove, plenty of plates, bowls, pots, skillets, and utensils, and even a new electric refrigerator instead of an icebox, but no provisions. There was no telephone. The women hired a taxi and went for lunch in downtown Buenos Aires. Erika told Kay to ask the waiter about a grocery store. From his directions, Kay led them a few blocks to a small food store where they bought several bags of groceries and necessities such as toilet paper and other toiletries. They hailed another taxi and returned to the house.

That evening, Erika prepared them a dinner of pork chops smothered in sauerkraut, with sides of boiled Rotkohl (red cabbage) and grüne Bohnen (green beans). It surprised Kay that Erika knew how to cook anything at all.

"When can I call my husband?" Kay asked Erika as they ate.

"Soon, I hope."

"What does 'soon' mean?"

This time, Kathryn responded to Kay's question. "Kay, you're husband will find us and arrest Erika, Zhanna, and me if he knows our location. We might still face that future even if we complete the mission and return you safely to him."

Erika added, "The mission is now two-fold, Kay. We have to find out if Hitler is alive, and we now have to find out if the Soviets are bumping off Germans in this country. That's why we need Zhanna with us. If a German was involved with the concentration camps, or murdered civilians in Poland or Russia, he or she should be tried by one of the war crimes tribunals."

"Yes," Kathryn agreed, "but Otto Bergmann didn't deserve to be murdered just because he was in the Gestapo. He was a beat cop in Berlin before the war. When war broke out in '39 many policemen were reassigned to the Gestapo. They had no choice in the matter. Many in the Gestapo abused their power and deserve to be hanged, but Otto wasn't one of them. All he did during the war was remain a policeman and eventually ended up a detective investigating common civilian crimes—the same job I did."

Zhanna listened to all of this but remained silent as she continued to eat.

"What does all this have to do with me not being able to call Leroy and let him at least know I'm still alive?" Kay asked.

Erika: "Kay, you know very well that the CIA can trace any call. It's especially easy if the call originates from another country because it has to go through a series of operators."

Kay: "I can call from a pay phone. There's no telephone in this house, anyway."

Erika: "They can still trace it to the pay phone. We can't let your husband know we are back in Buenos Aires just yet. Besides, your husband most likely is not in Washington. He's likely in Guatemala. He would be able to trace us to Guatemala City because of the airplane tickets we had to buy."

Kay: "I can call Major Reid or someone else assigned to his office."

Erika: "It doesn't matter who you call, the call will be traced. You know that. I'll tell you what, Kay. We'll be here in Buenos Aires tomorrow, but the next day we'll probably be leaving this city. I'd like to talk again with Ernst Roth, he might know more than he claimed to know about Hitler's supposed escape, but when I visited his apartment he was scared and packing to leave. We'll never find him. He helped train Kathryn and me at Quenzsee—that was the German spy school just outside Berlin. Herr Roth knows all the tricks on how to successfully go underground. We need to pursue information by other means.

"Between the money we got off the drug dealer in Puerto Barrios and the big sum that El Búho gave us, money is no longer a concern. We have plenty of it. Banks aren't open tomorrow; it's Sunday. It will be Monday morning before we can get to a bank and convert it to Argentinean currency. I can't let you make a phone call, but if you want to return home, we'll take you to the airport Monday after we get the money converted and buy you a ticket to Washington. We'll make sure you're on the plane when it takes off. You won't be able to make a phone call until the refueling stop in Panama City. That will give us about a twenty hour head start, which is plenty of time. We'll ask El Búho's man to be our translator, or supply us another one."

"You won't tell me where you are going, of course," Kay said.

Erika smiled. "Of course not. I know you don't like me, Kay, but surely you don't consider me an idiot."

"And if I decide to stay with the team, what happens then?"

"I'll let you make a phone call just before we leave this town. You'll tell whoever you speak to the truth—that you're okay, and that I gave you the opportunity to return home but you decided to stay with us. If Leroy is not there, as I suspect, your message will be relayed to him."

There was a long pause as Kay returned to eating. Eventually, she said, "I'll stay on one condition. That I'm not treated like a child in tow. If I'm a member of this team I want to be treated as such."

Erika looked at Kay. "If you're saying you want to be trusted, it comes with responsibility. Leroy gave you the option of not coming with us but you decided to do it. That tells us you are not a coward, but I don't want a hasty decision, Kay. You have until Monday morning to decide. I will warn you that, with this latest turn of events, this assignment is unlikely to end up being a cakewalk with low danger risk as all of us originally believed. Things might get messy in a few days."

"As long as you agree to consider me an equal partner in the team," said Kay, "I won't change my mind."

Erika looked at Kathryn and Zhanna. "I'll leave this up to you," she told them.

Both women looked at Kay and eventually nodded their heads.

"So, where are we going when we leave here Monday?" Kay asked.

"We're going to Patagonia. It's in southern Argentina."

Puerto San Julián, in southern Argentina, was the place that Ernst Roth had told Lorelei and Róta the story about two U-boats dropping off people two months after the war in Europe ended. Both Erika and Kathryn considered this their only lead.

Erika looked at Zhanna. "Should we let El Búho's man know we are leaving Buenos Aires?"

"This man won't betray us," the former Russian assassin answered. "Doing so would also betray Demetri, who told him I'm a personal friend. The man knows he is a dead man if he does that. Still, I will call Demetri to see what he recommends we do. We don't want to hire a plane or go by any public transportation. Unlike in Guatemala, Argentina requires identification for any long distance public transportation, even if paying in cash. Mr. Carr would find out quickly where we go. Demetri will help us."

# Chapter 29

## Buenos Aires
## Monday, 18 August 1947

The four women rose at six-thirty this morning. It was Kay's turn to cook. She put together a breakfast of scrambled eggs, Argentinean bacon which resembled Canadian bacon more than American but was spicier than either, and fried potatoes and onions. Toasters, which were now in most American homes, were still uncommon in Argentina. Kathryn helped out by slicing bread from a round loaf, buttering it, and toasting it on an iron skillet.

Over breakfast they discussed tactics. Traveling by automobile to where they wanted to go—Puerto San Julián in Patagonia—would take too long. It would require a day and a half drive on rough roads, and even a train would take that long because of the myriad stops along the way. Yesterday morning (Sunday), Zhanna had contacted Demetri Mikhailov and told him they needed a flight out of Buenos Aires. She also asked him if she should tell his man in Buenos Aires of their journey.

*"No, keep your plans to yourselves, Zhanna, I'll send my plane and pilot,"* Mikhailov had said over the phone. Zhanna's old comrade told her he would dispatch his pilot and plane immediately. Having left Guatemala yesterday, the plane should arrive in Buenos Aires around noon today.

After Zhanna's phone call to Mikhailov, Erika called their local driver and told him they would only need transportation around Buenos Aires Monday morning.

"When El Búho's man arrives at nine o'clock, we'll have him take us to a bank," Erika said to the other women. "Then we'll have him drop us off downtown. We'll tell him we're going to do some shopping and that we'll call him when we're finished. We'll never call, of course. We'll hail cabs to take us to the airport. It will take two cabs for all of us and our gear."

## [same day—Puerto Barrios, Guatemala]

Because they had no other leads, Leroy Carr and Al Hodge were still in Puerto Barrios. They had called on El Búho three more times in the past two days. Each time they came away with nothing. More problems pressed on Carr's shoulders. When CIA Director Roscoe Hillenkoetter found out that Carr and Hodge had gone without authorization to Guatemala, he was livid. He assigned a team of assets in that Central American country to find Carr. When located, Hillenkoetter chastised Carr over the telephone, but when Carr explained everything about Kay, Hillenkoetter, who adored Kay, agreed to let Carr remain on the pursuit as long as he immediately left Guatemala.

*"Things are not safe there, Leroy. I can't have my assistant director running around Guatemala,"* Hillenkoetter said over the phone when he spoke with Carr.

"I understand, Admiral," Carr told him. "We've run into nothing but dead ends here, anyway. Lehmann is an expert at covering her tracks. Al and I will depart for Buenos Aires as soon as possible. That's where the original mission was based. Hopefully, we can get a break there." Carr wished he were more optimistic about his words. He knew trying to chase down Erika Lehmann when she didn't want to be found was a daunting if not impossible task.


## [later that morning—Buenos Aires]

As was their plan, the women had their driver take them to a bank where they exchanged the Guatemalan quetzals for Argentinean pesos. After that it was downtown for shopping where they bid El Búho's man farewell. Knowing the weather could be much harsher in southern Argentina than in Buenos Aires this time of year (where they were going was only 1,000 miles from the northern islands of Antarctica), they each bought a scarf and gloves, a sweater, and other clothes for layering underneath their jackets.

When they finished gathering what they needed. Erika told Kay she could call Washington. The call from a phone booth required many coins be dropped, but Kay finally reached her husband's office. Erika had demanded that Kay leave the booth door open.

At last, Kay heard from the other end: *"Assistant Director Carr's office, this is Major Reid. How may I help you?"* The Shield Maidens stood near the telephone booth, listening to what Kay said.

"Sheila, this is Kay. Is my husband there?"

*"No, Leroy is not here. Where are you, Kay?"*

"I'm back in Buenos Aires." Again, everyone knew the call would be traced making it useless to lie. "Where is Leroy?"

Erika grabbed the receiver out of Kay's hand and heard Sheila say, *"Kay, he and Al Hodge are on their way to Buenos Aires."*

"Sheila, this is Erika."

*"Erika, what's going on?"*

"We've learned some additional information that forced us into deep cover. The mission is still ongoing. I'll give you back to Kay."

Kay took the receiver. "Tell Leroy I'm okay, Sheila. Erika offered me the chance to return home, but I decided to stay. It was my decision." Kay hung up the phone before Sheila could ask more questions.

They found a taxi stand where four parked taxis lined up waiting for passengers. They hired two of the taxis and arrived at the Buenos Aires airport just a few minutes before noon. From a terminal window, they spotted El Búho's gray Cessna T-50 sitting quietly on the tarmac. The gray color made it easy to spot, as most Cessnas came painted white from the factory.

The Shield Maidens and Kay took their bags to the plane but it seemed to be empty. After several knocks on the fuselage door, the Night Witch finally opened it.

"We thought for a moment that no one was onboard," Erika said in Russian.

"After refueling in Lima, I had a strong tail wind over the Andes," the woman said. "I arrived about four hours ago and caught up on a little sleep." The pilot with no name let down the three steps and the women climbed on board with their luggage.

The Night Witch had checked the oil and refueled as soon as she landed, so all that was out of the way. She fired the engines. It took her about twenty minutes to check her gauges and navigation maps. There was no co-pilot or navigator onboard, unlike what she had been accustomed to during the war. The former Russian bomber pilot now served as her own navigator.

When the wheels of the T-50 finally left the ground, the women settled in for the six-hour flight. Kay rarely smoked. Kathryn, Zhanna and Erika lit Guatemalan cigars courtesy of El Búho. He had told Zhanna the cigars were hand-rolled on the thighs of virgins. Surely an exaggeration, she knew, but then her friend Demetri could display a sense of humor on occasion. Conveniently, each seat had an ashtray in an arm of each chair.

About an hour into the flight, Zhanna went to the cockpit and sat down in the empty co-pilot's seat. She sat in silence for a few minutes as she finished the cigar.

It was the Night Witch who broke the silence. "I know who you are," she said to Zhanna in Russian. "Colonel Mikhailov told me. You're Zhanna Rogova, our country's sniper with the most verified kills during the war."

"If you know who I am, it's only fair I know your name," Zhanna replied. "Demetri told us you were one of the famous Night Witches, and that you served in our county's 587th Bomber Regiment."

"I don't know how famous we were; most people outside of our motherland and the Germans we bombed never heard of us by that name. Yet, it is true I was a Night Witch. My name is Lyudmila Solokova. I'm from Syktyvkar in Siberia."

# Chapter 30

## Puerto San Julián, Patagonia, Argentina
## Next day—Tuesday, 19 August 1947

Yesterday, Lyudmila Solokova returned the wheels of the Cessna T-50 to earth at 1730 hours Puerto San Julián time (5:30 p.m.) which was only one hour ahead of Washington, D.C. time. As the southern part of Argentina was west of the northern part, they had gained back an hour since leaving Buenos Aires.

"There will be no one meeting you here at the airport," Lyudmila Solokova told them after she taxied to where the lone ground crewman directed. When he signaled her to stop, she cut the engines. Solokova took out a small index card from her shirt pocket and handed it to Zhanna who still sat beside her. "This is for you. It's from Colonel Mikhailov. On the card is the address of a house you can use while you're here. Any taxi driver will be able to find the address. On the back of the card is the name of a man who can help you, but the colonel told me to tell you to call this man only in the case of an important emergency."

Erika sat in the seat directly behind the pilot and heard everything. "Are you staying the night here?" she asked El Búho's pilot in Russian.

"Yes. I will need sleep before I begin the return journey to Puerto Barrios."

"You're welcome to stay the night with us."

"I never leave my plane at a strange airport. I have weapons."

"It might be a chilly night."

"I have plenty of wool blankets, and I'm from Siberia. In Siberia, this is a balmy day."

Erika and Zhanna laughed. "Then it's time to say goodbye," Erika said. "Thank you for all you have done for us."

"If you need me again, Zhanna Rogova, call Colonel Mikhailov. Otherwise, farewell.

The women stepped off of the plane into 37° F air, but a strong breeze off the Atlantic made it feel much colder. Solokova

125

disembarked with them. She would prep her airplane and refuel now so she would be ready for takeoff when she awoke. As the CIA team walked toward the small terminal, Erika looked back and saw the Night Witch climbing onto the starboard wing to check that engine's oil.

They did not hire a taxi to take them to the house. Erika thought that a bad idea. If Leroy Carr managed to somehow trace them to Puerto San Julián, cab company logs could be accessed and cab drivers would probably remember four Caucasian women hiring two cabs to take them to the same location. Instead, in the airport terminal they bought a map of the city and picked up a bus route schedule. Everything was in Spanish, of course, so Kay was in charge of finding a bus that would pass a car dealership. She asked questions at the terminal counter and came away with the answers.

When the women boarded the bus, Erika had Kay speak to the driver and offer him a generous tip to let them off where they wanted to go. Even though doing so would require him to deviate slightly from his standard route, the bus driver was happy to do so for the gratuity.

The bus dropped off the women and their bags at a car-lot. Kay did the talking. The owner told her they were about to close. Kay told him they would pay cash and had every intention of buying a car then and there if they found one suitable. This enticed the man to stay open.

The man had only eight cars on his lot and they were rusting jalopies in poor condition with balding tires. Kay told the man none were acceptable. He doubted these women had enough money to buy it, but he led them to his garage. He pulled a tarp off a black, 1937 Buick sedan. This was his best car. The women looked it over. The keys were in the ignition and Kathryn jumped in, started it, and checked the miles. The odometer read only 1500 miles. "The guy is a crook," Kathryn said. "He's turned back the odometer." Both Kathryn and Erika knew the mechanics of automobiles and how they should sound when idling.

"This car need points and plugs," Erika said. "Also better tires."

Kay translated.

Kathryn said, "Ask him how much he wants for it, Kay."

Kay spoke to the man for several minutes, haggling in Spanish. When finished she turned to her three partners.

"He wanted 14,000 pesos, that's $700 American. One could buy a brand new sedan in the States for a couple of hundred more. I told him we'd give him 7,000 pesos ($350) and that includes the tune up and better tires. He accepted. His mechanic has left for the day, so we'll have to bring the car back in tomorrow."

Erika complimented her. "Good job, Kay."

Erika paid the man and the women loaded into the car. All of their luggage fit in the large trunk except for one suitcase which was placed in the backseat between Kathryn and Zhanna. Erika drove with Kay beside her in the front. Even though they had a map, they weren't exactly sure where in the city they were, and, not wanting to ask the car dealer for directions, they stopped at a gasoline station a few blocks away. There, Kay asked for directions of the gas jockey filling their tank. They arrived at the house address at 7:30 p.m. only to find out it was a duplex in a drug ridden area of town. A large group of drug dealing hooligans had set up shop on the nearest corner, conducting their business in the open with seemingly no concern about the local authorities.

Kay was somewhat taken aback at the location of their hideaway but the three Shield Maidens didn't mind. The location was good cover.

Inside their small half of the duplex, it was easy to tell that the place had not been used in some time. Furniture was covered with dust sheets, and, like the house in Buenos Aires that El Búho had arranged for them, the place was void of any food. The single bathroom did have a half roll of toilet paper sitting on the sink beside the toilet. There were two bedrooms, each with one queen-size bed. Erika would have to decide who slept with whom. In the kitchen was a small gas stove with just two burners. Beside the sink sat an old-fashioned ice box with no ice—they would have to order some. Unlike the safehouse in Buenos Aires, here there was a telephone in the living room.

They would buy provisions tomorrow. Tonight they would find a restaurant. After depositing their luggage in the living room, they took their weapons and all of their money with them. If the drug gang who controlled the neighborhood, or one of the dope addicts that roamed the street considered breaking and entering while they were gone all that they would come away with was ladies clothes.

"It was wise of Demetri to place us here," Zhanna said. "He knows we can protect ourselves, and it would be extremely difficult for anyone to find us here. I would be willing to wager that even the police avoid this area."

Erika nodded. "I agree, but we have to park the car on the street so we'll have to make a deal with the gang that rules the neighborhood so our car will not be stolen or the tires slashed. We'll do that when we return from dinner."

◊ ◊ ◊

Using the telephone book that the living room phone perched upon, along with the city map they had bought at the airport, Kay found a restaurant in the town square. As they drove, she gave directions to Erika.

After dinner they returned to their temporary home. The sun had long ago disappeared. The only street light was on the corner, about a half-block from the house. Six members of the neighborhood's Mafia-wannabes still occupied the corner, continuing the everyday drug business with their addicted customers.

"Time to buy some car insurance," Erika said after they parked on the street in front of the duplex. "Kay, we'll need you to translate."

The four of them began walking the half-block to the corner. As they got nearer, the six thugs spotted them. They began hooting and making obscene gestures with their hips. Two women, dressed like prostitutes, stood nearby.

As the four-woman CIA team reached the group of young men, Erika told Kay to translate exactly what she would say.

"Good evening, boys," Erika said. "We just today moved in down the street and we love our car. How much will it take to keep it safe?"

The men laughed. "Americanos?" one of them asked.

"None of your fucking business," Erika answered. "How much will it take to ignore our car?"

Kay translated exactly, including the curse word.

The smile left the thugs' faces, replaced by frowns. The one who asked her the question seemed to be the leader and he did the talking.

"We start out with sex for all of us then, depending how good you are, we'll decide how much money you pay us."

The Shield Maidens had not rehearsed it, but almost if on cue, they drew weapons from underneath their jackets. Before the thugs had time to react, Erika pointed her handgun at the leader's privates. Kathryn slapped the cigarette from another thug's lips and replaced the cigarette with her gun barrel that she shoved into his mouth. At the same time, moving like a striking jungle cat, Zhanna repositioned herself behind another man and held a dagger to his throat. Kay had not drawn her revolver, but after seeing the example set, she drew it out and pointed it at another one of the six.

The two prostitutes shrieked and took off running. The two men who were not covered drew knives.

Kathryn told Kay, "Tell them to drop the knives or I'll send every rotten tooth in this lowlife's mouth out of the back of his head."

After Kay spoke, the leader told the men to drop their knives.

"We're trying to be nice. How much money, you stupid motherfucker?" Erika said angrily to the leader.

Kay repeated the exact words in Spanish and the man started talking. Kay told Erika, "They want 900 pesos a day."

"That's too much," Erika said. "Tell him we'll pay 300 a day ($15) or I'll make him a eunuch. And the deal includes leaving our house alone, as well as the car." Erika lowered her gun enough to fire a round into the brown brick sidewalk, causing all the men to jump. She then returned the Beretta to her original aiming point.

Zhanna addressed the gang leader for affect. "Please say no so I have an excuse to open this podonok's throat."

Kay didn't know the Russian word for bastard. She winged it and used the word 'escoria', the Spanish word for human waste.

After Kay translated, the leader said, "Okay, okay!" That required no interpretation.

**[same day]**

As soon as he and Al Hodge landed in Buenos Aires, Leroy Carr called Sheila Reid for any updates. The Army major filled him in.

*"Kay called from Buenos Aires yesterday, Leroy."* The connection with Washington was not good. Sheila had to talk loudly so Carr could understand. *"Kay said that Erika offered her the chance to come back to Washington, but that she—Kay—decided to stay."*

Carr's heart sunk. "Al and I will check the Alvear Palace Hotel. That's where the team stayed the first time they arrived here. We'll get a room there, Sheila, so call me immediately if you hear anything more. If we're out, leave a message at the desk and I'll call you back as soon as I return to the hotel. And find out the exact phone where the call came from, Sheila." Carr hung up the airport pay phone. Hodge stood next to him.

"Al, Kay called my office from this town yesterday. Sheila will trace the call, but Lehmann is too cagey to make the blunder of letting Kay call from a place where they could be tracked down."

"That also means they are probably no longer in Buenos Aires," Hodge added. "I doubt that Lehmann would let Kay call unless they were leaving this city."

Carr nodded slowly.

Hodge asked, "Do you think Lehmann could have forced Kay to say she was staying of her own free will?"

"No, not even Erika Lehmann could force my wife to say that. Kay is still with them because she wants to be. Why, I don't know."

"We'll find them, Leroy, and Lehmann will get what she deserves."

Carr looked at his old friend but didn't comment.

# Chapter 31

## Puerto San Julián, Patagonia, Argentina
## Next day—Wednesday, 20 August 1947

Erika had decided that she and Zhanna would bunk together, with Kathryn and Kay in the other bedroom. She felt Kay would probably be uneasy sleeping in the same bed with her. Regardless, last night Kay lay awake most of the night. That she had drawn a gun and pointed it at another human being haunted her. Also, she was disturbed at the ease of which the three women she was associated with could seemingly draw forth such extreme viciousness at the drop of a hat. What type of people were these women that surrounded her?

Kay now knew of Zhanna's background as a sniper for the Red Army and later a cold-blooded assassin. Zhanna's personality was straightforward. As for Erika . . . well, Erika was Erika—the She-Wolf who allowed in her circle only women who were as cunning and ruthless as she. Under her surface lurked a level of ferocity that she could seemingly flick on like a light switch.

Yet, Kathryn was the hardest for Kay to figure out. Kathryn was personable and seemed so normal. She could be your next-door neighbor's friendly wife. But last night on the street corner, Kathryn had, without blinking an eye, instantly shifted into a level of brutality on par with Erika and Zhanna. It was unnerving for Kay. Much like Erika, Kathryn also seemed under the spell of a Jekyll and Hyde personality.

They skipped breakfast this morning. There was nothing in the house to prepare and they didn't want to take the time to eat in a restaurant. Instead they took the car back to the dealer for the tune up and tires. As they waited inside the car dealer's office for the mechanic to complete the work, Kathryn said, "Kay, that was brave of you to draw your gun yesterday on the corner." They were alone in the office. The owner was outside on the lot hawking his jalopies.

"Yes, it was," Erika affirmed. "Would you have pulled the trigger if one of the men who we couldn't cover rushed toward you?"

"I couldn't sleep half of the night thinking about that, and other things," Kay responded. She thought for a moment then answered the question. "I think I might have. I would have probably missed, but I would have pulled the trigger. I hate drug dealers to begin with, and for that reason it would have made the choice easier. God forgive me."

After a two hour wait, the mechanic knocked on the office door and told the women their car was ready. All four of them followed the man to the garage where Erika and Kathryn inspected the car. The tires weren't new, but better than the originals, that was for sure. Not trusting the man, Erika checked the oil. The level on the dipstick indicated the oil pan was full and the oil looked clear. Kathryn started the engine; it sounded much better.

"Unlike your boss, you are an honest man," Erika said to the mechanic. "Do you have children?"

Kay translated.

"Yes, my wife and I have four children."

Before they left the house that morning, Erika had divided the money equally between them all. Each woman was now rich by Argentinean standards.

"Give him a generous tip, Kay."

Kay reached into her pants pocket (none of the women carried a purse) and gave the man a 1,000 peso bill (a $50 dollar tip). The man's eyes widened. It was more than he made in a week.

"Buy something for your wife and children that will make them happy," Erika told the mechanic. Kay translated as the women loaded themselves into the Buick.

◊ ◊ ◊

The women had decided on the plan for that afternoon. Zhanna and Kay would go shopping for food and other necessities. For example, the house had a kitchen drawer full of eating and cooking utensils, pots and pan inside the white metal cabinets, but there wasn't a dinner plate to be found anywhere. Towels were also needed.

Erika and Kathryn would remain at the house, going through the telephone book. Puerto San Julián was many times smaller than

Buenos Aires and the phone book was not nearly as thick, but if they could spot even just one name they recognized it would at least give them someone to call on and question.

Zhanna took the wheel so Kay could put her attention to the city map. However, Zhanna, who had driven a car only three or four times in her life, proved to be a terrible driver. She was constantly grinding gears when she shifted, and she weaved all over the road. After just a few blocks, Kay had to take over. This forced Kay to pull over every few blocks so she could check the map.

"So you are Mr. Carr's wife. Are you happy with him?" Zhanna asked as they drove.

"Yes."

"He is a good husband and lover?"

"Yes."

"That is good."

Last night, after the women showered, Kay had for the first time seen Zhanna without her ever-present neck scarf she wore during the day. Kay saw the wide, gruesome scar that encircled the Russian's neck, but she didn't feel comfortable asking this strange and menacing woman about it.

Back at the house, Erika and Kathryn sat side by side slowly flipping the pages of the Puerto San Julián telephone book.

"Kathryn, I can't help but feel guilty about getting Zhanna involved in this."

"Why?"

"She seemed at peace at the nunnery in Honduras. She told me she was even considering becoming Catholic." Both Erika and Kathryn were Roman Catholic and, despite the violence their jobs sometimes required, both tried to hold tight to their faith.

"After you talked with her at the convent, you told her not to come, Erika. You didn't force her. Zhanna has to make herself feel like we do, that what we do is no different from what a soldier is required to do during a war. A soldier can keep his faith while being bound by duty to kill the enemy. Both of us supported the Reich during the 1930s and the early years of the war. We thought our country was doing only right. It wasn't until we found out about the KZs (concentration camps) that we wavered and lost faith in our leaders. The United States is far from perfect, but it is certainly a country that offers people a better life than what Zhanna had under Stalin, or our lives under Adolf Hitler. I don't feel guilty about being a soldier for a country I can believe in."

"Still, I feel guilty about bringing Zhanna back into our world."

They returned to perusing the telephone book. Puerto San Julián was a small town with a large number of people living in nearby fishing or farming communities. Only half of the households had telephones, so it didn't take the two women long to get through the phone book. There were a significant number of German names, but neither Erika nor Kathryn recognized the name of anyone they knew.

The only thing of interest for their purposes was a listing for a German singing club, the Germania Gesangverein.

"We'll have to start there," Erika said.

# Chapter 32

## Puerto San Julián, Argentina
## Same day—Wednesday, 20 August 1947

After Kay and Zhanna returned after gathering groceries and other items, the women threw together a quick dinner of ham sandwiches with American-style potato chips as a side.

"Apparently the house attached to ours is unoccupied," Erika said as they ate. "I've seen nothing that would indicate that someone lives next door."

The other women agreed that they had seen no one coming or going from the other half of the duplex.

"It's 1900 hours (seven o'clock)," Erika said. "Let's finish eating quickly so we can get to the German singing club before it gets too late. We'll do the dishes later."

They bundled up and stepped out of the house under clear nighttime skies. The half-moon was directly overhead and the stars of Orion shined bright. Nevertheless, the 30° F temperature was made to feel much colder to the skin by the wind moving north from Antarctica.

"I wonder how close those stars are to your God's throne." Zhanna wondered.

"I don't know, but the Bible says the stars shine for Him, not us." Erika said. "We're told that each night the stars shout happily, 'Here I am, Lord!'"

The Germania Gesangverein was located on a street named Urquiza just a block from the bay. Erika drove. Luckily, they found a spot to park in the nearly full gravel parking lot beside the building. Resting in the lot were American and German cars (a Horch and several Mercedes-Benz). Most of the cars were pre-war but Erika and Kathryn spotted two brand new Mercedes.

The building was constructed by Germans shortly after the First World War and had served as a beer hall and restaurant open to the public. Now it was a private club. The Ratskeller was on the main floor with a large festival hall upstairs.

"This definitely looks like some of the beer halls back home," Kathryn said to Erika. No one stopped them at the door, but as soon as they found a table a large, overweight man approached. The veins in his bulbous nose gave it a purple hue. He wore Lederhosen topped off with an Alpine hat complete with feather. He spoke in German.

"I have not seen you here before; are you guests of a member?"

"Nein," Erika said. "What is your name?"

"Hupprecht, but they call me 'Huppi.'"

"Where are you from, Huppi?" Erika asked with a smile and friendly tone.

"I lived in the Sudetenland." This was an area of Czechoslovakia inhabited primarily by Germans. "But enough about me. You speak as a native German, where was your home?"

Erika told the truth. "I was born in Oberschopfheim, a small village in Baden. Later, I lived in Munich and eventually Berlin."

"These women with you, they are all German, yes?"

Erika knew lying wouldn't work. Zhanna spoke acceptable German but with a Russian accent; Kay's German was limited to 'tourist' German and her American accent undeniable. Erika made introductions.

"This is Kathryn. She's from Berlin."

"Wie geht es Ihnen?" Kathryn used the formal phrase for 'How do you do?' which Germans preferred for those they were meeting for the first time.

Now Erika had to start combining the truth with lies. "This is Zhanna; she's Russian but fought for our side during the war."

The man frowned.

"This is Kay; she's an American. We met her in Buenos Aires. She speaks fluent Spanish, which the rest of us do not speak. We hired her to be our interpreter."

"A Russian and an American." Huppi grumbled to Erika and Kathryn. "You should not have brought them here, Fräuleins, especially the Russian."

"As I told you," Erika said, "Zhanna was on our side. As far as Kay, her last name is Becker. Her ancestors are German. Her father was a member of the German-American Bund that supported the Führer in the United States before the war."

"Nevertheless, this is a private club for those born in the Fatherland. Even you and Fräulein Fischer will have to be approved for membership by our committee. The Russian and American cannot join. I will let you stay as my guests for as long as you wish tonight. You can order and pay for your beer or wine at the bar. We serve Berliner as well as several Bavarian beers. Our wines are from the Rhineland. If you come back do not bring the Russian and American with you. If you return, you can then fill out a membership application and speak to our leader, Oberst Graf (Oberst was a military rank—a colonel). He will decide if your application will be reviewed by the committee."

After the man walked away, Erika said to Kathryn, "I think we found the right place."

◊ ◊ ◊

The women had read the sign beside the bar that told the hours. It closed at two o'clock in the morning each night—closed on Sunday. The four women of the CIA team drank beer (slowly, and in moderation) until midnight. The club was busy but they remained to themselves; the other drinkers ignored them or looked on with suspicion.

They returned four hours later after the club shut down and everyone had left. It would be their time to burglarize the office.

Zhanna was assigned as lookout. Kay was brought along just in case they were pulled over by the local police because of the odd hour when there were few cars on the road. A freezing Kay Carr stood in the shadows breathing into her hands outside the club with Zhanna.

It took Kathryn a couple of minutes to pick the back door lock. When eventually successful, she and Erika entered the club's storage area.

Using only small penlights for illumination, Erika found the club office. She held the light for Kathryn as she again picked another door lock. Inside the office was a desk and chairs with several filing cabinets on a side wall. Some of the file cabinet drawers were unlocked; three were locked. The two women ignored the unlocked cabinets. Kathryn went to work. The file cabinet locks were much simpler than the door locks and this time it took the former Gestapo officer only seconds to open them.

Using the pen lights, Erika and Kathryn worked together going through the files. In the last cabinet Erika withdrew a folder containing a ledger with a list of all of the club member's names.

Erika held the penlight in her teeth and slowly thumbed through the hand-written ledger with Kathryn looking over her shoulder to also scan it. Erika stopped at a page and used an American expression: "Bingo. Kathryn, hold the light for me."

From a pocket, Erika drew out a small Leica microcamera. Known as the 'spy camera' it was the same type she had used on missions for Abwehr and it was also standard CIA issue. While Kathryn held the penlight, Erika took photographs of several of the ledger pages.

# Chapter 33

**Puerto San Julián, Argentina**
**Two days later—Friday, 22 August 1947**

On the pages of the ledger that Erika had photographed during their break-in were the names of all the club members, the town or area in Germany they hailed from, and their wartime occupation. If they had been in the military, the ledger included rank and service group. Many names had 'farmer' or 'factory worker' listed, but nearly all of these people came from an area that was now in East Germany. Those Germans had fled to avoid living under the communism, not because they fled justice.

Included were also names of SS and Gestapo, many of whom served in occupied countries during the war as was noted on the pages. Also the word ODESSA appeared associated with some of the names. This meant that they had been helped to get out of Germany with help from the SS who, after the war, set up the ODESSA organization to aid hunted Nazis flee to South America. As they stood over the ledger, Erika and Kathryn committed as many names to memory as they could because they reasoned that they would have a difficult time getting the tiny and special film developed in such a small town.

That assumption proved to be correct. Yesterday afternoon, after the women had gotten some sleep, Kathryn left the house to investigate, taking Kay with her for any necessary translations. Only one small photography shop existed in the town and it was owned and run by a German who was a member of the German singing club. He spoke in German so, in the end, Kay was not needed. Obviously, there was no way they could risk having the film developed there.

Knowing Leroy Carr was not in Washington, this morning Erika mailed the film to Sheila Reid. They used a fake return address. The postmark would tell the CIA the city the package came from but it couldn't be avoided—the film was too important. Sheila was one of them, a Shield Maiden, but she was also an American Army major. Her oath of duty would force her to contact Carr with the location, and

Erika respected that. However, the two weeks it would take the package to make its way to Washington should hopefully give them the window they needed.

Last night—the night after their early morning break in—Erika and Kathryn left Zhanna and Kay at the house and went to the German club by themselves. The man that Huppi had referred to, Colonel Graf, was not at the club that night, but the women filled out a membership application and were told the colonel always came to the club on Friday.

So tonight the two Germans arrived early, ordered a pitcher of Berliner (a popular Berlin beer) and sat at the bar. Again tonight, Zhanna and Kay stayed behind to avoid problems.

Huppi wasn't a bartender but he was never far from the bar, always carrying his large ceramic beer stein.

"I'm sorry, Fräuleins," Huppi said. "Women aren't allowed to sit at the bar. You must have not seen the sign." He pointed out the sign behind the bar.

"We saw it," Erika said, "and promptly ignored it. We're here to see Oberst (colonel) Graf, Huppi."

One advantage of the two-day delay from their first visit on Wednesday was the time it gave Zhanna to call El Búho, who still maintained contacts in the Soviet intelligence community. He could check out Graf's background. Neither Erika nor Kathryn had heard of Graf. This morning, Zhanna again called El Búho to see if he had found out anything. Zhanna's former SMERSH comrade told her that Graf was Totenkopf-SS and had been stationed in Prague for the first half of the war where he worked under Reinhard Heydrich until Heydrich's assassination by Czech partisans in 1942. After that, Graf served under Ernst Kaltenbrunner, Heydrich's replacement.

Yet, it wasn't Graf who was their main interest. As Erika went through the club membership ledger during the break-in, two names stood out: Eric Bauer, who was the captain of U-260, the U-boat that had taken her across the Atlantic to America for her mission in that country, and another, much more nefarious name—Axel Ryker. Ryker was a man who was supposed to be dead. Erika had killed him; or at least, that's what she thought.

"When can we the Oberst about our membership application?"

"He just arrived and is in his office. I will ask him if he will see you."

"Thank you, Huppi," Kathryn said as he walked away.

Huppi returned in a few minutes. "The Oberst says you should return next week. He's busy."

Erika told Huppi some information she and Kathryn had not included on their applications. "Huppi, tell the Oberst that I was an Abwehr field agent, and that Kathryn was a Gestapo officer."

Huppi looked at them with doubt on his face, but eventually walked away again.

When he returned, the heavyset German told them, "The Oberst will see you now."

Huppi led them to the office that, unknown to Graf or anyone else, Erika and Kathryn had burglarized. He opened the door and led them in. Behind the desk was a man of perhaps sixty years with full but silver-gray hair. He was dressed casually in a brown, long-sleeved shirt. He wore reading glasses because his attention was directed to some papers on his desk. When Huppi brought in the women, the man looked up and removed the eyeglasses.

"Oberst Graf," Huppi said to him in German, "here are the women you agreed to see."

Graf looked the women over. "Thank you, Huppi. That will be all for now."

Huppi exited and closed the door behind him.

"Please take a chair, ladies."

"Danke," Erika replied. She and Kathryn sat down in two wooden chairs across from his desk.

"So," Graf said, "I have your application here. Are you singers? This is a simple German singing club."

"Yes, we can sing," Erika answered.

"Your application mentions nothing about the information you gave Huppi about your occupations during the war. Why is that?"

"We wanted to make sure we have come to the right place."

"And what place would that be?"

"Oberst Graf," Erika said, "we didn't come here to play games. I am wanted for murder in the United States for a mission I conducted for the Fatherland during the war. My friend Kathryn was a Gestapo Kriminalkommissar; that alone is enough to get her arrested by the Allies."

Graf looked at Kathryn. "It was very unusual for a woman to rise to the rank of Kriminalkommissar in the Gestapo."

"Yes it was," Kathryn replied. "Yet it is true in my case."

"Where did you work?" Graf asked Kathryn.

"Gestapo headquarters at 8 Prinzalbrechtstrasse in Berlin."

"Who was you immediate supervisor?"

"Heinrich Müller."

Graf turned to Erika. "Tell me about the Abwehr. Where were you trained?"

"Oberst, you know very well that all Abwehr agents were trained at Quenzsee west of Berlin."

Graf smiled. "Who were your supervisors at Quenzsee?"

"I had several. Of course we all eventually reported to Admiral Canaris, but two of my most notable supervisors at Quenzsee were Major von der Osten and Ernst Roth. Now, Oberst Graf, in all due respect, if we have successfully completed your lie detector test, I will tell you my father and I were personal friends of the Führer, and I am a close friend of Otto Skorzeny. My question to you is: 'Have we come to the right place?'"

Graf looked them both over for a long moment.

"We have ways of checking your stories, but as I said, this is just a simple German singing club. Come back on Monday evening at seven o'clock. Do not be late."

# Chapter 34

## Puerto San Julián, Argentina
## That weekend and Monday

The weekend that Erika and Kathryn had to wait until reporting back to the Germania Gesangverein on Monday was not uneventful. A young family of four moved in next door in the other half of the duplex. On Sunday afternoon, the husband and wife knocked on their door.

Zhanna answered. Erika and Kathryn were drinking coffee in the kitchen.

"We just moved in next door," said the wife in Spanish. Zhanna immediately called for Kay, who was nearby.

"How do you do?" Kay said.

"I'm Sofia," said the wife. She held a cake. "This is my husband, Guillermo. On behalf of us and our two children we wanted to bring you this cake. We hope to be good neighbors."

"You have two children?" Zhanna asked as Kay translated. "Why did you move into this rat hole of a neighborhood?"

The women seemed taken aback. "We . . . we could not afford anything else."

Kay took the cake and thanked the woman.

After the couple left, Zhanna said to Kay, "Let us take a walk to the corner."

After the half-block walk, Zhanna and Kay drew near the corner thugs. This time there was only three of them, the leader and two others.

"A family has moved into the half of the building next to us." Zhanna addressed the gang. "The deal we have to leave our possessions alone covers that family. Do you understand?" The Russian assassin spoke in her heavily-accented English; Kay did her part.

"That will cost you extra," said the gang leader.

Zhanna quickly drew her knife and swiped it across the man's nose, causing blood to squirt like a geyser.

"I will assume our current deal stands," Zhanna said.

**[Monday, 25 August 1947]**

The next evening, Erika and Kathryn walked through the doors of the Germania Gesangverein a half-hour before the time Colonel Graf had ordered them to report at seven.

Over the weekend, Erika told the other women about one of the names on the club's ledger, Eric Bauer, the captain whose Unterseeboot had delivered her to the shores of North Carolina in 1942. Her mission was to infiltrate a naval shipyard in the Midwest and gather intelligence on LSTs, a new kind of ship the Americans were building.

However, she had not mentioned the other name in the ledger that stood out. Now, since they had some time to wait for their appointment with Graf, they ordered beers and Erika opened up to Kathryn.

"It wasn't just Kapitän Bauer whose name I recognized in the ledger, Kathryn. There was another name—Axel Ryker. He was Gestapo. Have you ever heard of him?"

"I'm familiar with the name. He had appointments with Himmler now and then, but I never met him and know nothing about him. Who is he?"

"Ryker mainly served in the Reich's occupied territories. He worked solely for Himmler and reported only to him. Ryker's main responsibilities were to eliminate anyone suspected of subversion. He was a horrible man, a cold blooded killer, and very good at his job. Himmler sent him to the United States to kill me during my mission there."

Kathryn seemed surprised. "Why would Himmler want you cancelled?"

"It's a long story, and we don't have time now. I'm just telling you this in case we were to run into Ryker here."

"Did he find you in America?" Kathryn asked.

"Yes, in Evansville, Indiana. That was where my mission was based."

"What happened?"

"I killed him."

"You killed him? So do you think the name in the ledger is just someone using Ryker's name? That happens, as you well know."

"I hope that's the answer. He was a tough man and very hard to kill. He almost got the best of me. I hope that I don't have to deal with him a second time."

Huppi finally fetched them and took them to Graf's office. The Oberst stood this time when they entered.

After they all sat down, Graf said, "You're claims seem to have checked out, Fräuleins. Just a couple of more questions. If you are truly who you say you are, you will of course know the secret codenames for Kathryn Fischer and Erika Lehmann. What are they?"

"Mine was Róta," Kathryn replied.

"Lorelei," Erika said.

"So you are the famous Lorelei. I thought as much."

Graf stared at them both for a moment. "I think we can bypass the membership committee in your cases, Kriminalkommissar and Sonderführer. Welcome to the Gesangverein.

"A reception will be held for an important man on Saturday. I'll make sure you're both on the invitation list. You will need appropriate attire for this formal affair."

# Chapter 35

**Buenos Aires**
**Tuesday, 26 August 1947**

After a week in Buenos Aires, Leroy Carr had run into one dead end after another. Carlos, his CIA asset, had not seen the women since they left two weeks ago on a trip they would later find out was to Guatemala. Nobody at the Alvear Palace Hotel—the hotel manager, the concierge, desk staff or bellmen—knew anything that might help them establish a clue as to the women's whereabouts.

Although, Carlos had unknowingly added credence to Carr's theory that Erika had taken her team there to find Zhanna Rogova. Carlos had told Carr and Hodge about the rumors swirling around Buenos Aires that the Soviets had hit squads in South America hunting former members of the SS and Gestapo.

"I don't care what that lying Soviet colonel, or former colonel I should say, in Guatemala told us, Al. Erika was there looking for Zhanna. Zhanna would be a necessary asset if the Soviets were involved." Carr and Hodge shared a hotel room at the Alvear Hotel. Room service had just delivered hot coffee and pastries. "I know that guy is in cahoots with the women, or at least with Zhanna. He and Zhanna have past history together, and the fact that Erika took the team to Puerto Barrios is too big to be a coincidence."

"You won't get an argument from me, Leroy," Hodge said right after he poured both of them a cup. "I know that drug-dealing Russky was lying his ass off, no matter how calmly he did it. But do you still think we can do any good here in Buenos Aires? We've been here a week and have diddly-squat. They could be anywhere. They might be in Europe."

"No way. One thing Lehmann has never done is abandon a mission. She couldn't live with herself. After a week of coming up short here, it appears they are no longer in this city, but they're somewhere in this country or Uruguay, the other hot spot for Germans fleeing justice."

"How long do you think Hillenkoetter is going to let you stay down here?" Hodge asked. This was a question that had gone through both men's minds.

"If I have to quit the CIA to stay here, that's what I'll do," Carr said firmly.

"Come on, Leroy. You know that would be counterproductive. If you leave the agency you'll lose all the resources you now have to search for Kay. If Hillenkoetter eventually orders you back to Washington, you can leave me here. Hillenkoetter won't counteract your authority to do that. I'll bring down two or three of my men, and you can send me Marienne Schenk."

Carr said, "Marienne's pregnant."

"Oops, forget that idea," Hodge replied.

Marienne Schenk had been a top notch investigator for the OSS during the war and had earned the reputation of that agency's top shadow. It seemed Marienne could tail anyone, anywhere, without them knowing it, even if they were wary of being tailed. Carr had offered her a job with the CIA but Marienne had married and wanted to move on. She still accepted occasional, clandestine jobs if Carr called upon her, but she had made it clear that the jobs couldn't interfere with her family life.

Hodge continued. "Anyway, Hillenkoetter isn't going to allow you to remain down here indefinitely, Leroy. You need a plan. As I said, you have authority to leave me here. I'll bring down a couple of my best guys and that Army Ranger, Stephen Floyd."

Carr refused to think about leaving Argentina with his wife still in danger. "Let's not talk about that now."

147

# Chapter 36

**Puerto San Julián, Patagonia, Argentina**
**Wednesday, 27 August 1947**

The day after the episode when Zhanna sliced open the nose of the neighborhood gang leader to protect the young family next door, she phoned Demetri Mikhailov and told him the story. Zhanna also told the other Shield Maidens about the incident.

Yesterday, the street corner gang leader showed up on the Shield Maidens doorstep with a heavily bandaged nose. Erika answered the door and called for Kay to join her for interpretation.

"I am here to apologize," said the visibly worried man. "You should have told us you were friends of El Búho." He handed Erika an envelope.

Erika, surprised that Mikhailov's influence reached so far from Guatemala, took the envelope. Inside was money.

"It is the money you paid us for protection," said the man with the sliced nose. "If you would have told us you were friends of El Búho, the money would have not been requested."

Erika milked the man's fear. "When we move from here, we want you to ensure the family next door and their possessions are protected for as long as they live in this shithole neighborhood. That is if you and your comrades wish to continue breathing. Is that understood?"

"Yes, Señorita."

"Good." Erika closed the door in the man's face.

At their simple lunch that afternoon, Kay watched Erika hand Zhanna a ring.

"This is the Valringr you left behind with your letter when you disappeared," Erika addressed Zhanna. "It's time you reclaim it."

Kay watched Zhanna take the ring, look it over for a long moment, then put it on the ring finger of her right hand.

"I've noticed that you and Kathryn wear the same ring," Kay said to Erika. "What does it mean?"

Erika looked at her and answered. "It is the Valringr, or in English the *Ring of the Slain.* It's a ring that was worn by a select few Viking warriors that had already proven themselves as courageous in battle. The Norse believed that if they wore this ring and died nobly in battle, the ring would make it easy for the Valkyries to find their bodies and escort their souls to Valhalla."

## [that evening]

The young couple next door had invited them to dinner. The Shield Maidens accepted. This invitation had taken place before the gang leader showed up at their door earlier this day.

Because the family was poor, the dinner was simple: mostly fried vegetables on a tortilla with a smidgeon of chicken. The Shield Maidens and Kay had brought to the dinner two bottles of wine and a bottle of tequila.

"This is delicious," Kathryn commented of the simple meal. This seemed to lighten greatly the spirits of the hostess. Kathryn refilled everyone's glass of wine.

The couple's two children also sat at the table. One of them, the oldest was a girl about the same age as Erika's daughter, Ada. Erika took special interest in that child.

"We are happy to have nice neighbors," the husband said.

Erika, not one to mess around with etiquette amongst strangers, cut to the chase. "You told us you moved into this neighborhood because you could not afford a better place. We understand that. Zhanna has ensured that you will be not bothered for as long as you live here. Nevertheless, this is no neighborhood to raise children."

Erika looked at Zhanna who took a wad of Argentinean pesos equal to $4,000.00 American. She handed it to the husband.

"That is enough money to buy a house in a much nicer neighborhood in this town. Move out as soon as you can."

The husband and wife looked at each other dumbfounded. "Why are you doing this?" the husband asked. "It is very nice of you, but we don't need charity."

"It doesn't matter why we are doing it," Erika answered. "Just do what we request. You know it would be best for your children."

The man looked at his wife and kids, swallowed his pride, and took the money.

## Chapter 37

**Puerto San Julián, Argentina**
**Thursday, 28 August 1947**

Despite giving over half of their money to the couple next door, more than enough of El Búho's money was left for the shopping Erika and Kathryn had to do.

The town of Puerto San Julián was far from being capable of offering a shopping Nirvana equal to New York's 5th Avenue, or the Kurfürstdamm in Berlin. Nevertheless, with its share of rich ranchers in that area of southern Patagonia whose wives demanded upscale attire for their parties and receptions, the town did have one store with formal wear. Kay accompanied them to translate. Zhanna tagged along only because she had grown bored of being cooped-up at the house. She could have entertained herself with a flower garden; she had enjoyed gardening at the convent, but it wasn't the time of year for flowers. It was currently 33° F with gunmetal gray skies and a strong sea breeze that again made it feel much colder.

After looking around the women's dress shop, Erika and Kathryn tried on gowns until they found two that would not require alterations. Because of the time of year, full-length wraps would be a necessity. Before they decided on the gowns, they made sure the store had wraps that would match or compliment the dresses.

The shop's owner, a petite, gray-haired Latin lady, had been watching her new sales girl. When the woman realized that she might have some high-paying customers in the store, she stepped in and took over from the teenage girl.

Erika decided on a chiffon, champagne-colored V-Neck gown with lace cap sleeves. The fur wrap she chose was snow-white. Both set off her bright blonde hair. Kathryn's gown was also chiffon but a rose blush color. Her long, full length fur wrap was a very pale pink that augmented her gown's blush color. High heels were also purchased.

This left only one item—jewelry.

"Kay, ask her about jewelry," Erika said.

"Joyeria?" Kay asked the woman.

After a brief conversation with the shop owner, Kay told Erika and Kathryn, "She doesn't sell jewelry, but she says if we'll come back tomorrow morning she can have someone here with some fine pieces that can be purchased from him."

"Tell her we'll be back at nine o'clock tomorrow morning. Let's pay for these clothes and get out of here so we can find someplace to eat. I imagine all of us are hungry; I'm starving."

# Chapter 38

## Puerto San Julián, Argentina
## Friday, 29 August 1947

With their appointment for Erika and Kathryn's jewelry at nine, the women rose at 7:30 that morning. None of the four felt the desire to cook a big breakfast, so they each ate a banana and left it at that. They would find lunch after that morning's business was finished.

At nine, all four of the women walked into the ladies' fashion store where the previous day Erika and Kathryn had purchased their gowns. Waiting was a man in his thirties with jet black hair and a scraggly black beard. The shop owner met them and introduced the man. She then locked the shop door and turned over the closed sign. This told Erika, Kathryn, and Zhanna that the man's goods must be black market. The only one not realizing this was Kay, who thought the woman locked up the shop to safeguard the expensive jewelry.

The man opened his large, black case to reveal a sparkling array of diamond chokers, bracelets, earrings, and brooches. There was also a tray of rings.

"I can offer you ladies fine prices," the man smiled. His teeth were yellow with several missing, making his smile that of a bearded jack-o-lantern.

"May I use your loupe, please?" Erika requested.

"Of course, Señorita." He handed her the small magnifying glass that jewelers and watchmakers use.

Erika put it to her eye and expected every piece. "Your diamonds are real," she told the man, "but not of great quality." Erika picked out a choker and a bracelet. Kathryn did the same and both women chose earrings. "How much for all of this?" Kay had translated the entire conversation.

"Six thousand pesos," the man answered.

"That's ridiculous," Erika scoffed. "One could buy a small house for that sum in this town. Don't take us for fools. The quality of these diamonds doesn't warrant that price. We'll pay you 1500 pesos, and that's generous. We won't be cheated. If you're wise; you'll take it."

The man shook his head no. Erika grabbed his jacket, pulled him down on the counter, and punched him in the side of his head, bloodying his ear. The shop owner lady shrieked.

"We could take everything and not give you a peso." Erika told the man sharply. "We're willing to pay a fair price. My offer is more than fair for your stolen merchandise. I'm sure the local police would be interested in looking through your case."

The man quickly agreed to the much fairer price. Kay paid the man his 1500 pesos. After they walked out of the store, Erika said to Zhanna, "Our funds are growing low. We have enough for this weekend, but can you contact El Búho and request more? Maybe he can wire it to a local bank."

"Yes, I will contact him," Zhanna answered.

Next on the agenda was to find a place that would be open tomorrow (Saturday) for Erika and Kathryn to get their hair done for that's night's soirée.

"I can do your hair," Kay said in the car. "We just need to buy what I will need."

So their last stop before they went to lunch was at a store that sold hair and makeup supplies.


**[Same day, that evening]**

Having been instructed by Colonel Graf to be at the Germania Gesangverein by seven that evening, Erika and Kathryn again arrived early to sit at the bar and have a beer or two. Drinking beer came as natural to the two Germans as eating. Beer in Germany was considered a food. Factories had beer breaks for the workers twice a day, usually one at ten in the morning and one at three that afternoon.

Warsteiner Dunkel, a dark beer, was their choice this time, brought to them in gray ceramic steins. The formal clothes they had purchased earlier this day were back at the house. Tonight they both wore slacks and button blouses of different colors. Their makeup was light.

On weekends, a German brass band played in a corner of the Ratskeller, accompanied by a group of the club's singers. The mini-concert was going on now. Both Erika and Kathryn enjoyed the familiar German songs they had loved while growing up.

Huppi had greeted them with a merry, "Good evening, Fräuleins," when they had entered but left them alone until seven o'clock, when he approached. "You may report to the Oberst now. He is expecting you."

Erika and Kathryn knew the way. When they entered Graf's office he was just hanging up the telephone.

"Please take a seat, Fräuleins," Graf said. He looked them over. "If you are to be members of this club, we will need to find some dirndls for you." The dirndl was the traditional German dress with an apron and bust suspenders.

Both Erika and Kathryn had worn dirndls many times, but that was years ago.

"I'm afraid our dirndls were lost during the confusion at the end of the war when we had to escape the Fatherland," Kathryn replied.

Graf nodded. "I was just being lighthearted. All that is a trivial matter now, isn't it?"

The colonel didn't wait for, or care about a response. "I trust you will be dressed appropriately for the event tomorrow night."

"Yes," Erika replied. "You told us it would be a formal affair. We found gowns and accessories this morning."

"Money was not a problem?" Graf asked.

"No," Erika answered. "After Stalingrad, both Kathryn and I began depositing sums of money in a Swiss bank in Zürich whenever we could."

Graf felt like he should chastise them for their lack of confidence that Germany would win the war after the debacle at Stalingrad, but in good conscience he could not. He, and many of his colleagues, started depositing money in Swiss banks after Stalingrad. In the end, Graf admired the women's cunning (even though he didn't know the entire Swiss bank story was a calculated lie from Erika).

Graf downed a shot glass of Jägermeister and offered them one. Known as *Göring Schnapps* in Germany in the late thirties and during the war, Jägermeister was a favorite of the Luftwaffe chieftain. The women accepted. After pouring them a small glass, Graf continued.

"About the gala tomorrow evening, there will be some of our former comrades who are now residing here in Argentina. Perhaps you might run into someone you know. That would be nice, ja?"

"Ja, that would be nice," Kathryn replied.

"Where will the affair be held" Erika asked.

Graf smiled and did not answer. "Report here tomorrow evening at six o'clock. The three of us will be taken there. This is an honor for both of you because of your service to the Reich."

## Chapter 39

**Puerto San Julián, Argentina**
**Saturday, 30 August 1947**

Early this afternoon, Kay began working on Erika's and Kathryn's hair. Everything needed had been purchased the previous day, including clips for finger waves, pin curls, and rag ties. Kay didn't want both hair styles to look similar. Kathryn's hair was a little longer than Erika's so for Kathryn she put some gentle curls and let her hair remain down. Kay piled Erika's blonde hair up in Rita Hayworth style, leaving the back of her neck exposed.

"Where is this party?" Zhanna asked as Kay worked.

"The Oberst wouldn't tell us, which makes sense as a safety protocol. He said we would be taken there."

"You'll need backup," Zhanna said. "Kay and I will follow you."

Kay looked up suddenly.

"No, Zhanna," Erika said. "We can't take the chance that someone would see you following us. Our cover is secure. We told Graf only what is true about my service with Abwehr and Kathryn's position with the Gestapo. If this is a turnout of true Nazis, as Graf has implied, we should be welcome with open arms. We're not in danger."

"Still, I don't like it," Zhanna added. "I thought you found me because you needed my help. I have done nothing but sit on my ass and eat Mexican food."

"We're not in Mexico, Zhanna," Kathryn said with a smile. "Nor are we in Guatemala or at your convent in Honduras. This is Argentina."

"What's the difference? Everybody speaks Spanish, they all eat peppers, and you can't find a bowl of Borscht anywhere."

Kathryn, Erika, and even Kay laughed.

Erika reminded her, "I wanted you along in case we find out the Soviets have hit squads roaming South America looking for certain Germans. Maybe we can get some leads about that at this gala. Besides, you've already been a big help, Zhanna. You helped us take care of the gang on the corner—twice."

157

"That's no gang. They're just a group of sleazy bastards. If they want to see what a real gang is like I can show them some in Moscow and Leningrad. A Russian gang would eat those dickheads for lunch and spit out their bones. I know you're team leader, Erika, but Kay and I are backing you up tonight. Do you really think I would be spotted tailing you? Apparently you Germans still enjoy insulting us Russians. I'll remind you that we in SMERSH went through much tougher times than your Abwehr."

Erika saw that Zhanna was determined. The Russian was one of them—a Shield Maiden. Not only that, but she was right about what she implied—the former Soviet SMERSH agent was a skilled and seasoned spy.

It was Kay who was the concern. "Okay, Zhanna. We'll work on a plan later this afternoon. You'll be in charge of Kay's safety." Then she addressed Kay, who stood behind her working on her hair. "Kay, you'll do everything Zhanna tells you to do to the letter. Agreed?"

Kay didn't appreciate Erika's comment about the need for Zhanna to protect her, but at last Kay had a feeling of being considered a team member (thanks to the Russian assassin). Kay was tense but hid that feeling from the others. "I understand," she said. "And I agree with Zhanna. You need backup."

**[that evening]**

The town of Puerto San Julián had a minimal number of street lights scattered about helter-skelter. So through mostly dark streets, Kay Carr drove. Nobody wanted the terrible driver, Zhanna Rogova, behind the wheel so she was assigned to ride shotgun. Erika and Kathryn, wearing their gowns and wraps, sat in the back seat. Kay pulled the Oldsmobile into the parking lot of the Germania Gesangverein just before six o'clock, the time that Graf had told them to report. After Erika and Kathryn got out of the car, Kay drove away.

Erika and Kathryn walked through the doors of the German singing club at five minutes before six. Huppi was waiting.

"You're late," he scolded.

"We are not late," Erika said. "The Oberst told us to be here by 1800 hours. Check your wristwatch, Huppi."

Huppi didn't need to check the time. He knew they weren't late. "You might not be late, but you are the last to arrive, follow me."

He led them to a back room. "All of the other invited guests except for the Oberst left several minutes ago," Huppi told them. "When the boat returns, I will come get you. Stay here."

The mention of a boat surprised Erika and Kathryn. Apparently the gala was taking place somewhere offshore.

◊ ◊ ◊

The wait for Zhanna and Kay was a cold one. Kay had turned off the engine to conserve gasoline. The 30° weather quickly turned the car into a refrigerator.

In accordance with the plan they had worked out that afternoon, Kay parked the car on a hill three blocks from the club where, with binoculars, they could look down at anyone coming and going (Zhanna and Kay had left the house that afternoon to purchase the binoculars, which they found at a duck and geese hunting store).

Finally, Zhanna saw Erika and Kathryn, easily recognizable in their formal wear, being escorted out of the club by two men who led them to a car. "I see them," Zhanna told Kay. Kay started the engine but waited for Zhanna's instructions.

The German club on Calle de Urquiza was a mere block from the bay. Zhanna watched the car drive to a dock where her two Shield Maiden partners and one of the men emerged from the car and walked up a gangplank to board a cabin cruiser where they disappeared inside.

"This will make things more difficult," Zhanna told Kay. "Drive to the dock."

# Chapter 40

**Bay of San Julián, Argentina**
**Saturday, 30 August 1947**

By the time Zhanna and Kay drove to the dock, the boat carrying Erika and Kathryn had sailed. Lights of the cabin cruiser were already growing dim as it moved away into the enormous bay. Similar in size to the Chesapeake Bay, a boat could still be in the bay of San Julián but the crew felt as if they were already far out to sea as no land was visible.

Many boats of all types and sizes were tied up at various docks of the large port. Zhanna told Kay they would have to steal a boat, but as they ran trying to find one suitable they spotted a small fishing trawler with a light on in the wheelhouse.

"Looks like someone is on the boat," said Zhanna. "We'll offer them money."

The two women walked up the short gangplank and stepped down onto the boat's deck. Near the bow was the wheelhouse where they had seen the light. Zhanna banged on the door and kept banging until a young Latin man opened it. Seeing two women standing there made the surprise in his face evident.

Kay said in Spanish, "We'd like to hire your boat."

"My father owns this boat and he doesn't hire it out. It is our family livelihood. We are fishermen. The only reason I'm here is because I am replacing some bulbs in our radio. We're heading out to our netting area at dawn."

"We'll pay you, handsomely," Kay countered then she explained the conversation to Zhanna. The young man heard the English.

"I speak English, Señorita."

"Good," Zhanna replied. She was about to say more when Kay boldly took over.

"We'll pay you 200 pesos an hour ($10)."

The young man couldn't take his eyes off Zhanna. The jet-haired Russian was a beautiful woman, her looks marred only by the hideous scar on her neck, which was covered.

Perhaps Zhanna's appeal, plus the substantial offer, convinced the young man to agree.

"We have to hurry," Zhanna said. "We want to follow a boat and it's almost out of sight."

The young man fired up the engine; Zhanna and Kay helped him untie from the dock. As the trawler pulled out into the bay, Zhanna stepped outside the wheelhouse. With the binoculars she could just barely see the waning light of the boat her comrades were aboard.

She came back into the wheelhouse and instructed the young man to proceed at full speed with all lights off.

Zhanna and Kay split time with the binoculars watching the lights of the boat they pursued. The winter wind over the water made standing outside the wheelhouse for more than a minute or two dangerous. The trawler certainly wasn't a fast ship, but at full speed they slowly gained a little ground on the cruiser. They could now watch from inside the wheelhouse. As they sailed through the bay, the young fisherman divided his time between steering the trawler and looking at Zhanna. The Soviet sniper/assassin realized what was happening and she milked it for all that it was worth.

"What is your name?" Zhanna asked him.

"Lautaro."

"How old are you?"

"Nineteen," he told Zhanna.

"You're a handsome young man, Lautaro."

"And you're a very beautiful woman."

Zhanna smiled, drew near to him, and put her hand on his shoulder.

Kay rolled her eyes. *Good Lord!* She thought to herself. *The kid is smitten by the Russian killer. He'd be better off having a rattlesnake for a companion or a crush on Lizzie Borden.*

◊ ◊ ◊

In the enormous bay, a half moon shed enough illumination for Erika and Kathryn to see several small islands that rose from the black waters as the cabin cruiser passed by; most of the islands were dark and looked uninhabited, but as the boat approached one of the islands, the German women could see light in the distance coming from what looked like a mansion or large chateau.

They soon realized that was their destination when the boat altered its course and headed toward the lights.

As the boat grew near the island, the captain cut the engines and let the boat slowly drift toward the dock. Men stood on the pier using flashlights to help the captain know where to tie up. Whoever the captain was (the women had not met him), he expertly guided the cruiser into position without bumping the pier. The men with flashlights quickly helped the boat's crew secure the ropes and install a gangplank.

Erika, Kathryn, and Graf disembarked. Graf was dressed in a tuxedo underneath a long black leather greatcoat—a coat quite familiar to Erika and Kathryn. Before and during the war, many members of the Gestapo and SS officers wore such a coat. A Mercedes-Benz waited to take them the half-mile to the mansion.

"This estate is owned by a man high in the Peron government," Graf told them as the car pulled into the lavish mansion's red gravel circular driveway. "He has proven to be a true supporter of the Reich."

The driver pulled up and stopped in front of the manor's front door. The building looked more like a castle than a mansion or chateau. Several men in suits, overcoats, and hats were stationed outside; one hustled to open their car door. Two other cars that were used to shuttle guests from the dock to the mansion sat parked and empty. "We must be among the last to arrive," said Graf. Two life-sized statues of matadors stood proudly at the end of the stone walk. With their capes, the concrete bull fighters directed the Totenkopf Colonel, Erika, and Kathryn inside.

# Chapter 41

## Island in the Bay of San Julián, Argentina
## Same evening—Saturday, 30 August 1947

Doormen held the wide, double doors for Graf, Erika, and Kathryn as they entered the huge mansion. In the vestibule, a main in a suit stood beside a table where two middle-aged ladies dressed in gowns sat.

"Willkommen, Oberst Graf," said the older looking of the two women.

"Danke sehr, Frau Beck."

The second woman said nothing as she checked off Graf's name on papers before her.

"Who are your lovely companions?" Frau Beck asked.

"Erika Lehmann and Kathryn Fischer," Graf answered. "Their names will be on your lists of invited guests. I called the general and informed him about them two days ago."

The list was arranged with normal German efficiency in alphabetical order. The other woman quickly found the names and checked them off. The man, apparently a guard, opened the inside door of the vestibule for the trio.

They entered a grand room that would remind someone of a posh hotel lobby complete with a fountain surrounded by potted flowers. Yet grabbing the eye first were the long swastika flags festooning from the thirty-foot high mural ceiling, and a large portrait of Adolf Hitler that hung on the wall at the bottom of a blue-veined marble staircase descending from the second floor. Expensive Chinoiserie burgundy wallpaper covered three walls. Several tapestries hung here and there. In a back corner, a string quartet currently played the prelude to Richard Wagner's *Tristan and Isolde*. A young man dressed in a white SS lieutenant tunic and black trousers took Graf's coat and the women's wraps. On the lieutenant's upper sleeve was the red swastika armband. When Graf shed his leather overcoat, both Erika and Kathryn immediately noticed the small NSDAP pin on his tuxedo's lapel, signifying he was a member of the Nazi Party.

Several groups of people milled about the room. Some of the groups were small—three or four people. Some groups were larger. The SS attendant told them in German that formal festivities would begin in about an hour.

"When it is time," said the lieutenant, "concomitants will escort you. For now, please enjoy yourselves. Waiters are passing through with champagne or will take your drink orders if you prefer something else. The food is on a table along the far wall."

After the lieutenant walked away with their coats, Graf said, "I just spotted an old friend I haven't seen since the war. If you'll please excuse me ladies."

Both Erika and Kathryn were glad to get rid of Graf. Now they could talk freely. A waiter walked by with flutes of champagne; both women took one from the silver platter then scanned the room looking for anyone they might recognize.

"There's Eichmann," Kathryn said. "The man wearing glasses talking to the group near the fountain." Erika had heard of Adolf Eichmann but had never met him. During the war, Kathryn saw him often and had spoken with him on several occasions at the SS/Gestapo headquarters on Prinzalbrechtstrasse in Berlin. Eichmann had been a lieutenant colonel in the SS and also served in the Gestapo. He was not in uniform but, like Graf, his Nazi Party membership pin was attached to his tuxedo's lapel.

"He's the guy who deported Jews to the concentration camps, right?" Erika asked.

"Basically, yes, he was in charge of the railway systems that deported Jews, Gypsies, homosexuals, and other people who our government deemed Untermenschen (less than human) to the camps.

"I wonder how many war crimes tribunal lists include *his* name?" Erika asked tongue in cheek.

"How many lists do they have?" Kathryn responded with a disapproving smirk as she looked at Eichmann. She also pointed out a couple of more minor Gestapo officers and gave Erika their backgrounds. Kathryn was better suited to identify people at a gathering such as this; she had worked in Berlin in the building that served as the hub for the Gestapo. Erika, on the other hand, had spent most of her time during the war on missions outside of Germany.

Erika spotted only one person she immediately recognized. His name had been on the list she and Kathryn saw when they broke into Graf's office at the singing club. Eric Bauer had served as the captain of U-260.

"Kathryn, at the food table is the U-boat captain who took me across the Atlantic to the U.S. in 1942—the tall man with the graying beard. Let's go talk to him. I'm curious as to why he's here. Unterseebootmänner are not considered war criminals as far as I know. I spent two weeks on his U-boat where he impressed me as a stern, but patriotic and fair man."

Holding their glasses of champagne, the attractive women in their formal gowns walked toward Eric Bauer, all the while being followed by the roving eyes of many of the men in the room.

"Kapitänleutnant Bauer," Erika interrupted him as he was finishing loading his plate of food from the buffet, "you might remember me. You took me across the sea to American back in 1942."

Bauer's eyes grew large. "Ja, ja, you are the Abwehr agent, Lorelei. I remember exactly." Bauer had never been told Erika's real name. He sat down his plate of food and, in standard Prussian etiquette, bowed as he shook her hand.

"My name is Erika Lehmann, and this is my friend, Kathryn Fischer."

Bauer extended his hand to Kathryn and again bowed.

"Why are you here, Kapitänleutnant Bauer? Surely you didn't have to flee Germany like Kathryn and me."

"You were forced to flee?" Bauer asked.

"It's a long story, but yes."

"It is true," Bauer said, "I did not have to flee the Fatherland but I had nothing left there. My home in Dresden was completely destroyed by American bombs, killing my wife and child. Dresden ended up in the Soviet sector and the Soviets confiscated every. I got nothing for the land."

"I'm sorry to hear about your family. So many of us lost close family members during the war. I lost my father; Kathryn her sister. Where are you living now?" Erika asked.

"In Santa Cruz, I found a job working in the stables on a ranch."

It bothered Erika that this noble warrior who had done nothing wrong other than be loyal to his country now worked as a stable hand. She said nothing, knowing any comment she might make could embarrass him. So many of her fellow countrymen, not unlike her and Kathryn, didn't find out about the atrocities until very late in the war, or after the war ended.

"Tell me, Herr Kapitänleutnant, have you heard the rumors that the Führer survived the war and is now here in Argentina?"

"Yes, I have heard the rumors but I know nothing other than that."

Erika believed him. "Well, it is certainly wonderful to see you again, Herr Kapitänleutnant. I wish you the best."

Bauer again bowed to both women before they walked away.

# Chapter 42

## Island in the Bay of San Julián, Argentina
## Same evening—Saturday, 30 August 1947

Graf had been mingling with a large group that grew larger when Adolf Eichmann and his entourage joined them. Eichmann had been a lieutenant colonel so Graf outranked him. That put the onus on Eichmann to join Graf and not the other way around.

One of the SS waiters approached Erika and Kathryn.

"Fräuleins, Oberst Graf is requesting that you join him." He clicked his heels and walked away.

The two Shield Maidens crossed the floor. Graf saw them approaching.

"Comrades," Graf announced to the large group, "let me introduce you to these guests of mine." Unlike Bauer, who had simply shaken their hands, Graf took Kathryn's hand and kissed the back of it. "This is Kriminalkommissar Kathryn Fischer of the Gestapo."

The group of twelve people seemed impressed.

"Guten Abend," Kathryn said. Everyone returned the greeting or nodded.

Graf released Kathryn's hand and moved to Erika. After the hand kissing, he said, "This is Sonderführer Erika Lehmann, she is the daughter of Karl Lehmann, a close friend of the Führer. Fräulein Lehmann served in the Abwehr and conducted three dangerous missions for the Reich."

Before Erika could offer a greeting, Eichmann said, "Karl Lehmann's daughter? There was a well circulated rumor at Prinzalbrechtstrasse that Karl Lehmann's daughter was the famous spy, Lorelei."

Graf chuckled. "Yes, all of you are meeting Lorelei. I have brought two special guests, have I not?"

Everyone in the group stopped drinking or talking and looked at Erika with astonishment. Graf introduced those in the group to Erika and Kathryn. Other than Eichmann, neither of them recognized any of the names. Besides the few minor officials Kathryn had already pointed out, Eichmann was the only person in the room that she recognized. Erika even less. Besides the U-boat captain, Eric Bauer, Graf was the only person present that she knew, and in Graf's case she had met him for the first time at the German singing club.

After that, the two women were treated like celebrities. Word circulated quickly through the room and for the next thirty minutes, men and their wives (if the wives were present) approached Erika and Kathryn eager to exchange a few words. Erika would eventually steer all the conversations to the rumor about Adolf Hitler surviving. Many seemed to have heard the rumor but claimed they knew nothing.

Both women were hungry. They finally managed to break away from their admirers and make their way to the buffet table. Before them were German delicacies such as wild boar. Neither Erika nor Kathryn had eaten wild boar since before the war and they both took a generous helping. On the long table were more common German foods such as Bratwurst, Mettwurst, other assorted sausages, and Leberknödel (liver dumplings). Roasted carrots and boiled baby potatoes did their duty as the vegetable sides, and there was an abundance of hearty breads such as rye and Schwarzbrot. For dessert the table offered several types of strudels and cakes, including Kirschtorte (cherry cake).

"Kathryn, Kirschtorte was the Führer's favorite dessert. When my father and I visited the Berghof there were always several of those cakes sitting around."

"Lots of people like Kirschtorte, Erika. It doesn't mean the Führer is here."

"True, but the Führer also had a taste for Leberknödel. The reports of him being a strict vegetarian are wrong."

"Interesting," Kathryn replied. "I didn't know that. Could it be true, Erika? Could the Führer still be alive?"

Erika paused. "I don't know."

A few small tables stood at the end of the buffet. There were no chairs. The high, round tables were designed so guests could stand while eating. All of the tables were taken. Kathryn spotted one where two men stood eating. At the table was room enough for two more. The women approached.

"Würdest Sie erlauben?" Kathryn asked the men (Would you allow?). In Germany, it was considered proper etiquette in restaurants for people already seated to allow strangers to share their table if no open tables were available. The men had been among those who had earlier approached them and offered their admiration.

"Of course, Fräuleins. You would honor us," one of them said. A waiter came by with a tray of champagne flutes. Erika and Kathryn both told him they would prefer a German beer. Going along, the men abandoned their champagne and also requested beer.

"Our vineyards along the Rhine are not yet up to capacity," the same man said. "The champagne is from Yugoslavia. "It is acceptable wine but it's not from the Fatherland. I commend you for choosing German beer."

Both women were more interested in eating than talking, but they calmly answered questions and responded to comments from the men. The waiter delivered the beer in clear pint glasses.

"Horst and I saw the Führer in a parade once, but we were never privileged to meet him like you," the talkative man said to Erika. "I'm sure it was an extreme honor for you to meet him. Tell us, what was he like in private?"

"He was always kind to me," Erika answered. She wasn't lying. Because she was the daughter of an old friend, Hitler always treated her well. She eventually changed the conversation from answering questions to asking them.

"So tell us what you two did during the war."

The man who had so far done most of the talking said, "We were both Totenkopf-SS guards at Treblinka. I was just a corporal and my friend here, Horst, was a private."

Erika and Kathryn avoided looking at each other; both had learned after the war about the horrors that had taken place inside the infamous extermination camp in Poland.

"What were your duties there?" Kathryn asked.

"We patrolled outside the fences with dogs. We are proud of our service to the Fatherland."

Remaining on mission, Erika said with no hint of sarcasm, "Yes, I'm sure you must be proud."

Both of the men raised their beer mugs. "Prost!" said the Death's Head corporal. "Here's to the Fatherland." Erika and Kathryn raised their mugs and clinked them together with the two men.

"Ja," said Erika, "Prost to the Fatherland and the Führer. Have you heard the rumors that the Führer is still alive?" Erika asked the men after everyone had taken a healthy swig of beer to confirm the Prost.

Both men looked at her dumbly. "No we have not heard any such rumor. You two Fräuleins were much higher up than us. What are you saying? Could it be true?"

"It's just an odd rumor," Erika replied. "Never mind." She knew these low-ranking enlisted men would probably know nothing but she had nothing to lose by asking.

Both Erika and Kathryn had hearty appetites. Both returned to the buffet table and grabbed seconds on the wild boar and picked out a dessert.

They were nearly finished with their second helpings when suddenly a man asked loudly for the crowd's attention. He stood two steps up on the staircase.

"Damen und Herren (Ladies and Gentlemen)," the man spoke loudly. "I am Kriminalsekretär Weiss." Kriminalsekretär was a Gestapo rank one level below Kathryn's rank as Kriminalkommissar. So Kathryn would have outranked this man during the war. Weiss continued, "It is my great privilege to introduce our honored guest for the evening." Erika knew if it was Hitler, a higher ranking Party member like Graf would be doing the introduction. Nevertheless, both she and Kathryn held their breath as a man and his wife appeared on that balcony and began descending the stairs.

"Mein Gott," Kathryn said to Erika quietly. "It's Müller."

Heinrich Müller, referred to as 'Gestapo Müller,' had served as chief of the Gestapo. His only superiors during the war were the Führer and Heinrich Himmler. Kathryn, as a Kriminalkommissar, had had many interactions with him.

The Gestapo officer continued, "I give to you Gruppenführer (general) Heinrich Müller and his wife, Frau Müller!"

The crowd cheered and clapped loudly. Müller and his wife descended the steps where he stopped to shake hands with Weiss.

After a moment, three other men appeared at the top of the steps and began descending. One of the men was Axel Ryker. Erika and Ryker locked eyes when he was only halfway down the stairs.

It was a rare occasion that Erika Lehmann felt dread.

# Chapter 43

## Island in the Bay of San Julián, Argentina
## Same evening—Saturday, 30 August 1947

"Kathryn, I told you about Axel Ryker," Erika said as Ryker and the two other men reached the bottom of the stairway and began mingling with the guests fawning over Heinrich Müller. "That's him at the bottom of the steps—the large man with the smashed nose."

"You mean the guy who looks like the Missing Link is the guy you thought you killed?"

Erika nodded and took a drink of beer.

"So what problems will we have with him, Erika?"

"I don't know. I do know by all rights I should not have gotten the best of him. I got lucky. My question is, 'Why was he upstairs with Müller?' He was just a murderous henchman for Himmler."

Kathryn offered a theory. "He followed the Gruppenführer and his Frau down the stairs. Maybe he's a bodyguard."

"Perhaps."

◊ ◊ ◊

Axel Ryker could not have been less interested in the conversation taking place around Heinrich Müller. As he walked down the stairs, he had spotted Erika Lehmann in the crowd. As quickly as possible, he broke away from Müller's entourage and began walking toward Erika.

"Here he comes," Kathryn said. "Will we need our knives?" Both women had a slim stiletto in a sheaf holstered to the inside of their left thigh. It was the only weapon they could conceal under their tight fitting gowns.

"No," Erika answered. "Ryker is too cagey and too professional to try anything here."

When Ryker reached Erika, he said, "I was told you would be here."

"I don't know if that is a greeting," Erika retorted, "but I thought, and hoped, you were dead."

"You nearly succeeded, Fräulein Lehmann. However, your dagger to my throat did not cut deep enough—a mistake on your part."

In 1943, during her mission in the States, Ryker was sent there on Himmler's orders to kill her. Their confrontation came to a head on a bridge over the Ohio River. Climbing the iron work of the bridge with Ryker in pursuit, she was in an awkward position when she struck him with her dagger. Because of that, it was now obvious that she had not penetrated deeply enough into his thick and sinewy neck.

"I heard that your body was found in the river that runs by Evansville."

"Luck was on my side. I found a hobo living under the bridge who was approximately my size. I cut his throat in the same fashion you cut mine, only I made sure the knife was successful. It was his body they found."

"You were always resourceful, Herr Ryker," Erika commented.

Ryker was a grizzly man in appearance, looking like an apparition from a nightmare. His wide, muscled frame, smashed nose underneath a protruding brow and thick dark eyebrows that barely separated gave him the countenance of something created by a mad scientist. But Ryker was no mindless automaton; he was intelligent, cunning, and multilingual.

Ryker looked at Kathryn. "You must be Kathryn Fischer, the Gestapo Kriminalkommissar."

"That's right," said Kathryn.

Ryker turned back to Erika. "Gruppenführer Müller has assigned me the task of investigating the Soviet threat to our comrades here in South America. When Oberst Graf informed the Gruppenführer that you two were now in Argentina and in this area, the general issued orders that you will work with me on my mission."

Erika leered at Ryker. "You and the Gruppenführer expect me to simply forget that you were sent by Himmler to the United States to kill me?"

"Exactly," Ryker sneered. "Just as I have been ordered to put aside the fact that you slit my throat and left me for dead, you Canaris whore."

173

# Chapter 44

## The Gala on the island in the Bay of San Julián, Argentina
## Same evening—Saturday, 30 August 1947

Ryker returned to the group surrounding Heinrich Müller and his wife.

Kriminalsekretär Weiss, Müller's adjutant and the man who had announced the general's entrance, again asked the guests for their attention.

"Gruppenführer Müller will now speak!" Weiss announced loudly.

Müller climbed back up three stairs so everyone could easily see him; the people in the room went silent.

"Thank you all for coming," Müller said. "It is pleasant to see some old comrades, and Frau Müller and I want to meet all of our new comrades. I know all of you were loyal to the Reich or you would not be here tonight."

Müller rambled on for about fifteen minutes, saying not much of interest, at least to Erika and Kathryn. He mentioned that the Third Reich would live on and one day would rise again.

"We must teach our children well," Müller stated. "They must learn to love the Party as all of us do. Now, if you'll join me in saluting the Führer." The general walked back down the three steps and turned toward the portrait of Hitler. He raised his hand in the Nazi salute and the crowd did the same. Erika and Kathryn followed suit.

"Sieg," Müller barked.

"HEIL!" the crowd shouted in unison. This was repeated two more times.

◊ ◊ ◊

Zhanna had instructed Lautaro to circle the island, staying far enough offshore to not draw suspicion from the shore guards. She wanted to find a place where she and Kay could get themselves on land, but the shoreline was mostly rocky cliffs. The few places that did have a small beach were guarded by men with dogs.

"We'll have to sit offshore for now," Zhanna told Kay and Lautaro.

"Why do you have any interest in this place?" Lautaro asked.

"We just wanted to see it, but there is obviously a party going on so we don't want to barge in uninvited."

"You wanted to see it at night?" Lautaro asked with amazement. "Would not during daylight be better?"

Zhanna grabbed the young man gently by the jaw, turned his face toward her and kissed him on the lips. Then she patted his face. "You're so curious and sweet," she said.

Lautaro, struck dumb by the passion of the kiss, returned to manning the wheel without asking any more questions.

*Men are so easy,* thought Kay.

Zhanna told Lautaro to position the trawler where they could see the lit-up mansion, but as far away as possible. The binoculars allowed them to station the boat two miles offshore. At that distance, and with all lights off, they could remain unseen by the men patrolling the dock.

◊ ◊ ◊

After the salute to Hitler's portrait, people who had never met Heinrich Müller formed a line and paraded past the Gestapo general, stopping for a very brief chat and then moving on.

"It's like a line of people meeting the Pope," Kathryn quipped about the reception line.

"Or, like people paying their respects to the family at a funeral," Erika countered.

The meet and greet went on for over a half-hour, maybe forty-five minutes. Ryker had disappeared. Finally, Müller stepped out of the room, disappearing through a white door a few steps from Hitler's portrait.

Just a few minutes later, Kriminalsekretär Weiss approached Erika and Kathryn.

Weiss bowed before he said, "Sonderführer Lehmann and Kriminalkommissar Fischer, Gruppenführer Müller is asking for a moment of your time. Please put down your drinks and follow me."

He led them through the crowd and opened the white door. "Please step inside." Weiss did not follow them into the room.

When they entered, Müller was relaxing on a sofa in a room that looked like a study. In a chair sat Axel Ryker smoking a cigar. The walls of the room were dark oak or varnished to give that appearance. A fire blazed in a stone fireplace. The swastika flag and the flag of Argentina stood side-by-side, hanging limp from standards in one corner. There were no windows.

"Ah, please come in," Müller said without standing. "Kriminalkommissar Fischer, it is nice to see you again."

"I assure you I feel the same way, Gruppenführer," Kathryn said.

Müller looked at Erika. "And the famous Lorelei. Unfortunately, we have never met, but fate has brought you here. Please, have a seat Fräuleins."

As the two women sat down in chairs opposite Müller and Ryker (who had spent his time during Müller's greeting puffing on his cigar and glaring at Erika), Müller pointed to a bottle sitting on the coffee table that separated them. Besides a bottle of German brandy, also on the table was a bottle of Scotch, some snifter glasses, a humidor of cigars, and a pack of cigarettes.

"I've been told you have an affinity for Asbach, Sonderführer Lehmann. Again, as providence would have it, there are several bottles in the wine cellar. Please help yourselves." Müller ignored the common courtesy of pouring a drink for the women. "Also, help yourselves to a cigarette if you wish."

"Thank you, Herr Gruppenführer," Erika said. She stood up and poured a brandy for herself and Kathryn. "We would prefer a cigar to a cigarette. May I?"

Müller smiled. He could never recall seeing a woman smoke a cigar; then again, these women were much more than ordinary.

"Of course."

Erika took two cigars from the humidor because she saw an opportunity to get under Ryker's skin.

"Herr Ryker," Erika said, "would you please snip these for us and give us a light?"

It worked. That Ryker fumed was obvious, and he made no move at the request.

Müller looked at him. "Herr Ryker, where are your manners? Please prepare the cigars and give the Fräuleins a light."

With hate in his eyes, Ryker took the cigars and snipped the ends with the cigar guillotine and handed them back to Erika. Then he rose, pulled a gold lighter from his suit pocket and held the fire to Erika's and Kathryn's cigars as they puffed to stoke them. As he was lighting Erika's cigar, she took a deep puff and blew the smoke in Ryker's face.

She smiled at the Gestapo henchman. "Thank you so much."

Kathryn now took the lead since she had had a working relationship with Müller. "Gruppenführer, Herr Ryker told us your orders are that we work with him on a mission. Please give us more details."

"That's correct, Kriminalkommissar. There are rumors that Stalin has sent members of his NKVD here to Argentina to assassinate any of those they can find who were members of the Gestapo or SS during the war. As I said, fate has brought you here. Both of you have superior investigative skills, as does Herr Ryker. You three will work together. Herr Ryker will be in charge and you will obey his orders. He will report directly to me. Ryker has a couple of leads that he will share with you once your work gets underway. You will spend the night here in the mansion and Oberst Graf will accompany you tomorrow morning to wherever it is you are staying so you can collect your things. Do you have any questions?"

Erika looked at Ryker who was now smirking. Neither woman asked a question.

"Gruppenführer Müller," said Erika, "I must ask you what is on everyone's lips. Did the Führer survive the war? You are aware that my father was a trusted, longtime friend of the Führer, and I was very good friends with Fräulein Braun, or perhaps I should say Frau Hitler if reports of their marriage are accurate. If they are alive and here in Argentina as some seem to believe, I would like to see them." When she finished, she took a big drag of her cigar and again blew the smoke in Ryker's direction.

"I am aware of your connection to the Führer," Müller stated, "but if I knew, I could not divulge such information."

Neither Erika nor Kathryn knew what to make of his ambiguous statement.

"You may return to the reception," Müller said.

Erika and Kathryn rose from their chairs.

"One last thing," said Müller, "do either of you speak Spanish?"

"I'm afraid not," Erika answered.

"Neither does Herr Ryker. I will find you a translator we can trust."

"We have a translator," Erika said quickly. "We met her in Buenos Aires. She is a German-American and is sympathetic to our cause. Her family was from Germany and her father was an important member of the German-American Bund in Cincinnati, a city in America. We can trust her."

Müller took a moment to think it over. "I know about Cincinnati and our Party's support there. Before the war, we had regular contact with that city's Bund. It wasn't until after the war started with America that we lost contact."

Erika said, "The Bunds in the United States were outlawed shortly after the Japanese struck Pearl Harbor and the Führer declared war on the Unites States."

"I am well aware of that, Sonderführer. I was in charge of keeping open communication with the American Bunds before those events occurred. I will consider this woman you speak of, but I want to meet her before I give my approval."

"Of course, Gruppenführer. I also know of another woman who could be of service to us. I'm sure you have heard of Zhanna Rogova?" Erika had entered into an extreme gamble.

Both Müller and Ryker lost all expression and stared at Erika.

"Are you referring to the Russian sniper who plagued our troops in the Soviet Union?" Müller asked.

"Yes."

"What is the meaning of this?" Müller asked sharply.

"Herr Gruppenführer, surely one at your position in the Reich knows that Rogova is being pursued by the Bolsheviks as a traitor. She is with us here in Argentina, and as a Russian, could be of great help to us on this particular mission. She still has contacts in Soviet intelligence who she can trust."

Müller did indeed remember the reports about the famous Russian sniper and her falling out with the powers in Moscow.

"Why is Rogova with you, Sonderführer?"

"She is on the run, as are all of us. Kathryn and I ran into her at a club in Central America. Of course, we did not know her, but I overheard her speaking Russian. I speak that language and I approached her. I suspected she was on the run, but we didn't find out she was Zhanna Rogova until later, after we saw her neck scar. You spoke of fate bringing the Kriminalkommissar and me to you. Could this be fate that brings Zhanna Rogova to us?"

Ryker now inserted himself into the conversation. "Consorting with a Soviet is grounds to have you both shot as traitors to the Party."

Müller held up his hand to silence Ryker. Erika, who was as cunning as Ryker, had worded her pitch for Zhanna wisely. Müller was a firm believer that providence played an important role in one's life.

"I'll have a boat that brought you here take you back to Puerto San Julián early tomorrow morning. Instead of Oberst Graf, Herr Ryker will accompany you. I'll order the boat's crew to wait for you at the city dock. Bring Rogova and this translator to me tomorrow but wait until darkness falls for security reasons. Now, you're dismissed, Fräuleins." He redirected his attention to Axel Ryker. "Herr Ryker, I need a moment with you after the Fräuleins leave the room."

Erika and Kathryn left the room not knowing what Müller had in mind.

# Chapter 45

## The Gala on the island in the Bay of San Julián, Argentina
## Same evening—Saturday, 30 August 1947

For three hours the fishing trawler set offshore. Zhanna decided not to drop anchor because it had to be retracted by hand, which would take too long in case they spotted something on shore that required them to respond. The boat would drift slowly toward the island, but Lautaro used the engine on low to return the boat to the desired location.

The young boat pilot stayed in the wheelhouse to keep the boat in position. Despite the cold, Zhanna and Kay both stood outside on the stern watching the mansion and dock area. A light snow had started falling but so far it was not sticking to the deck.

Things ran smoothly until Lautaro lit a cigarette.


## [15 minutes later]
The Gestapo general and Axel Ryker were still in the study. Müller was instructing his henchman how to proceed with the investigation. He also discussed the surprising news that Zhanna Rogova was in the picture.

"I don't like this situation," Ryker said, not addressing Müller by rank. Axel Ryker was too much of a brute to concern himself with protocol. "I don't trust Lehmann, and Rogova should be eliminated immediately."

"Perhaps you are right," Müller replied. "It will take some thought. Lehmann is supposed to bring the translator and Rogova to us tomorrow evening. I will let you know my decision after I speak with them. If I decide to eliminate the Russian, or all of them, that would be the time to do it. They'll be unarmed and trapped on this island."

Suddenly, Weiss, the adjutant, burst into the room without knocking. "Gruppenführer! One of our shore guards spotted a light offshore. The guard commander used the telescope and identified it as a fishing trawler that is sitting about three kilometers from the island. It seems to be stationary."

"No one would be sitting in one place dropping nets, especially at night," Müller said. "Send out a boat. Bring one person back for Herr Ryker to interrogate. Kill everyone else onboard and sink the boat. Be sure their bodies are placed somewhere under the deck so they don't float to the surface."

Weiss clicked his heels. "Yes, Herr Gruppenführer."


**[on the trawler]**
It was Kay's turn to put her eyes to the ice cold binoculars.

"Zhanna, three men just loaded into one of the speed boats and it looks like they're headed this way."

Zhanna took the binoculars and looked.

"Damn that cigarette!" Zhanna exclaimed. When she saw Lautaro using a match, she rushed into the wheelhouse and slapped the cigarette from his mouth. The Russian knew even the small light from a match or cigarette could be seen across a considerable distance over waters under a dark, cloudy sky. She ordered Lautaro to proceed at full speed away from the island then returned to the deck with Kay.

"They're gaining fast, Zhanna."

"I know. There is no way this old tub can outrun that speedboat. The best we can hope for is to get far enough away from the island so gunshots can't be heard."

"Gunshots?" Kay gulped.

"Yes, Kay. I doubt they are sending out a welcoming committee. Get below deck and find a place to hide."

"I will stay up here with you."

"No you won't! I have orders to protect you. You'll do what I say."

With the trawler running at full speed, Lautaro managed to get his boat enough distance from the island that it had disappeared under the horizon by the time the speedboat pulled alongside. A bright spotlight lit up the trawler deck, settling on Zhanna who stood alone. By now, the sea wind was howling.

Using a bullhorn, a man in the speedboat shouted in broken Spanish with a German accent, "Cut motor. We come aboard."

The wheelhouse door was open. Lautaro, having no idea what was happening, heard and shut down the motor. The men in the speedboat were armed with what many Germans referred to as 'Dillingers' —American Thompson machineguns with a drum clip, the gun that the famous American bank robber was well-known for using. Zhanna was armed only with a handgun in the back of her pants, concealed under her shirt, and a dagger strapped to her ankle. Under this extreme disadvantage, she would first try and talk her way out of the situation. One man in the speedboat threw a line to Zhanna. She pulled it tight and secured it to the nearest docking cleat.

The boat driver stayed on the speedboat. The two others climbed onto the trawler's deck. The man who had talked through the bullhorn trained his machinegun on Zhanna. Then, in German, he issued orders to his comrade. The man went into the wheelhouse and brought Lautaro out onto deck.

"Why you sit offshore near our island?" the talker asked, again in broken Spanish. Apparently the other man spoke nothing but German.

"You're accent sounds German," Zhanna said in that language. "I am German."

The man was no expert on accents, but her German didn't sound native to him. "You don't sound German. Where are you from?

"Danzig. I'm a German from Danzig. The accent you hear is probably the Polish influence." Danzig was a former city in Prussia that ended up located in Poland after the Versailles Treaty following the First World War. Poland's refusal to agree to Hitler's demand for a Polish Corridor so Germans in Danzig could travel freely back and forth to and from Germany was an important factor in his decision to invade Poland in 1939, starting the Second World War.

The man gladly switched to German. "I'll ask you again, why were you out here sitting off our island?"

Zhanna put her arm around Lautaro. "My boyfriend lives with his parents and we have no place to make love other than on his boat. We stopped off your island because it was the only island with lights which allowed him to control drift."

"Why did you flee as we pursued you?"

Zhanna answered, "Lautaro's parents are very strict Catholics and would not approve if they were to discover why we are out here."

Lautaro stood there looking dumb. He didn't understand a word of what was being said.

The leader was almost ready to believe Zhanna's story. Perhaps they were indeed just star-struck lovers who simply picked the wrong location. Still, he had his orders.

He nodded to his comrade. "Search the boat."

First, the man looked around the small wheelhouse then he went down the deck hatch.

"If what you say is true," said the leader, "we'll take you back to the island where you'll be asked a few questions and then released." He understood his orders to kill everyone on the boat except one person, but if these were the only two aboard he would take them both back. He was a Totenkopf-SS sergeant during the war and he knew two people to question were better than one. After that, the Gruppenführer could decide their fate.

Not ten minutes had passed before the other guard dragged Kay up onto the deck.

"Ah," said the SS sergeant, "so you have lied to me."

"They hid this one for a reason," he told his comrade. "We'll take her back to the island for interrogation. Kill these other two." The man holding Kay threw her roughly down on the deck."

Both men raised their Thompsons. Zhanna knew she couldn't get both men but she'd take at least one with her. In the blink of an eye she snapped the handgun from the back of her pants and shot the leader through the heart.

The Germans had made a mortal error. Confidently armed with their Thompsons, they had neglected to search either of the women for weapons.

The second man trained his machinegun at Zhanna, but before he could pull the trigger, Kay, still lying on the deck, yanked the Smith & Wesson revolver from the back of her pants. Using both hands she took aim.

Leroy Carr's wife pulled the trigger.

# Chapter 46

## The Bay of San Julián, Argentina
## Same evening—Saturday, 30 August 1947

Kay had aimed at the side of the man's chest when she pulled the trigger, but her hands shook so badly she was lucky to strike him at all. The .38 caliber bullet entered the side of the man's knee. He dropped to the boat's deck like a stone. This gave Zhanna time to react. With her handgun, the Russian rushed over and sent a bullet through the man's heart and another through his right eye.

Zhanna picked up the man's Thompson, ran to the boat's rail, and with uncanny accuracy with the bucking and usually less than accurate machinegun, chopped up the remaining man in the speedboat. She would have liked to preserve the fast boat for their use, but several shots from the powerful American weapon penetrated the hull. Water began flowing in and Zhanna knew the speedboat was lost. Using her knife, Zhanna cut off a long piece of rope attached to a fishing net, jumped into the slowly sinking boat and tied the dead coxswain's hands to the wheel so his body would not surface after the boat sank.

Kay felt sick, turned away, and vomited on the deck.

Zhanna climbed back onto the trawler's deck and told Lautaro she needed some sort of weights to ensure the two other bodies never made it out of Davey Jones' locker. The young fisherman, also nauseous, went below to fetch some fishing net weights.

During the time Lautaro was below deck, Zhanna put her hands on the sides of Kay's face and kissed her on both cheeks. "You saved my life," Zhanna told her.

Kay didn't respond.

Zhanna then added, "I have to kill Lautaro. We cannot leave any witnesses behind. I've watched what the boy does to drive this boat. We'll take over."

Kay was shocked. For a brief moment the thought passed through her mind to point her gun at Zhanna, but she was shivering from cold and shaking from anxiety. She knew she had no chance of intimidating the coldblooded Russian assassin. Kay couldn't believe that standing before her was a woman who had contemplated becoming a nun.

Instead of raising her gun, she said to Zhanna. "There is no reason for the boy to die. He doesn't know where we live. He doesn't even know our names. Anyone who might question him will find out nothing. You just said I saved your life. You can repay me by sparing him. He is no danger to us."

The most feared Soviet assassin during the Second World War looked at Kay poker faced.

# Chapter 47

## Nazi controlled Island, Bay of San Julián, Patagonia, Argentina
## Next morning—Sunday, 31 August 1947

At 7:30, someone knocked on Erika's and Kathryn's door. They had spent the night in one of the mansion's guest bedrooms on the second floor. Kathryn answered the knock. A young maid wearing a traditional maid's uniform (black dress, white apron, and white maid's cap) stood in the hallway.

"May I please have your breakfast order?"

"We're not eating downstairs?" Kathryn asked. She and Erika had assumed they would have breakfast with Müller and Ryker to further discuss Müller's assignment.

"Ma'am, all I know is I was told to take your orders and that the food is to be brought to your room."

"Okay, thank you," Kathryn said. "We'll have some scrambled eggs and some rye toast if you have it, and perhaps some cheese slices and a piece of fruit. You're very kind. Are you from Austria? I'm guessing because of your accent."

The young woman, who couldn't be over sixteen years in age, wasn't used to guests being polite to her. "Yes, I'm from Linz."

"I love Linz," Kathryn said pleasantly. "I'm sure you often visited the Hauptplaz." She referred to the famous medieval square in Linz.

The girl smiled. "Yes, my father took me there often."

Kathryn was curious. "So what brings you to South America?"

"My father was SS and is currently in an American detainment camp. Mother brought me here a year ago after the Americans asked her to testify against my father. She refused, of course, and she felt it best to leave Germany, at least for a time. We hope we can return someday, or that Father is released and can join us here. The Odessa helped us with our journey."

"Where is your mother now?"

"She works in a bakery in Puerto San Julián."

"I wish you and your family the best of luck, Fräulein," Kathryn said."

The young maid curtsied and said, "Danke schön."

◊ ◊ ◊

The young maid and an older woman who, from her attire, appeared to be a cook delivered the food to their room on a cart about a half-hour later. As soon as they left, Erika and Kathryn finished the food off quickly. They assumed Axel Ryker (per Müller's orders) would call on them soon that morning to return to Puerto San Julián to fetch Zhanna and Kay. The wait was longer than expected, but finally, Ryker banged loudly on their door at noon.

He barged into the room, not waiting to be invited. Erika and Kathryn had been ready to go for three hours.

"We have a situation," Ryker told them. "Last night, our shore guards spotted a fishing trawler apparently watching the island from off shore. We sent a boat out to investigate and it never returned. The trawler has disappeared. The rumor about the Soviet killing squads must be true. Who else could it be? I see you are ready; we will go now to San Julián and get your two comrades. The Gruppenführer is eager to talk to them, especially the Bolshevik bitch."

(Erika knew who else could have made the boat and men in it disappear—Zhanna.)

Heinrich Müller believed in fate, but he didn't follow it blindly. He had decided all four of the women would be cancelled on the island if he wasn't convinced that Zhanna Rogova could be trusted.

Looking forward to killing them, the sly Ryker had decided to play the part of putting old grudges with Erika aside and present himself as their comrade.

### [CIA headquarters, Washington, D.C.]
When Erika mailed the film of the German club's ledger containing the names of members to Washington, she was told at the post office that the package would take two weeks to reach its destination in the States. It took only eight days. Late this morning, Sheila Reid received the package at the CIA offices on E Street. She found herself torn

between her loyalty to the Shield Maidens and her allegiance to the United States. As an Army major, she had sworn an oath to only one. She called Leroy Carr at his hotel in Buenos Aires. Neither Carr nor Hodge were in their rooms so she left a message at the desk for Carr to contact her.

# Chapter 48

## Puerto San Julián, Argentina
## Same day—Sunday, 31 August 1947

At full speed, the cabin cruiser crossed the enormous bay in half the time it took Lautaro's slow fishing trawler.

Axel Ryker knew how to play his part. He could not come across as affable; the Abwehr spy knew how much he hated her. Any sort of friendly demeanor would draw her suspicion. Instead, he would convince her and the Gestapo Kriminalkommissar that he was willing to put old animosities aside for the sake of the assignment. Then, once back on the island, he would kill them as soon as he received Müller's nod. He would simply shoot the other three, but for Erika he had a special death planned. He would hang her slowly using piano wire.

◊ ◊ ◊

The heavy clouds of the previous night had raced away, transporting the snow farther inland. Now, in the afternoon, a blue sky smiled down from overhead allowing only a few pure white, puffball clouds (scattered about helter-skelter) to complete the heavenly mural. The temperature, happy for the friendlier sky, had strengthened itself to a much more sociable 48°F. Not bad for the dead of winter in southern Argentina.

Thanks to Kay, Lautaro was still alive. Zhanna thought it best to kill the young man, but Kay had called in her marker for saving Zhanna's life. That left Zhanna few options when one factored in the previous night's confrontation in the bay with the island guards. Adding all that together, Zhanna had no other option than to instruct Lautaro to take them back to the dock in Puerto San Julián. There they would wait. If Erika and Kathryn were not brought back to the mainland sometime today, they would sail out to the island again tonight. This time they would find a way to get on the heavily guarded islet despite the risk.

Last night, while sailing back to the town, Lautaro was frantic that the significant amount of blood on the deck had to be cleaned off before his father came aboard at dawn for their fishing plans for the day. The trawler reached its pier three hours before dawn and Zhanna, Kay, and Lautaro spent well over an hour scrubbing and swabbing the deck.

When the father showed up at first light, he took a look at the women onboard and began scolding his son. Lautaro told his dad that the women had hired the boat at 200 pesos an hour. Totaling up the hours the boat had already been chartered was already equal to $300 American, with more to come. That initial sum in itself was more than the family made in a month.

"How do you know these women will pay?" the father asked his son.

Kay overheard, took out the amount of pesos already owed, and handed the money to him. "We'll pay the rest at the end."

The father pocketed the money, patted his son on the back, and left to tell his wife and younger children of their good fortune.

That happened seven hours ago. It was nearly two in the afternoon when Zhanna spotted in the distance the cabin cruiser heading toward the dock.

The Russian went inside the wheelhouse and retrieved her binoculars.

It was obviously the same boat that took Erika and Kathryn away last evening. The boat eventually docked several piers away. A car awaited. Erika and Kathryn walked off the boat followed by a large man. The boat driver remained on the vessel.

"It's time to leave," Zhanna said to Kay. "Get in the car and start it. I'll be right behind you."

Kay jumped off the boat and onto the dock. She headed toward their car that was parked less than a block away.

Zhanna handed Lautaro another 1600 pesos to cover the additional hours since their earlier payment. "This is for you, my darling," Zhanna said and again kissed the young man on the mouth.

Lautaro wanted to say something but could not. He watched Zhanna jump off the ship and run away.

The young man would never know that the woman who bewitched him would have killed him if it wasn't for Kay.

# Chapter 49

**Puerto San Julián, Argentina**
**Same day—Sunday, 31 August 1947**

"The restaurants in this town are closed on Sunday," said Axel Ryker. He sat in the back seat alongside Kathryn, keeping Erika in front of him next to the driver. "This is some bizarre tradition in this country. What can I say? Almost everyone in this country is a Catholic. We'll dine with the general when we return to the island with your two comrades." Ryker wore a dark brown business suit. Erika and Kathryn were still in their gowns and wraps. Not expecting to stay overnight, they had brought no change of clothes to the island.

◊ ◊ ◊

Zhanna told Kay to stay at least a block behind the car driving Erika, Kathryn, and the large man, only speeding up if the car ahead turned a corner. After a turn, when they were again in sight of the car, Zhanna had Kay again drop back. Eventually, both women realized where the car was heading. When it pulled over to the curb in front of their house, Zhanna recognized the man and told Kay to keep driving.

"Drive to that little grocery store down the next block where we buy our groceries," Zhanna told Kay.

Kay had struggled to keep control of herself ever since she had shot the man on the trawler then watched Zhanna brutally finish him off. Both her hands shook and she felt like a sleepwalker going through the distracted motions of life. During the war, Zhanna had seen this reaction by inexperienced comrades many times—the shaking hands and glassy look in the eyes.

"Things will be alright, Kay. You'll get used to it."

"I will never get fucking used to it!" Kay said loudly. "I'd rather die than get used to it! How can you live with yourself?"

Zhanna said, "There is the store. Pull over quickly."

◊ ◊ ◊

The ever present drug gang on the corner had watched the formidable women get out of the car, followed by a man. Axel Ryker turned his head to look at the gang. This alone was enough to intimidate the drug dealers and they quickly looked away.

Once inside the house, Ryker wasn't happy that Lehmann's and the Kriminalkommissar's comrades were not home. Ryker was a man with a very low level of patience and he abhorred waiting.

"Where could they be, Lehmann?" Ryker didn't bother with the *Fräulein* in front of the surname.

"I don't know, but I'm sure they'll be back soon," Erika answered. She had no idea where Zhanna and Kay were. She knew they had surveilled the singing club yesterday and had probably watched her and Kathryn get on the cabin cruiser. Other than that she knew nothing. She suspected Zhanna might have something to do with the missing men and boat Müller referred to last night but couldn't be sure. Müller's assumption might be right; maybe the trawler sitting off shore was a Soviet cover to allow them to monitor the island.

Ryker scowled, "They wouldn't be welcome at the singing club, especially the Russian. Where are they?"

"You already asked me that and I just told you I don't know, Ryker."

A minute later, Zhanna and Kay walked in, each carrying a bag of groceries.

"Ah, groceries," Kathryn said. "We needed those." She had a feeling Zhanna and Kay held the bags of food as a cover.

Zhanna and Kay had seen the man at the dock and watched him get out of the car in front of the house. Zhanna didn't recognize him at the dock; he was too far away. But when she saw him step out of the car at the house, she immediately knew who he was. That caused the detour to the grocery store.

Zhanna played her part. "I see we have a guest."

Kay just stared at the fiendish looking man with her mouth half open.

"Herr Ryker," said Erika "this is Kay, the interpreter we told you about that Kathryn and I met in Buenos Aires. And this is Zhanna Rogova. Ladies, we've been invited to a dinner tonight."

"Take off your scarf," Ryker snarled at Zhanna.

Zhanna smirked at Ryker and removed the scarf. "We have met before, *Herr* Ryker.

Ryker looked at Zhanna's neck scar for confirmation. "Yes, we certainly have met before. We briefly crossed paths in Bulgaria during the war. You assassinated our head of Gestapo in Sofia and were captured. I began my interrogation but somehow you managed to escape the next day."

Zhanna laughed. "Interrogation! That is a soft word for torture."

Ryker undid the top button off his shirt, revealing his own neck scar. His scar wasn't as gruesome as Zhanna's, but eye-catching, nevertheless.

"I also have a scar," Ryker growled. "Courtesy of your slut Abwehr comrade, Fräulein Lehmann."

Erika and Kathryn, both taken by surprise, watched Ryker and Zhanna glower at one another.

# Chapter 50

**Back to the Present**
**Islet in the Bay of Puerto San Julián, Argentina**
**Sunday, 31 August 1947**

Müller's orders to Ryker included returning to the island with the women under the cover of darkness. They didn't have to wait long. This time of year darkness came early to Puerto San Julián, a town barely over a thousand miles from the outer islands of Antarctica. In late August, darkness fell just shortly after four o'clock in the afternoon.

Ryker insisted they drive to the dock in one car. Kay drove. Erika sat beside her because Ryker wanted her in front of him. That left Ryker, Kathryn and Zhanna to squeeze into the back seat of the narrow sedan. The wide and muscular Ryker took up nearly half the seat so Zhanna ended up being crowded up against Kathryn, nearly sitting on her lap.

As were his orders, the cabin cruiser pilot had waited patiently at the dock. This journey across the bay would be more comfortable for the women. Erika and Kathryn no longer required formal gowns and high heels, and Zhanna and Kay would not have to stand outside on the freezing, windblown deck of a fishing trawler. The women had come dressed in operative clothes including sensible, soft leather shoes with good traction. Their pants were American blue jeans they had brought along from D.C. Blue jeans had become popular in the United States because of the John Wayne westerns in the '30s. They all wore matching gray men's long-sleeved shirts and medium weight jackets that were enough since they would be inside the boat's heated cabin during the trip across the bay. All were armed. Ryker had okayed the bringing of weapons. The wily Ryker knew if he insisted the women be unarmed it would raise their wariness. They would be disarmed when they arrived at the mansion. His only goal was to get them on the island where he could kill them as soon as Müller gave his go ahead.

Shortly after the cabin cruiser left the pier, they passed a fishing trawler retuning to the Puerto San Julián dock. Kay looked. It was Lautaro's fishing trawler. Apparently he and his father were returning from a day of netting. Kay turned away, just thankful the young man was alive. She had gotten her shaking hands under control but her nerves were still on edge.

◊ ◊ ◊

After the boat docked and the group was driven to the mansion, Ryker followed the four women into the large atrium where the reception had been held the previous evening. The swastika flags and Hitler portrait were still there. The band and guests were not.

The only people in the room were two men in business suits who Erika recognized from last night. Then, they had been dressed in their SS lieutenant uniforms and had served as waiters. Both men looked to be in their early thirties. Both were over six-feet tall with granite jaws. They looked as if they jumped off of a Nazi propaganda poster of the perfect Aryan fighting machine. One had blond hair, the other brown.

"Fräuleins and Herr Ryker," said the blond man, "I have to ask you to hand over your weapons. We are part of the general's protection squad, and this we do for the general's safety."

All this had been set up before Ryker left the island that morning. He told the guards to also disarm him to allay suspicions. All of them handed over their handguns. The brown-haired SS man checked the guns to make sure the safeties were engaged. Kay's .38 Special was the only revolver, which has no safety, so the man opened the cylinder and dumped out the cartridges.

"Knives, as well, please," the blond man said.

They all handed over their hidden knives. The women's had been strapped to their ankles—Ryker's, under his jacket.

"You will dine privately with the general at seven o'clock (it was now getting close to five). Fräuleins, until then, you can wait in your rooms. The general plans to invite you to stay here tonight."

Erika and Kathryn glanced at each other.

Ryker disappeared, and the women were escorted upstairs by the Nazi poster clones and given two large bedrooms. Erika and Zhanna would take one, Kathryn and Kay the other. Once they were left alone they gathered in Erika's room. Erika, Kathryn, and Zhanna searched the room for bugs but didn't find any. Nevertheless, Erika turned on the radio and told everyone to speak softly. They huddled closely. Kathryn, Zhanna, and Kay crowded onto the divan. Erika pulled up a Queen Ann chair that had sat at the vanity. This was the first time a private conversation between them was possible since Erika and Kathryn had been taken to the island yesterday. When they had been reunited today at the house, Ryker was there. Erika and Kathryn knew nothing about the fishing trawler incident.

Erika spoke sotto voce. "Zhanna, when you got to the house shortly after us this afternoon, you and Kay were carrying groceries. So I know you were following us from the dock. Fill me and Kathryn in."

Zhanna also used a soft undertone to tell them about the fishing trawler and the confrontation with the men from the island.

Zhanna ended with, "Kay saved my life."

Erika was impressed and looked at Kay. "Are you alright, Kay?"

"No, I'm not alright with shooting a man! Leave me alone. Just tell me what I need to do from here."

"You have to keep your voice down, Kay," Kathryn said.

Kay felt like voicing a vulgarity, telling them all what to do, but she held her tongue. "None of us are prepared to stay here overnight."

"You'll sleep in your under garments like Kathryn and I did last night," Erika replied. "A housemaid will bring you makeup in the morning, if that matters to you."

"I'm not talking about that," Kay said impatiently. "Do you think I give a damn about my makeup? I'm referring to the facts that we are unarmed and this entire thing sounds fishy to me."

Erika replied, "Just play your part at the dinner, Kay. You're an American who was a supporter of the Führer. That's all you have to do." Then she addressed the group. "What Müller said about forming a team with Ryker might be true, or this could very well be a trap because of Zhanna. Zhanna, at dinner tonight you have to convince

Müller that my suggestion to bring you in on this investigation is in his interests. It will all be up to you."

"What if Zhanna doesn't convince him?" Kay asked.

"Then we're dead," Erika said bluntly. "For me, my only wish is to kill Ryker before I die even if I have nothing but a table knife. I couldn't kill him with a dagger to the throat, so my chances of succeeding with a simple table knife are minute to say the least, but I'm willing to die trying. The rest of you should make a run for it as best you can. Perhaps you can get to one of the speed boats."

"We are sisters, none of us will abandon you with Ryker," Kathryn said.

"Kay and I agree with Kathryn, right, Kay?" Zhanna stated.

Kay nodded, "Yes." Apparently the Russian now felt Kay was a friend and equal. Kay considered the Russian assassin at least half insane if not totally. As subtly as she could, Kay grabbed her left hand which had once again begun shaking.

# Chapter 51

## Islet in the Bay of Puerto San Julián, Argentina
## That evening—Sunday, 31 August 1947

At ten minutes before seven o'clock, the brown-haired SS lieutenant, still wearing a suit, escorted the four women to the dining hall. No one else was present once they got there. A crystal chandelier sparkled over the long mahogany table that could easily seat forty guests. The lieutenant showed the women where to sit and held their chairs for them one-by-one. They were all seated at one end of the table with one seat left open on the right side of the empty head chair at the end. Each placing was already set with fine porcelain china rimmed with gold, spotless silverware, a water glass already filled, and an empty red glass goblet with a black swastika on the side. Without further comment the SS man left. Less than a minute later a tuxedoed butler with an NSDAP pin on his lapel escorted in a waiter who filled the goblets with white wine. Neither of them spoke.

The women sipped their wine for several minutes. Finally, at ten minutes after the hour, Heinrich Müller walked in followed by Axel Ryker and a waiter with another bottle of wine. Müller took the head chair, of course. Ryker sat down beside Kay with the three Shield Maidens opposite him. Erika sat directly across from Ryker, then Kathryn and Zhanna beside her. Kay, sitting next to the apparition of horror, put her hands under the table.

As soon as he seated himself, Müller said in German, "Welcome again, Sonderführer Lehmann and Kriminalkommissar Fischer. Please introduce your comrades." Müller already knew who was who but asked anyway as the waiter filled his and Ryker's goblets. Before Erika could speak, Müller looked at the waiter. "Bring another bottle of wine and leave it on the table. We'll pour our own glasses. Tell the kitchen people to serve us now. That will be all." The waiter bowed and left.

"Next to Kathryn is Zhanna Rogova, Herr Gruppenführer," Erika said. "Sitting next to Herr Ryker is Kay Becker, our Spanish translator I spoke to you about who supports our cause. I'm afraid Kay doesn't speak German but I will translate for her when necessary."

Müller looked at Kay for a long moment, and then at Zhanna.

"Before we dine and talk business," Müller said, "let us toast the Reich." He raised his goblet. "To the Führer and the greater German Reich."

Everyone raised the goblets and repeated, "To the Führer and to the Reich, Prost!"

The food was brought in and scooped onto the plates by two footmen. Each diner was given a piece of white fish, five or six shrimp, and three large scallops. All the seafood had been baked in a white wine sauce with herbs. Asparagus handled the duty as the vegetable du jour. A platter of assorted breads and cheeses was placed where everyone could reach.

"The seafood is all from the bay or just off the nearby coast," Müller commented. "By the way, the wine we are drinking is from the vineyards near Rüdesheim on the Rhine. Generalissimo Peron imported it before the war. The wine cellar here at this estate is quite impressive. By the way, the wine goblets were a Christmas gift to my wife and me from Reichsführer Himmler."

"I'm surprised to see the asparagus this time of year, Gruppenführer Müller," Kathryn said.

"It's a favorite of mine, Kriminalkommissar. I have it brought down from Brazil."

"So this is now your permanent residence?" Kathryn asked.

"It is for now. The Generalissimo has invited me to stay as long as I wish. I expect to be transferring to a different location if this investigation into Soviet activity to murder our comrades proves to be true. That's why we are here tonight—to discuss."

Kay hadn't understood a word; Erika had yet to translate any of the conversation.

Müller paused for a moment as everyone began eating. Then he turned his attention to Kay.

"So, Fräulein Becker, tell me about yourself," Müller said as he locked eyes with her. Erika translated.

For much of the day, Kay felt herself teetering on the edge of a nervous breakdown. *What type of people are these? What type of world do they live in?* She had played a part in killing a man. Now she sat at dinner with a man who was arguably one of the top five most powerful Nazis before and during the war, and a grizzly Gestapo killer who enjoyed torturing people. Then there were the Shield Maidens who were no more hesitant to mete out violence than they were to pass the salt at dinner. Kay felt as if she were going mad.

"I'm not an interesting person, General," she replied, holding herself together. "I'm just an American who supported the Party and the Führer. I still do. That's why, when I met Erika and Kathryn in Buenos Aires, I accepted the job Erika offered me to work as their Spanish translator."

"I'm told your father was a member of the American Bund before the war."

"Yes, both my father and mother where enthusiastic supporters of the cause in Cincinnati."

Erika was impressed. She had been prepared to alter the translation if necessary, but didn't have to now. She translated exactly. The bottle of wine was passed around to refill the goblets.

Neither Ryker nor Zhanna had yet to speak. Müller now turned his attention on Zhanna. "Comrade Rogova, I'm told you speak German."

"Yes, I speak your language," Zhanna rejoined without looking up from her meal. "Please don't bother me now. I'm eating." She cut one of the huge scallops in half and forked it into her mouth.

Ryker started to rise from his chair, but Müller reached over and put his hand on Ryker's forearm. "Please sit back down, Herr Ryker."

Müller smiled at Zhanna. "I see you are the Zhanna Rogova from legend—the fireball. Tell me; are you as skilled as the rumors would have us believe?"

"Skilled at what?" Zhanna asked, again without looking up from her food.

"In eliminating people?"

Zhanna finally looked at Müller. "Yes, but especially Germans."

Erika and Kathryn knew Zhanna was handling this perfectly. She was being herself. If the Russian were to come across as too friendly and accommodating, Müller would immediately recognize the act.

Still addressing Zhanna, Müller said. "You are the reason our men and boat disappeared last night, am I right?"

"Yes, they're all at the bottom of the bay. And, of course, it was you who sent them to kill me and Kay, not knowing we were with Erika and Kathryn."

Müller smiled. He respected anyone who had defied death so many times over the years by fighting bravely, even if they were the enemy. The Russian could be a great aide in this mission involving the Soviets. "Herr Ryker, return the Fräuleins' weapons to them after dinner." Then the Gestapo general addressed them all. "Your investigation begins tomorrow morning."

Rage swept over Ryker's face.

# Chapter 52

## Puerto San Julián, Argentina
## Next morning—Monday, 01 September 1947

The cabin cruiser returned the four-woman rogue CIA team and Axel Ryker to the Puerto San Julián dock at nine o'clock this morning. Erika Lehmann had hoped to convince Heinrich Müller to include in their Soviet investigation a search for Hitler (the reason she and Kathryn were in Argentina in the first place), but she could not suggest this at dinner last night. Müller had been very ambiguous about what he knew about the Führer's fate, but one thing she did know, the Gestapo chieftain would never allow a Russian to be involved in seeking out Adolf Hitler. Because of Zhanna, Erika's suggestion was never aired.

Axel Ryker was another story. Now she and the other women had to contend with him.

As far as Ryker's thoughts, he felt betrayed by Müller but had few options other than to keep himself in the general's good graces. He would like nothing better than to kill all four of the women, but he knew if he did so without good cause that he could present to Müller, he would be on the run for the rest of his life, not only from the Soviets and the war crimes tribunals, but then also from Müller and the general's extensive South American web of faithful Nazi underlings. He would play along with Müller's orders, all the time looking for a reason to eliminate the women that would be acceptable to his Gestapo general overseer. Ryker didn't like it but knew it was a situation forced upon him. Müller had now replaced the dead Heinrich Himmler as Ryker's boss and there was nothing he could do about it.

The women would stay at their house. As for Ryker, no soul on Earth intimidated the menacing brute, but even Axel Ryker had to sleep. He didn't trust Erika not to shoot him in the head while he slept, so he would not overnight with the women. Instead, he would sleep in a small, upstairs room at the Germania Gesangverein.

◊ ◊ ◊

**[that afternoon]**
Yesterday, Leroy Carr had spoken to Sheila Reid about the microfilm from Erika that had been mailed from Puerto San Julián. The plane carrying Carr and Al Hodge touched down just outside the fishing town in Patagonia shortly after one o'clock.

**[that evening]**
Ryker, now the team leader, ordered Erika, Kathryn, and Zhanna to report to the singing club at 7:00 p.m. Their instructions were to sit at the bar and wait. Kay would not be needed at the German-speaking club and she was ordered to stay at the house.

"Huppi," said Erika in German to the rotund bartender, "all three of us will have a Warsteiner Dunkel."

"Very well," said Huppi, "are you here to see Oberst Graf?"

"No, we're meeting a man who is supposed to be staying here—a Herr Ryker."

Immediate fear flashed in Huppi's eyes. He had met Ryker for the first time that afternoon.

"Would you tell him we are here?" Erika asked.

Huppi hesitated. "I will tell Oberst Graf. The Oberst is here tonight." It was apparent that Huppi wanted nothing to do with Axel Ryker.

When Huppi returned, he led them into a side room. Inside, Ryker and Graf sat around a large table used by club members who could request the room for private dinners. Graf stood when the women entered; Ryker did not. Huppi closed the heavy door behind him and returned to the bar.

Five minutes after the three women disappeared from the bar into the side room, Leroy Carr and Al Hodge walked into the club.

## Chapter 53

### Germania Gesangverein, Puerto San Julián, Argentina
### Same evening

Inside the club's private room, the colonel gave Ryker the floor. Everyone spoke in German.

"We have two leads," Ryker began. "The first one is that four Russians arrived in this area four days ago. Fellow comrades informed us of their arrival. The next day, I followed them for several hours. They definitely have the look of NKVD."

The Soviet NKVD was Stalin's secret police. The organization was more or less the Russian version of the German Gestapo. Zhanna had been a member of the NKVD after Stalin disbanded SMERSH shortly after the war.

Ryker continued, "These men are staying on a ranch just a few miles west of this town. I've already researched the background of the ranch owner. In the 1930s he and his wife were Communist sympathizers. The man got in trouble at a demonstration, was arrested, and sentenced to six months in jail, but his wealthy father's lawyers got him out in less than a month."

"What's the second lead?" Erika asked.

Ryker glared at her. "We'll travel one road at a time, Sonderführer. That is, if it's okay with you." The disdain in his voice was clear.

"So, what is our assignment on this *first* lead?" Erika asked. "Or do we have to suffer through more boredom before you get to the point?"

"You and your two comrades will break into the ranch house in the dead of night and confiscate all documents and anything else of interest. I know you speak Russian, Sonderführer, but it's my understanding you cannot translate Russian Cyrillic script on paper. Is that true?"

"Yes."

"That is why your Russian comrade is still alive," Ryker said without glancing at Zhanna. "The Gruppenführer sees this as an opportunity for your Bolshevik friend to earn our trust. Your orders

205

are simple. After you have the documents, kill everyone in the house: men, women, children, servants—everyone except one of the NKVD men who you will deliver to me for interrogation. I will dispose of him when I feel I've extracted all of the information I can get. After that, we will proceed from there."

◊ ◊ ◊

When they arrived in town earlier this day, Carr and Hodge landed without any leads other than that the package Sheila Reid received was mailed from here. Leroy found out there was a German singing club in Puerto San Julián and, with nothing to lose, decided to visit the club. It was a place where he thought native Germans would be comfortable. Perhaps Erika and Kathryn had been here. Carr knew that Erika could have mailed the package right before they left for a different location, but if they had been in the club in the past few days it would at least point to the fact that they *might* still be in the area.

Leroy Carr spoke pretty good 'tourist' German but was not fluent. He could, however, order a beer. Carr looked at the taps and ordered for himself and Al. "Zwei Berliner, bitte."

Huppi looked at Carr. The man ordering the beers spoke with an American accent; that much was undeniable. "This is a private club," Huppi said in German. "You must be a member, or guest of a member."

Neither Carr nor Hodge understood what the bartender said. "Jeder hier spricht Englisch?" Carr asked (anyone here speak English).

Huppi looked around the Ratskeller and spotted a member who spoke English. He got the man's attention by calling out loudly, "Herr Böhm!"

The man sat with his wife; he turned toward the bartender when he heard his name shouted. Huppi waved him to the bar.

◊ ◊ ◊

Herr Böhm translated a brief conversation between Huppi and the two Americans. Huppi excused himself from behind the bar then proceeded to the private room where he walked in on the meeting between Graf, Ryker and the women.

"What is it, Huppi?" Graf asked impatiently.

"Oberst Graf, I apologize for interrupting you but I thought this information you would want to know."

"What is it?" Graf barked.

"There are two Americans sitting at the bar. They speak little German, but Herr Böhm is here tonight so I asked him to translate. The Americans claim to be college professors who have come to Patagonia to research the region's history."

"What college?" Graf asked.

"Some college in the American state of California is what they told me. They said they have received some sort of government grant for their research."

"Did you get their names?"

"Yes, Oberst. They are a Professor Grayson and a Professor Taylor."

"What excuse did you give them for your absence from the bar?"

"I told everyone at the bar that I had to change the keg of Berliner. It was not yet empty but, nevertheless, I will exchange it when I return.

"Very good, Huppi," said Graf. "Return to the bar and make sure you exchange the keg for them to see. Herr Ryker will come out shortly to talk to them."

Huppi extended a proper German bow and left the room.

# Chapter 54

## Germania Gesangverein, Puerto San Julián, Argentina
## Same evening—01 September, 1947

Leroy Carr and Al Hodge both saw Ryker enter the Ratskeller bar area.

"Good Lord," Hodge said. "Look at that guy. He looks like the bastard son of Boris Karloff and Bela Lugosi."

"Last I heard, two men can't have a child together, Al."

"Well, if they could, that's what he'd look like."

Ryker walked up to the end of the bar, several chairs away from Carr and Hodge. He ordered a double Jägermeister from Huppi. Before he downed the drink, he looked at the two *professors*.

"Ah, I see we have new friends." Ryker lifted the glass and gave a prost. The two CIA men returned the salute with their beers. Ryker downed the strong schnapps in one quick gulp and walked over to the men. He moved away a stool beside Carr so he could stand.

"Huppi, bring me another and bring our new guests another beer. I will pay." Ryker turned back to Carr and Hodge. "My name is Schmitt."

(Leroy Carr knew about Axel Ryker from Erika's past history from her file, and in his conversations with her after the war ended. But a photograph of Ryker wasn't available. Carr wasn't aware that Ryker stood next to him).

"My name is Herman Grayson," Carr said in German. "This is my colleague, Ralph Taylor. I understand a bit of German and could make out what you said, but I'm not fluent."

Ryker switched to English. "I speak pretty good English. I can tell from your accents that you are Americans, yes?"

"That's right, Herr Schmitt. Thank you for your efforts to speak in our language."

"No thank you necessary," said Ryker. "I'm always ready to practice and improve my English. So, what brings two Americans to our humble little club?" Ryker acted like the information from Huppi had never reached his ears.

"We're college history professors here to study the history of Patagonia. We'll deliver a series of talks about our research, not only to our students but at other universities."

"A noble task," Ryker replied.

**[back in the private room]**

Oberst Graf," Erika said. "While we wait for Herr Ryker to return, I would like to use the toilet room."

"Of course, Sonderführer. Do you know where it is?"

"Ja."

There were two doors that entered the private room. One opened into the Ratskeller; the other into a corridor by the kitchen. Erika used the door opposite the kitchen. From a dark corner of the hallway she looked out into the bar area.

After a moment, Erika returned to the private room, pulled her Beretta out of the back of her pants and used the butt of the gun to knockout Graf.

"Those two *college professors* Huppi mentioned are Carr and Hodge," she said to Kathryn and Zhanna. "Ryker is talking to them."

Kathryn and Zhanna both stood up and drew their handgun.

Erika continued, "The package containing the microfilm must have arrived in Washington sooner than expected. If Leroy or Al asks Ryker if a blonde and brunette have been here, he'll know our stories are fake. He'll kill Leroy and Al then come for us."

Graf, who had fallen out of his chair onto the floor, moaned and started to wake up. Erika put him back to sleep with another blow, this one harder and to the jaw.

**[at the bar]**

It was Al Hodge who posed the questions after summoning Huppi over.

"Herr Schmitt, would you please translate for me?"

"Of course," Ryker said.

Hodge looked at the bartender. "You said Huppi is your name, right?"

Huppi waited for Ryker to translate then said, "Ja."

"We have some interns who were supposed to meet us when we arrived and we've not seen them yet. Since this seems to be a popular meeting place, I was wondering if you had seen them here. There are three of them. One is a blonde woman, the two others are brunettes." Hodge was referring to Erika, Kathryn and Kay. Although he and Carr suspected Zhanna might be with them, they weren't sure. "One of the brunettes is an American who accompanied the others down to act as their Spanish translator."

The bartender looked nervously at Ryker, picked up a signal, and said, "No, I don't recall any such women."

Huppi was a lousy actor. Carr caught the nervous check with *Herr Schmitt* and knew the bartender was lying. He also now suspected he knew the real name of the brutish man standing next to him.

Carr turned to Hodge. "The weather is much milder than we expected, don't you agree, Ralph."

Hodge heard the code phrase and said, "Indeed."

## Chapter 55

### Germania Gesangverein, Puerto San Julián, Argentina
### Same evening—01 September, 1947

Erika, with Kathryn and Zhanna behind her, again peeked around the corner of the kitchen corridor.

"They're gone!" Erika told the others. "All of them: Carr, Hodge, and Ryker."

No one needed instructions from Erika. They all ran out into the bar with guns drawn ss if they all knew what to do by instinct. Kathryn and Zhanna covered the crowd and Erika confronted Huppi. The band stopped playing.

"Where are Ryker and the two Americans?" Erika shouted as she pointed her gun at Huppi's face.

Huppi's eyes rolled back in his head and he fainted, falling heavily to the floor behind the bar.

When Kathryn saw Huppi keel over, she grabbed the nearest man to her and put her gun to his head. "Where are the three men?"

"I don't know! They left!"

"What do you mean 'they left'? They left the room?"

"No, they left the building!"

Kathryn pistol whipped the man for good measure. The woman sitting next to him, presumably his wife, screamed. Zhanna shot her in the foot needlessly.

"Let's go!" Erika shouted. The three women sprinted out of the building. They quickly looked around for Ryker's car but didn't see it, so they raced to their car.

"Leroy and Al are probably already dead," Erika said as the women loaded into the car. "We have to grab Kay and get to a different location before Ryker can get to her. He'll kill her just because he would consider it fun."

Erika turned the key but the engine didn't start. She tried several times until the battery became weak. She jumped out of the car and popped the hood. The spark plug wires had been cut.

Erika realized they would have to steal a car. "Kathryn, go back into the club and make sure no one gets on a telephone to call the police. Zhanna and I will find a car."

Kathryn ran back into the club with gun in hand.

Erika and Zhanna split up and raced around the parking lot until Zhanna found a Chevy with unlocked doors. All three of the women had in the past hot-wired cars. Even Zhanna, the terrible driver, had undergone the training on stealing cars at the Army intelligence base at Fort Huachuca. She jumped behind the wheel and went to work.

They didn't have a flashlight so it was hard for Zhanna to see under the dashboard. Five minutes passed by, then ten.

"Hurry up, Zhanna!" Erika exclaimed.

For a moment Zhanna forgot her English and exclaimed, "Der'mo (Russian for human excrement). I'm doing the best I can! I can't see under here. I have to feel around for everything."

It took a good twenty minutes, but finally the car started.

"Erika said, "I'll drive. Go get Kathryn!"

Zhanna ran into the club and in an instant she and Kathryn came running out. Once everyone was in the car, Erika put the Chevy into reverse and spun the back wheels in the gravel as she backed out of the parking space. Then she jerked the gearstick on the steering column into first gear and spit gravel with the tires as they pulled out of the Germania Gesangverein parking lot.

Erika drove at least twice the speed limit on the way to the house. Puerto San Julián had no stoplights, but she shot through several stop signs along the way. When they finally reached the house, it was at least thirty minutes, probably a little more, since Ryker, Carr, and Hodge had disappeared from the club.

Ryker's car was not on the street in front of the house. That might be good or bad news. Perhaps Ryker had decided Kay wasn't worth his trouble, or, on the dark side, he had already been here and kidnapped or murdered her.

Erika squealed the tires as she came to a stop in front of the house and they all jumped out.

"Kathryn, go around to the back door! Zhanna, go to a side window. I'll go in the front door. Count to ten and we all enter together. Go!"

Kathryn and Zhanna ran into the nighttime shadows beside the duplex. After a count of ten, Erika kicked open the front door, Kathryn shot the door knob off the back door, and Zhanna hurled herself through a locked bedroom window.

# Chapter 56

## The House, Puerto San Julián, Patagonia, Argentina
## Same evening—Monday, 01 September, 1947

Erika was the first to see Kay sitting on the living room sofa, reading a Spanish version of *Time* magazine. Within a brief few seconds, Kathryn and Zhanna rushed into the room. All three women held their guns in hand as they quickly looked around the room. Zhanna's jacket and other clothes had presented a good shield as she hurled herself through the window glass. All that was visible was an abrasion on her forehead and a bleeding cut on her chin from which a few drops of blood ran.

Erika was relieved that Kay was still alive.

"Kay," Erika said, "we have to get out of here! Ryker might be on his way to kill you. Don't concern yourself with your clothes. Let's go!"

"Ryker and my husband have already been here . . . Al Hodge, too. They left about fifteen minutes ago. Sit down, all of you. We have some business to discuss."

Erika looked at Kay incredulously. "What are you talking about?"

"Sit down, all of you, please" Kay said again.

"I don't want to sit down," Erika replied. Neither did Kathryn nor Zhanna.

"Suit yourselves," Kay said as she tossed the magazine on the coffee table and lit up a Pall Mall cigarette from a pack just given to her by her husband.

"Cigarette?" Kay asked the three Shield Maidens.

"Cut the crap, Kay," Erika demanded. "What's going on?"

"Our mission is over, and it was successful," Kay said after she exhaled the smoke.

"What in hell are you talking about?" Erika asked loudly.

"Our real mission was never to search for Adolf Hitler. The FBI and other agencies from other countries are already doing that. They'll find him if he's still alive. Our mission was to find Axel Ryker. You've succeeded."

Erika lowered her gun. "I don't understand. We all thought that Ryker was dead, including Leroy."

"You believed that, but it's obvious that my husband had a reason to believe otherwise. He never told you because he knew you'd disappear to pursue Ryker. He and Al have Ryker now and are probably getting on a plane as we speak. Leroy wanted to separate you and Ryker for now while emotions run high. All of us will meet in my husband's office in Washington on Thursday morning. The four of us will fly out of here tomorrow morning."

"How are we going to do that?" Erika asked. "This town has no commercial airline service."

My husband made some sort of deal with El Búho. The Night Witch is on her way. She'll fly us to Panama. There we'll board a U.S. Air Force plane that will take us to Washington."

Now Erika sat down, suddenly overcome with fatigue that was much more mental than physical. Kathryn and Zhanna remained standing but both leaned back against a wall as flabbergasted as Erika.

"So what happens now?" Zhanna asked.

Kay looked at the Russian. "Zhanna, the Night Witch will take you back to the convent in Honduras on our way to Panama, or you can rejoin the CIA with no prejudice. No charges will be filed. The decision is yours. Also, there will be no backlash for either Kathryn or Erika for going rogue since you were duped and the mission was a success."

"Leroy couldn't have been here at the house more than ten minutes," Erika was suspicious. "He told you all of this in the brief few minutes he was here?"

"I knew the real reason for the mission all along—before we left Washington. However, the decision to not file charges against you isn't my husband's idea. It's mine."

"Your decision?" Kathryn said. "How can we trust that?"

"You don't have much choice, do you? Unless you all want to disappear into some obscure convent in some forgotten place like Zhanna did. Maybe you want to do that. Personally, I don't care one way or another."

Erika asked, "So this stuff with your nerves on edge and your hands shaking was all acting?"

"No," Kay admitted. "Maybe at first I was acting, but when I shot the man on the boat and watched Zhanna kill him, after that I struggled. I thought I might go out of my mind before all this was over. You know, being around women like the three of you is not easy. Then when I finally laid eyes on that creepy Ryker, it frazzled my nerves even more. I'm not like you, Erika, and hope I never will be."

Erika ignored the slight. "It surprises me that Leroy would put his wife in this type of dangerous mission."

"It wasn't supposed to go this way. My husband thought this would be a low-risk assignment. He knew Ryker was in South America but didn't know where. He hoped that in our search for Hitler, we'd meet some influential Nazis because of your and Kathryn's backgrounds, and that I could report back to him before we got into trouble. His plan was to then recall us and send down Al Hodge and his men to pick up the investigation. He wasn't expecting you to go rogue and keep me from contacting him. Your finding Zhanna was something else he wasn't expecting. It's you who made it more dangerous than it had to be."

After a long pause while Erika tried to process all this, she finally asked, "What is Leroy going to do with Ryker?"

"He's already done it. He offered him a job. That's why Ryker left willingly with Leroy and Al from the German club.

"You three have the night to think things over. The three of you can all disappear from here and I'll fly back by myself; or Erika and Kathryn, you two can disappear and Zhanna can go with me back to the convent with assurances that the CIA will not pursue her. The other choice is for all of you to return to D.C. with me if you trust my word that my husband will not take punitive actions against you. If you don't trust me then I recommend you all disappear from here.

"Now, I'm exhausted and going to bed." She ground the cigarette into the ashtray on the coffee table, stood up, and left for the bedroom.

## Chapter 57

### Puerto San Julián, Patagonia, Argentina
### Monday, 01 September, 1947

The couple living in the other half of the duplex were not home when Kathryn shot the lock off the back door the previous evening, so they didn't hear the gunfire. Other neighbors ignored it. It was not uncommon for the holligans on the street corner to fire guns into the air for fun, especially after a bit too much tequila.

Lyudmila Solokova, the Soviet WWII "Night Witch," set down her Cessna T-50 onto the gravel runway outside Puerto San Julián just after two o'clock in the afternoon of this day. As was always the case, the first thing she did was refuel and add more oil to the engines. After nearly two years of working for the Guatemalan drug lord El Búho, she knew prompt takeoffs were many times necessary. By the time her taxi reached the house (her boss had given her the address), twilight waned. Luckily for her, total darkness had not yet descended, for no cabbie would drive his taxi into this area of town after dark.

Solokova knocked on the door. After a few moments, none other than her fellow Red Army comrade-in-arms, Zhanna Rogova, answered the door.

The Shield Maidens, the Night Witch, and Kay Carr sat down at the kitchen table and poured themselves a brandy. It wasn't Asbach, but still an acceptable brandy from northern Chile.

"I've been flying overnight and all day today," said Solokova in Russian. "I have to get some sleep before we can take off tomorrow."

"Of course," Zhanna said, also in Russian. "You'll stay here tonight."

Kay looked at Erika and asked, "What did they say?" Erika told her and Kathryn.

Erika didn't see any point in questioning the Russian pilot. She would not know anything about the assignment or any deal Leroy Carr had cut with her drug lord boss. Like the military pilot she had been during the war, the Russian simply flew an airplane and did what she was told.

Sleeping arrangements were rearranged. Kay would still billet with Kathryn, but Erika would for tonight sleep on the sofa and give the two Russians the other bedroom.

After about an hour, and two snifters of brandy, everyone retired for the night.

◊ ◊ ◊

Erika was suffering a fitful night on the couch, dozing off for a few minutes, then laying awake thinking of how Leroy and Kay Carr had deceived her. This was something that had never happened before. During her time serving in the German Abwehr or during her time affiliated with the American government, she had always been the one delivering the surprises.

Leroy Carr was a master of his craft, she had to admit that, and Kay had pulled off her part beautifully.

It was shortly after midnight that she rose, put on her robe, and walked to the kitchen to get another brandy, hoping it would help her sleep. Kay had given them all the option of disappearing. *Lorelei* could pull that off, but she knew she wouldn't flee. It might mean she would never see her daughter again. She would return to D.C. with Kay and face the music if Kay was once again deceiving them about her offer of no prejudice for going rogue. Even if she were in prison, her grandparents could occasionally bring Ada to the States to see her during visitation.

As far as Kathryn and Zhanna were concerned, Erika didn't know what they were thinking. Everyone had to decide for themselves.

**[next morning—Tuesday, 02 September, 1947]**
At nine o'clock, Erika took Kay along and knocked on their duplex neighbors' front door. The wife answered.

"We are leaving today," Erika told her and waited for Kay to relay in Spanish.

"My husband and I were going to come see you this evening after he gets home from work," she said excitedly. "We have found a house in a nice neighborhood only a block from the children's school. All of it thanks to you. How can we ever repay you?"

"When are you moving out?"

"This weekend."

"That's wonderful," Erika said. "So this is goodbye."

The woman started crying and hugged Erika and Kay.

When they stepped off the porch, Erika said to Kay, "We can't leave without saying goodbye to our friends on the corner."

When they reached the gang, Erika addressed them all.

"My friends and I are leaving today," she told them. "The couple who lives in the other half of our house should also be moving out soon, but for as long as they live there, you will make sure they are not bothered and their possessions are left alone. Do you understand?"

After Kay translated, the leader said, "Si, Si, Señorita!"

Erika finished with, "One more thing. The side of the house that we lived in has two busted door locks and a broken window. You will make sure those are repaired. If the couple is bothered, or if the repairs are not made, you'll be dealing with El Búho."

◊ ◊ ◊

At eleven o'clock, the team was aboard the Cessna T-50: Kay, Erika, Kathryn, and Zhanna. Lyudmila Solokova fired the engines one at a time, let them warm, and then taxied out onto the gravel runway. About ten minutes later, the Night Witch roared the engines, picked up speed, and left Puerto San Julián behind.

# Chapter 58

## Washington, D.C.
## Thursday, 04 September 1947

Tuesday morning when they took off from Puerto San Julián, Zhanna decided, after all, to return to the Cloister of Saint Flora and Mary in Honduras, telling Erika that because of her heavy sins throughout her life she found peace only there in the solitude and simple life.

"I'm not worthy to be a Sister, but I can tend the gardens in peace," the Russian told Erika, Kathryn, and Kay.

Zhanna's decision should have surprised Erika, but there had been too many bigger surprises in the past couple of days. Before she departed the plane, Zhanna hugged everyone and thanked Kay again for saving her life. It was both a sad and happy goodbye.

After dropping off Zhanna in Honduras, it was on to the U.S. controlled France Air Force Base near Colon, Panama. There they said goodbye to the Night Witch and transferred to an Air Force DC-3 ordered up by Leroy Carr for the flight to Washington. The DC-3, after a brief refueling stop in Miami, sat down at Andrews Air Force Base yesterday evening.

Now, north of the equator, it was a warm, late summer day. From Andrews, a car took Kay home to Annapolis. Another car, followed closely by a Jeep with three armed MPs, took Erika and Kathryn to a CIA safehouse in D.C. located on South Dakota Avenue NE, where they remained under guard through the night.

Today, at 9:00 a.m., the two women were taken under guard to the CIA headquarters on E Street and escorted to Leroy Carr's office. Carr and Hodge were waiting. Kay was not there, which prompted Erika's first question.

"Where's Kay, Leroy?"

"Kay's at home. She didn't want to see you, Erika."

"Why are you offering a war criminal like Axel Ryker a deal?" Erika said bluntly.

"None of your damn business. You have no right to ask questions after doing what you did—going rogue and endangering my wife. Besides, do I have to remind you I also gave you a deal?"

"I'm not a war criminal. You lied to Kathryn and me. You told us we were to search for Hitler. Why didn't you just tell us the truth?"

Carr laughed tersely. "You've got to be joking . . . with the track record between you and Ryker!?" He went on to basically repeat the same comment Kay had made in Puerto San Julián. "You're the one who went rogue and stopped Kay from daily contact with me. Not only that, you brought Zhanna Rogova into the picture. This mission never had to be as dangerous as you made it."

"So the rumors about Hitler and Eva surviving the war are untrue?" Kathryn asked.

"I don't know if there is anything to the rumors or not," Carr replied. "There are people in other agencies working on that case."

"Where is Ryker now?" Erika asked.

"Do you really think for a moment I would tell you that?"

(Ryker was already on his way to Fort Huachuca, Arizona for training and indoctrination. This was the same U.S. Army intelligence base where Zhanna was indoctrinated into CIA-style human intelligence gathering.)

"So Ryker is selling out to save his ass, is that what you're telling me, Leroy?"

"Axel Ryker's loyalties are flexible. That much is apparent. It took me only about five minutes talking to him at that German club in Puerto San Julián before he agreed. Ryker felt betrayed by Müller and knew as a hunted war criminal he was living on borrowed time in South America."

"Ryker can't be trusted, Leroy," Erika added.

"And it seems neither can you or Kathryn."

"Have it your way, Leroy. You're the boss. Where do Kathryn and I go from here? To prison?"

"My wife interceded on your behalf. Because of all that she went through, I have to consider her recommendations. Neither of you will be prosecuted, but your passports are revoked. Both of you are prohibited from leaving the United States, and both of you are suspended from further missions. Erika, you'll return to your job as a trainer at Camp Perry. If you want to see your daughter you'll have to make arrangements for her to be brought here to the States by your grandparents at their or your expense.

"Kathryn, you also are suspended from field duty. You'll return to your job as an instructor at the Naval War College in Rhode Island. As with Erika, if you wish to see family members who live in Germany, it will be at your expense to bring them to the States, and I will have to approve it beforehand, for both of you.

"And let me make this perfectly clear, you and Kathryn are to have no contact with each other. If I find out you have talked to each other, even if just on the telephone, your probation at my wife's generosity is revoked and I'll put you in jail."

"I want to see Kay," Erika said.

"No," Carr said firmly, "absolutely not. She doesn't want to see you."

Al Hodge, who had always had some conflict of one type or another with Erika, blurted out, "Just shut up, Lehmann, and count your lucky stars that Kay is being so gracious. She saved both of your asses, and Rogova's, too."

Erika turned back to Carr. "Does that mean Zhanna will be left alone, even though Kay knows where she is?"

"Yes," Carr answered. "I will not pursue her. It was part of an agreement I made with Colonel Mikhailov (El Búho) that I would leave Zhanna alone in exchange for his help getting Kay out of Argentina. I'll honor that agreement. I can't speak for the Soviet NKVD that still has Rogova on its Top 10 wanted list. That's totally out of my hands. Kay gave Zhanna the chance to return here with you two and Zhanna turned it down. That tells me all I need to know. I wash my hands of Rogova."

Erika changed the subject. "You can be proud of your wife, Leroy. She fooled us and is a brave woman."

"I don't care what you think of my wife," Carr said fiercely. Erika had never seen Carr this confrontational. "I know she's brave. She proved that during the war in Bath, England, with your buddy, Otto Skorzeny. I will never forget that you put her life in danger on this latest mission because you didn't follow my orders. Now get out! MPs will drive you to Camp Perry, Erika, and Kathryn to Rhode Island. Toe the line, ladies. Kay cannot save you next time!"

"I have more questions, Leroy," Erika stated.

"If you're both not out of my office in five seconds you'll be taken to the stockade at Fort Dix instead of to Camp Perry and Newport!"

# Chapter 59

## On the road to Conowingo, Maryland
## Friday, 05 September 1947

After two nights and a full day back home where Kay was now out of danger, Leroy Carr still worried about his wife. She had barely slept since she arrived home and still occasionally succumbed to the hand jittering. Kay was not herself.

Kay's family lived in Illinois, but Leroy grew up in Conowingo, Maryland, and many of his family members still resided there. Conowingo was a mere two-hour drive from Annapolis.

Carr left his office a few hours early on Friday so he and his wife could spend the weekend in Conowingo with family. His family adored Kay, and he hoped that would take her mind off of the past five weeks. However, this didn't keep Kay from bringing up topics from the mission during their drive.

"Leroy, why would the United States want to employ a man like Axel Ryker?"

"Kay, let's not talk about that nor the mission. I can tell you are still bothered by it."

"I want to talk about it. Why was all this about Ryker?"

Carr wanted to get his wife's mind off the recent weeks, but he felt he couldn't refuse to speak of it if she insisted. "As you know, Kay, our country is trapped in a vicious undercover war with the Soviet Union—a Cold War with countries behind the 'Iron Curtain' as Churchill phrased it. Sometimes we are forced to do unseemly things to protect Americans. Ryker speaks Russian and German fluently and as a native. An asset who can do that comes around vary rarely. Such a person is valuable. He could function as an asset for our country in both Moscow and East Berlin, blending in as a local citizen in either Russia or Germany."

Kay lit a Pall Mall. Since her return from South America, she had smoked twice the cigarettes per day than she did before the mission. "So is this the end of Erika and Kathryn as far as field missions?"

Carr couldn't lie to his wife. "I can never forgive Erika for putting you through what she did. If she hadn't gone rogue and instead followed my orders to allow you to keep me updated daily, the mission wouldn't have reach the danger level for you that it did. As for their future, both Erika and Kathryn speak German as a native, and Erika speaks fluent Russian and French. As far as I'm concerned, they deserve to have their tires removed and put on blocks for disobeying orders, but I can't say we won't have to ever use them again. Every mission for us that Lehmann has been on has been successful for us in one way or another, even if she didn't know the real reason for the mission like this last one."

"I understand. You should use her if it benefits our country, Leroy. Yet, I'm still confused about why you would make a deal with a drug lord."

"For that, my only concern was for you, Kay. I couldn't have Ryker and Lehmann on the same airplane for over a day. Colonel Mikhailov—El Búho—was the fastest way I could get another airplane to pick you up in Puerto San Julián."

For Carr, he wasn't concerned with the future for now. He felt nothing but relief and thankfulness to God just to have his wife back safe and sound after bouncing around Central and South America with the likes of Erika Lehmann, Kathryn Fischer, and Zhanna Rogova.

"How about some crabs from Hoppy's? You've always loved those," Leroy said as they drove north on the Susquehanna River Road in Maryland.

"Sounds fine, Leroy."

Hoppy's Crab Shack fit its name. It wasn't anything more than a small shack that sat just off the road in an area of Maryland called Port Flats between Port Deposit and the Conowingo Dam. Despite its humble appearance, Hoppy's was considered by the locals as serving the best blue crab and crab cakes in all of Maryland. Many claimed Hoppy's crabs were better than you could buy in any swanky Baltimore restaurant.

Leroy pulled into Hoppy's gravel parking lot. Kay waited in the car as her husband went to the walk-up window and ordered their meals.

In the pleasant early September sun, Leroy and Kay Carr sat at a picnic table on the edge of Hoppy's parking lot and ate their blue crabs in peace.

# Chapter 60

**Camp Perry, Virginia**
**Saturday, 06 September 1947**

After being kicked out of Leroy Carr's office on Thursday, Erika and Kathryn spent the rest of that day, and all day Friday being debriefed separately by Al Hodge. Early this morning, Kathryn was driven back to Newport, Rhode Island in a sedan driven by an MP. Erika, also riding in a sedan with an MP driver, was taken to Camp Perry, where she was dropped off before noon with orders to report to the Camp Commandant. The MP drove away without getting out of the car.

The commandant had been informed two days ago by Sheila Reid that Erika would be back at the camp sometime Saturday. Of course, the Brigadier General was informed of nothing to do with the recent mission, good or bad, so he had no reason to treat Erika as anything other than an instructor returning to her duties.

"You'll be assigned a new group of plebes on Monday, Agent Lehmann," the general said.

"Does that mean I'm off this weekend, General?" Erika asked.

"Yes, just make sure you're prepared for your new recruits on Monday."

◊ ◊ ◊

**[that evening—Williamsburg, Virginia]**
At eight o'clock, Erika walked into Lane's Tavern. She hadn't called ahead. Nick saw her walk in the door and was both surprised and obviously delighted to see her. She smiled at him and walked up and sat at the bar. Nick had already poured a beer from the tap and held it in his hand. He set it down quickly in front of a middle-aged man wearing overalls and a straw hat and quickly walked over to her.

"Erika! Are you back from Texas for good?"

Before the mission, she told him she was being reassigned as a typist at Fort Hood.

"Yes, I think so, Nick."

He leaned over the bar, took her hands, and kissed her.

"When do you get off work?" she asked.

"It's Saturday and I'm stuck here until closing."

"That's okay. I'll wait."

Nick said, "When I get off work, we'll go to that all-night diner we went to before."

With wolf-like eyes, Erika replied, "I'd prefer to skip the meal and go directly to your apartment."

# Epilogue
## The Hunt for Hitler

Josef Stalin was convinced that Adolf Hitler did not die in the Berlin bunker. He stated this opinion strongly to both Harry Truman and Winston Churchill at the postwar Potsdam Conference.

For years after the Second World War ended, many governments, including the United States and the Soviet Union, made investigations into the possibility that Adolf Hitler and Eva Braun did not die in the Führer Bunker below the Reichstag in April of 1945 as the Soviet Army took Berlin.

Rumors still swirl to this day. Many recent books have been written purporting evidence to support the claims that Hitler died a natural death in Argentina years after the war. Most of these claims present as evidence an FBI report of its investigation into the matter. However, many of these authors claim the reports prove Hitler survived the war. The author of this book has read these FBI reports and they simple state some of the details of the investigation without coming to any conclusion if, or if not, Hitler survived the war.

A confirmed fact is that two German U-boats did not surrender after Germany's capitulation in May of 1945. At least one of this rogue U-boats showed up off the coast of Patagonia in southern Argentina in July of 1945, two months after Hitler's purported death. There are witnesses who maintain that U-530 dropped off people near Puerto San Julián, including a man and a woman who resembled Hitler and Braun. These witnesses claim that Hitler had shaved off his famous moustache and Braun had changed her hair color.

In addition, there were two servants at the Eden Hotel in La Faldo, Argentina, who testified that they had seen Hitler at the hotel, surrounded by heavy guard, on at least two occasions: in 1947, and again in the early 1950s. One of these hotel employees was a waitress who claims she served Hitler tea. Here again, she testified that the Führer was sans his moustache, and also that his hair was thinning and graying.

The author of this novel does not contend that Hitler lived out his life at peace in South America, nor does he contend that Hitler died in the bunker. There is no hard evidence to prove either theory conclusively. For years, the Russians, who took the bunker in Berlin, claimed to have the skull of Adolf Hitler in a vault in Moscow (Stalin, during his lifetime, never believed it to be the skull of Hitler). Decades after the war, the Soviets finally allowed a team of American and British scientists to conduct DNA tests on the remains. It proved to be a skull of a woman in her forties, so it could not even be the bones of Eva Braun who was thirty-three years old in 1945.

It is up to the readers to field their own thoughts. Those interested in researching this topic, besides the several books written, there are a vast number of Internet posts, and many YouTube videos devoted to the investigation of Hitler in Argentina.

## Heinrich Müller

The fate of the Gestapo chieftain, Heinrich Müller, is as controversial as that of Adolf Hitler. At the end of the war, Müller's whereabouts were unknown. In the decades after the war, conflicting claims have been made that Müller's body had been found in various places, but none of the claims offered reasonable evidence and all have been disputed.

After Adolf Eichmann's capture in Buenos Aires in 1960, he told his Israeli interrogators he believed that Müller was still alive although he had no knowledge of his former boss's whereabouts.

# The Erika Lehmann Series

Book 1: *Invitation to Valhalla*
Book 2: *Blood of the Reich*
Book 3: *Return to Valhalla*
Book 4: *Fall from Valhalla*
Book 5: *Operation Shield Maidens*
Book 6: *Hope for Valhalla*
Book 7: *Search for Valhalla*

Other books by Mike Whicker:
*Proper Suda* (a novel)
and
*Flowers for Hitler: The Extraordinary Life of Ilse Dorsch*
(a biography)

All books are available in print copy from Amazon.com, bn.com, and electronically from Kindle. Signed copies are available from the author.

Author welcomes reader comments
Email:  mikewhicker1@gmail.com

**To learn more about characters in *Search for Valhalla* who have played significant roles in other Erika Lehmann novels:**

Zhanna Rogova: *Fall from Valhalla, Operation Shield Maidens, Hope for Valhalla*

Kathryn Fischer: *Return to Valhalla, Fall from Valhalla, Operation Shield Maidens, Hope for Valhalla*

Sheila Reid: *Fall from Valhalla, Operation Shield Maidens, Hope for Valhalla*

Axel Ryker: *Invitation to Valhalla*

Leroy Carr and Al Hodge: All Erika novels except *Invitation to Valhalla*

Kay Carr: *Return to Valhalla*

# Notes for Readers